ALL MAN

Novels by G.A. Hauser
Published by Phaze Books

ALL MAN
G.A. HAUSER

EXCEPTIONAL EROTIC FICTION

A Phaze Books Production
Phaze Books
an imprint of Mundania Press LLC
6457 Glenway Avenue, #109
Cincinnati, Ohio 45211-5222

To order additional copies of this book, contact:
books@mundania.com
www.mundania.com

Cover Art © 2011 by Debi Lewis
Edited by Stephanie Balistreri

Trade Paperback ISBN: 978-1-60659-597-8

First Edition • April 2011

Production by Mundania Press LLC
Printed in the United States of America

10   9   8   7   6   5   4   3   2   1

CHAPTER 1

"Go deep! Deeper!"

Hearing the shouting, Chase Arlington paused to watch as a football flew through the crystal clear fall morning air, to fall into the arms of a running man. In seconds the poor guy got smashed from behind and leveled into the dewy grass of Schoolhouse Park's football field.

He felt a tug on his arm. Peering down the leash, Chase said, "Yes? You have somewhere to go?"

His shepherd mix looked up at him, a pink tongue hanging out of his mouth while he panted.

"Hang on, Mutley. One more play."

The dog made a sound of impatience and tugged again.

Nine men, some approaching middle age, four on one side, five on the other, were covered in grass stains and mud, appearing to be having the time of their lives as they played football like college kids.

A pass from one tall handsome man connected to another. A cheer went up as they celebrated a touchdown.

Though he did not know them, Chase shared their elation for the accomplishment.

"Okay. You're obviously ready. Let's go." Chase resumed his jogging, Mutley keeping pace by his side.

The park was enormous, thirty-five acres of soccer field, baseball diamond, picnic grounds, and grass. Chase was glad he stumbled upon it. He was new to the area and still getting a feel for the neighborhood.

Kettering, Centerville, Washington Township, this was Middle

America, Ohio, corn country, the land of the chain restaurant and SUV. A far cry from his urban lifestyle in trendy Manhattan.

But his private practice had dried up. HMO's began making his work as a physical therapist one of misery as his fees became tied up in paperwork.

A friend e-mailed him the job listing for Wright-Patterson Air Force Base. Working for the air force had its perks. There was job security and he liked the idea of helping out the military. Liked it a lot.

Sweat pouring from his neck and face, Chase slowed down as he approached his silver Hyundai Tiburon GS. "Hang on, Mutt." He panted as badly as his dog to catch his breath from the last sprint.

Chase opened the trunk and set out a bowl for his pet, filling it with water. Once Mutley was lapping at it, Chase drank the rest of the bottled water himself.

Chase used his t-shirt to wipe at his perspiration. Mutley was recuperating as well, sitting, his tongue running with water.

He was attempting to duplicate their same routine from the Big Apple. Every morning Chase took Mutley out running in Central Park. The only addition here in Ohio was the use of car on weekends. They ran a route right from the front door of Chase's home on weekdays. Mutley already seemed to know the program but they were both adjusting to being on their own in a strange place.

Finally feeling less sweaty from the cool breeze that quivered the leaves of the changing trees, Chase made a move to enter the car. Mutley stood, staring at him.

Chase smiled at his sweet expression. "Come here." He patted his chest. Instantly Mutley stood on his hind legs and pressed his big paws into him.

Chase gave him a good ear scratching. "We'll get used to it, buddy. Hang in there." He avoided a lick to his face and nudged the dog back down. The car door tugged open, Chase adjusted the towels he used to cover the bucket seats and had Mutley jump into the passenger's side. The obedient pooch sat comfortably, waiting, licking at the window glass.

After he started the engine, Chase lowered the windows for Mutley to stick his head out and feel the wind as they drove.

❧

Once he was home and showered, he ate his breakfast and gave Mutley a slab of rawhide to gnaw on.

Sipping his coffee while reading the *Dayton Daily News*, Chase couldn't help but smile at the 'down home' coverage of the media, which included corn festivals and a spate of local burglaries.

Unfortunately nothing compared to the *New York Times* and its international flair. Chase simply didn't know if he could be happy here. Here. In corn country.

Mutley adjusted his paws on the strip of rawhide, making short work of it in his long canines. "You have a backyard, right?" Chase asked him. "You didn't have a backyard before."

Mutley moved his big brown eyes to meet his but didn't stop his chewing.

"A yard is a good thing. No more being cooped up inside all day while I'm at work."

Mutley let out a snort in disinterest, getting a better grip on his snack. It was down to a pasty hunk of goo in seconds, which Mutley began to stuff in his mouth to swallow whole.

Chase turned back to the newsprint under his elbows, as he recalled the men playing football. He'd love to get in on that game for *so* many reasons. He loved sports, and thought the men were exceptional.

"Are there gay men in Dayton? Aren't we all over the place?" He laughed, finishing is coffee. *Of course we are. Just gotta sniff us out.*

"Right, Mutley?"

The snack consumed, Mutley licked his lips neatly and gave Chase his undivided attention.

"Any suggestions as to what we should do today?"

The dog tilted his head curiously.

"We've got a yard, may as well use it." Chase rose up, set his mug in the sink and left through the back door, Mutley in pursuit. Finding his chewed up Frisbee, Chase tossed it to him, wishing he had already established a network of friends. It sucked living here, but he didn't want to have to change careers in order to move back to New York. He had to give this a try.

CHAPTER 2

Holding onto his patient's ankle, Chase stood at the end of the padded table and said, "Raise up your leg for me, Nick." With an effort, Nick attempted to push against Chase's hand. Seeing pain on the man's face, Chase asked, "How badly does it hurt?"

"It's only bad when I fully extend it. Christ, I really screwed up my knee, didn't I?"

"Yes. You did. But we can get you back to full strength again. It'll just take some determination." He requested, "Do it again for me." Chase studied Nick's expression to see how much pain he was willing to withstand. "Are you still taking the anti-inflammatory medication?"

"Yes," Nick replied with a grimace.

Chase let up on him. He took a closer look at the surgery scars on Nick's knee. "That's enough for today. I want you to keep working at it at home." Chase removed a printed paper from a stack on the counter with exercises described in detail. He handed it to Nick. "While you're sitting in front of the television, do these."

Nick took the paper and read it over.

"Don't overdo it, but push yourself a little more each time. I want this rehab to work for you and not frustrate you. If you're in agony after, ice it and take some ibuprofen."

"Okay."

He patted Nick's shoulder in comfort. "I'll see you next week. Just call if you have any questions." Chase helped him down from the table.

As Nick left, Chase watched him walk away, seeing how much he favored his good leg. After Nick had vanished, Chase wrote some notes in his file.

"Chase?"

He looked up to see his co-worker and fellow therapist, Thomas Russo standing next to him.

"How are you holding up with all the new patients?"

"Good. It's not any more or less than I had in New York." Chase knew Thomas was married, possibly nearing his mid-fifties. That was it as far as any information he had learned about him.

"Are you settled in? How did the move go?"

Finished with the file, Chase placed it on a counter, then crossed his arms over his chest. "The move was fine. Though I hate packing and unpacking, it's mostly done. I suppose I'm just struggling to get a social life going. It takes time to meet people."

"It does. I know. What are your interests?"

Chase shrugged. "I like working out, running…"

"Join a gym. There're bound to be people there your age to socialize with."

"I could. I've thought about it." He noticed another patient enter the rehab area. "Talk to you later," Chase whispered.

Thomas nodded in reply, meeting the man who had approached him.

Bringing the file back to the front desk, Chase looked at the schedule to see who he had coming in next. The receptionist smiled flirtatiously at him. He smiled sweetly in return. "Just seeing who's next."

"Mr. Brown."

"Thanks." Chase looked around the waiting area. "Mr. Brown?" he asked.

A man rose to his feet and followed him into the next room. Chase tried not to be anxious about a social life. Something was bound to happen to change things. He just had to be patient.

❧❧

Home again, three slices of his delivered pizza eaten, a can of dog food consumed by Mutley, Chase sat at his computer and tried to find a gay group of men in the area. Seeing mostly personal ads, Chase cringed. "It's worse than I thought."

Chapter 3

Rhodes nudged Devlin Young to get his attention as
dled with two other men before the next play.

hat?" Dev asked.

e guy with the dog is here again."

four of the men paused to look at the pair.

sus, he's hot," Gary said softy.

ou think he's gay?" Lewis kept staring at the tall man hold-

sh for large mixed breed.

Don't I wish." Gary licked his top lip.

Hey!" A shout was heard from the other side of the yard

nytime now!"

Ve're a man short. Ask him to play for us, Dev."

You ask him, Gary. Why is it always up to me?"

We're about to charge you guys a penalty!" Barry yelled,

v the ball!"

am stood tall and shouted back, "Hold your horses!"

What the hell's the hold up?"

ooking back at Dev, Sam asked, "Should I tell them?"

Dev glanced in the man's direction. "He's still there. If you

him to join us, Gary, now's the time."

No. I'm chicken shit. I can't ask him. Sam, you do it."

inally Barry stormed over. "What the fuck is wrong with

iots? How long does it take to decide pass or run the ball?"

ewis nudged Barry. "We were thinking of asking that good

g guy over there to play with us."

Barry took a peek over their shoulders. "Wow."

"I know." Gary shifted from side to side anxiously.

No gay clubs? No gay lounges? Gay locales? *I'm going to lose my mind.* He picked up his cordless phone and pivoted his chair side to side lazily as it connected.

"Hello?"

"Save me." Chase craved hearing a friendly gay voice.

"That bad?"

"Christ, Tyler, I feel like the only gay man in Dayton. No. Make that in Ohio." Mutley rolled to his side and splayed out on the carpeted floor next to his chair.

"I can't believe you actually moved there."

"You're the one who e-mailed me the job application." Chase laughed but was annoyed.

"Yeah, uh, it was kind of a joke. I had no idea you'd really go and live there. It's farm country."

"Shut up. Why did I call you? I should know better than to call a guy who used to plan weddings for a living." Chase rubbed his face tiredly.

"Ouch! That's a low blow, Chase. At least I've given that crappy job up. Hey, maybe you can find a corn farmer who likes corn-holing?"

"Are you finished, Mr. Holliday?"

"Or a hog farmer who likes eating sausage."

"You done yet?" Chase couldn't help but be amused.

"No. I can keep going. There are a million of them."

"It used to be so easy to get a date uptown. I need a kiss desperately." Chase gazed dully at the computer screen.

"You need to get laid, Mr. Arlington."

"That too."

"You into the ten hour drive? You could come and stay with me and Jordon for the weekend. We could bar hop with you. Help get you some action."

"Ten hours? More like thirteen. No. Never mind. I made my bed." Chase stared at Mutley as he slept.

"You work on an air force base. Chase, there must be dozens of gorgeous guys around there."

"No. Let me tell you something about the base, there are no gorgeous models like you floating around there. Believe me. Mostly jar heads too young to consider, or older straight good ole' boys. No way. And I won't even entertain the idea of coming out there."

"Back in the closet too? Jesus! Come back to Manhattan. There's got to be some hospital that needs a good physical therapist."

"Believe me, I'm considering it." He inhaled to calm down. He was growing unreasonably angry with himself for thinking this was a good idea. "It's October. I'll give it to the New Year. The housing market is in such a bad slump here that even though I picked up this house for a steal, my luck if I tried to sell it, I'd have to take a loss."

"Chase, Jesus, man. I'm really sorry. I feel like this is all my fault."

Not intending to give Tyler a guilt trip, he said, "Never mind. Let me go. I was just feeling lonely."

"Call me anytime. You know I don't mind."

"You're a good friend, Tyler. I miss you."

"I miss you too. Just take care of yourself out there in that godforsaken place."

"Godforsaken? Can't be! There's a church on every corner."

"Augh," Tyler moaned. "Just move back. Spare yourself the grief."

"January. By January if I'm still without a friend, I'm outta here."

"Good. I hope you do move back."

"See ya, Tyler. Thanks for letting me vent."

"No problem, buddy."

Chase hung up and stared at the phone. "January."

～≈≈

In bed, his hands behind his head, Chase thought about his life and where he envisioned himself to be in five years. The phone rang, startling him out of his thoughts. He reached over to his nightstand and picked up the cordless, saying hello.

"Hiya, sweetheart. Is it too late to call?"

"No. Hi, Mom. I'm not asleep. Just lying here thinking."

"Your father and I are so upset you moved away from us.

Was going so far away your only opti

"I thought we had this discussio his hand through his hair. It seemed a bad idea.

"We did. But now that you've b miss you."

"I miss you guys too." Chase heard first before his long muzzle rested on t ing at him, Chase gave him an affection to his neck.

"Is it horrible there?"

"No. Not horrible. Just not what having a yard." Chase stopped touching on the carpet next to the bed.

"Mutley liked having Central Parl chided.

"Look, if I still am unhappy here by

"Then you are unhappy."

They'd already had this debate be choice of words."

"Sweetie, all your family is here in the your sisters, your cousins…"

"What's your point, Ma?"

"Come back."

"You know what happened to my bankrupt. Can we just let it go for now? T

"Good. So you'll be back by January."

"Goodnight, Mom." He didn't need to

"Goodnight, sweetheart."

He hung up and let out a deep exhal missed. Maybe moving wasn't such a bad thing all the lights were off, Chase climbed out o making sure the doors were locked, too. Sati and called it a night.

No gay clubs? No gay lounges? Gay locales? *I'm going to lose my mind.* He picked up his cordless phone and pivoted his chair side to side lazily as it connected.

"Hello?"

"Save me." Chase craved hearing a friendly gay voice.

"That bad?"

"Christ, Tyler, I feel like the only gay man in Dayton. No. Make that in Ohio." Mutley rolled to his side and splayed out on the carpeted floor next to his chair.

"I can't believe you actually moved there."

"You're the one who e-mailed me the job application." Chase laughed but was annoyed.

"Yeah, uh, it was kind of a joke. I had no idea you'd really go and live there. It's farm country."

"Shut up. Why did I call you? I should know better than to call a guy who used to plan weddings for a living." Chase rubbed his face tiredly.

"Ouch! That's a low blow, Chase. At least I've given that crappy job up. Hey, maybe you can find a corn farmer who likes corn-holing?"

"Are you finished, Mr. Holliday?"

"Or a hog farmer who likes eating sausage."

"You done yet?" Chase couldn't help but be amused.

"No. I can keep going. There are a million of them."

"It used to be so easy to get a date uptown. I need a kiss desperately." Chase gazed dully at the computer screen.

"You need to get laid, Mr. Arlington."

"That too."

"You into the ten hour drive? You could come and stay with me and Jordon for the weekend. We could bar hop with you. Help get you some action."

"Ten hours? More like thirteen. No. Never mind. I made my bed." Chase stared at Mutley as he slept.

"You work on an air force base. Chase, there must be dozens of gorgeous guys around there."

"No. Let me tell you something about the base, there are no gorgeous models like you floating around there. Believe me. Mostly jar heads too young to consider, or older straight good ole' boys. No way. And I won't even entertain the idea of coming out there."

"Back in the closet too? Jesus! Come back to Manhattan. There's got to be some hospital that needs a good physical therapist."

"Believe me, I'm considering it." He inhaled to calm down. He was growing unreasonably angry with himself for thinking this was a good idea. "It's October. I'll give it to the New Year. The housing market is in such a bad slump here that even though I picked up this house for a steal, my luck if I tried to sell it, I'd have to take a loss."

"Chase, Jesus, man. I'm really sorry. I feel like this is all my fault."

Not intending to give Tyler a guilt trip, he said, "Never mind. Let me go. I was just feeling lonely."

"Call me anytime. You know I don't mind."

"You're a good friend, Tyler. I miss you."

"I miss you too. Just take care of yourself out there in that godforsaken place."

"Godforsaken? Can't be! There's a church on every corner."

"Augh," Tyler moaned. "Just move back. Spare yourself the grief."

"January. By January if I'm still without a friend, I'm outta here."

"Good. I hope you do move back."

"See ya, Tyler. Thanks for letting me vent."

"No problem, buddy."

Chase hung up and stared at the phone. "January."

In bed, his hands behind his head, Chase thought about his life and where he envisioned himself to be in five years. The phone rang, startling him out of his thoughts. He reached over to his nightstand and picked up the cordless, saying hello.

"Hiya, sweetheart. Is it too late to call?"

"No. Hi, Mom. I'm not asleep. Just lying here thinking."

"Your father and I are so upset you moved away from us.

Was going so far away your only option?"

"I thought we had this discussion before I left." Chase ran his hand through his hair. It seemed everyone thought this was a bad idea.

"We did. But now that you've been gone two weeks…we miss you."

"I miss you guys too." Chase heard Mutley's snuffling breaths first before his long muzzle rested on the bed next to him. Smiling at him, Chase gave him an affectionate petting from his head to his neck.

"Is it horrible there?"

"No. Not horrible. Just not what I'm used to. Mutley likes having a yard." Chase stopped touching him and Mutley curled on the carpet next to the bed.

"Mutley liked having Central Park as his backyard," she chided.

"Look, if I still am unhappy here by January, I'll come back."

"Then you are unhappy."

They'd already had this debate before he moved. "Poor choice of words."

"Sweetie, all your family is here in the New York area. Both your sisters, your cousins…"

"What's your point, Ma?"

"Come back."

"You know what happened to my business. I was going bankrupt. Can we just let it go for now? 'Til the new year?"

"Good. So you'll be back by January."

"Goodnight, Mom." He didn't need to hear this right now.

"Goodnight, sweetheart."

He hung up and let out a deep exhale. "Well, at least I'm missed. Maybe moving wasn't such a bad thing after all." Uncertain all the lights were off, Chase climbed out of bed, and checked, making sure the doors were locked, too. Satisfied, he washed up and called it a night.

CHAPTER 3

Sam Rhodes nudged Devlin Young to get his attention as they huddled with two other men before the next play.

"What?" Dev asked.

"The guy with the dog is here again."

All four of the men paused to look at the pair.

"Jesus, he's hot," Gary said softy.

"You think he's gay?" Lewis kept staring at the tall man holding a leash for large mixed breed.

"Don't I wish." Gary licked his top lip.

"Hey!" A shout was heard from the other side of the yard line. "Anytime now!"

"We're a man short. Ask him to play for us, Dev."

"You ask him, Gary. Why is it always up to me?"

"We're about to charge you guys a penalty!" Barry yelled, "Throw the ball!"

Sam stood tall and shouted back, "Hold your horses!"

"What the hell's the hold up?"

Looking back at Dev, Sam asked, "Should I tell them?"

Dev glanced in the man's direction. "He's still there. If you want him to join us, Gary, now's the time."

"No. I'm chicken shit. I can't ask him. Sam, you do it."

Finally Barry stormed over. "What the fuck is wrong with you idiots? How long does it take to decide pass or run the ball?"

Lewis nudged Barry. "We were thinking of asking that good looking guy over there to play with us."

Barry took a peek over their shoulders. "Wow."

"I know." Gary shifted from side to side anxiously.

"Yeah, but what will he do if he finds out we're all gay. The guy will freak." Barry kept glancing up at him.

"Jesus!" The rest of the opposing side approached angrily. "Christ! It's not rocket science. It's just football!" Chris, Kevin, Joe and Jerry began griping at the delay.

Gary said quietly, "We noticed that guy watching us last week. And we thought of asking him to join us. It sucks playing with a man down." He added, "Though us four are better than you five any day of the week."

"Screw you. You think you're better than me?" Barry pointed to his chest. "Pick one of us to go on your team, ya baby. We'll still beat you."

Gary glanced back at the good-looking man as they debated, seeing him and his dog jog away. "Forget it, guys. He's gone."

"Good. Now throw the ball!" Barry grumbled, walking back to their side of the field.

Sam smiled sadly at Gary. "He might be back next week."

"My luck he won't." Gary added, "Just throw the ball, Dev, when I go deep."

"You got it." Dev waited until they all got into formation. "Hep one, hep two, hep three!" Sam slipped the ball to Dev from between his legs, blocking Jerry's attempt to intercept as Gary and Lewis sprinted downfield.

❧❧

Chase still felt his cheeks burning in embarrassment. Jogging with Mutley at a fast pace, he couldn't believe the way they all stared at him as if he were an alien. "Christ, can't a guy watch a game? What the heck was that all about?"

He'd stopped to watch men play basketball in New York. No one blinked. Were there some unwritten guidelines here in Ohio? Don't stop to stare at men playing sport in a park they'll think you're a homo and gawk at you? Or worse, beat the crap out of you?

Chase began feeling like he was in some foreign place where only certain types of people were welcome. It was a sickening sensation.

Finally making his way to his car, Chase slowed his pace and noticed several Kawasaki motorcycles parked side by side. The brilliant gleam of chrome and enamel distracted him until Mutley tugged on his leash. He popped the trunk of his car and gave the dog his bowl of water.

"That's the last time I'm going to stop and watch them play, Mutt. I don't need the grief." Chase sucked down the rest of the water, wiping the sweat from his forehead.

As he and his dog cooled off, Chase stared back in the direction of the playfield. His chest ached with the loneliness he was feeling.

≈≈

Gary stood with the rest of the group as they kicked mud off their shoes and changed shirts. Glancing around the parking lot, he was hoping to catch sight of the man with the dog, but it seemed he was either still out running or gone. "I'm such an idiot."

Sam looked up at him as he tied his shoelace. "Don't worry. You'll find him."

"I doubt it. Not with my luck." Gary wiped his sweaty face with the shirt he'd taken off.

Dev stepped closer. "He obviously brings his dog here every weekend."

"True." Gary scanned around the parking lot again.

Lewis teased, "Just find your balls next time, Gary, and go talk to the guy."

"Shut up. You think it's easy?" Gary replied. "Like Dayton is West Hollywood and we're surrounded by gay men? You're a moron, Lewis."

"Hey, the guy was ogling us. Duh." Lewis tossed his dirty shoes in the trunk of his Honda. "He's gay."

Sam clipped his motorcycle helmet on his head. "He wasn't ogling, Lewis, he was just watching us. That's not an instant gaydar indicator."

"Thank you!" Gary gestured to Sam. "Now shut up, Lewis."

"Whatever. See you guys next week." Lewis climbed into his car and left.

Dev patted Gary's back in comfort. "It's only one week. You'll at least find out if he's game or not."

Gary nodded as he watched Sam climb onto his Kawasaki motorcycle, envious of his and Dev's relationship. They seemed to be the perfect couple.

"See ya, Gary." Sam waved.

"See ya." Gary waited as Sam and Dev sped off on their matching bikes. Pausing before he left, the last one of their group to go, Gary felt as if he had to keep searching the parking lot just in case that amazing man showed up. After a few minutes it felt more like a waste of time than a help. Sighing loudly, Gary finally sat behind the wheel of his car and drove home.

❧❧

Chase, a cup of coffee at his lips, zoned off into space as he recalled the odd feeling of being singled out at the park. Visions of being beaten up by a group of nine big brawny men almost caused him to cancel his weekend runs through Schoolhouse Park. "I'm being ridiculous." He placed the cup down on the table and rubbed his rough jaw stubble.

He checked the clock on the wall. It was only ten. What was he going to do all day on a Sunday? Go to a shopping mall?

"I'm in hell. Motherfucker. I'm in hell." Chase slouched in his chair and thought January may be optimistic. The way he felt at the moment, moving back to New York in a couple of days felt more promising.

The large pile of newsprint from the newspaper was at his elbow. Searching it for a weekend guide or some kind of entertainment section, Chase found a slim pullout pamphlet.

Oktoberfest, navy bean festival, harvest jamboree, black walnut festival.

Slapping the paper closed, Chase groaned in agony. "I have to get out of this place."

CHAPTER 4

Chase hooked up Mutley's collar to his leash and waited for the dog to hop out of his car. Another long, annoying, lonely week had past and he was back at Schoolhouse Park for his extended run. With his jaw clenched in determination, Chase was not going to stop this time to watch anything. No football, no men, nothing. Just his ten mile cross-country jog. That's it.

Damn if I'm going to let some homophobic assholes stop me from my run.

"You ready, Mutt?" Chase tucked his car key into his shorts' pocket. Mutley gave him a vigorous wag of his tail in reply. "Let's go."

Looping the leash around his forearm, Chase began their route trying to keep his annoyance about last week in check and his eyes on the trail ahead, not on the people around him.

Gary waited while Chris hiked the ball and looked for an open receiver. It was Gary's job to guard Barry, so he waved his hands around in front of him to block any attempt at a pass from Chris.

A man jogging by with a dog distracted Gary. "Shit!"

The football went sailing over Gary's head to Barry in a completed pass. Gary stood frozen in place as Barry sprinted to the end zone.

"What the fuck?" Sam yelled as he and Dev rushed over to Gary in exasperation. "Nice block, dildo!"

"Huh?" Gary felt his pulse quicken. "He's not stopping. Look."

"Who isn't?" Dev spun to look. "Uh oh. You're right."

"Go!" Sam pushed Gary.

"Go?" Gary dug in his heels.

"Go after him! You can't miss another opportunity." Sam used both his hands on Gary's back to shove him.

"What now?" Barry and the rest of the gang returned from the goal line to see what was going on.

"You're losing him, Gary," Dev warned.

"Fuck!" Gary felt petrified.

"You fucking chicken shit!" Chris laughed. "Nice. Here's Staff Sergeant Gary Wilson of the United States Air Force, petrified of a man with a dog. Good one, Gary."

Kevin drew closer. "What's Gary doing now? Still crying about our break up?"

At the jibe to his manhood, Gary glared at Kevin, "Fuck you," and took off running.

Behind him Sam cheered, "Go! Go!"

※※

Yes, they're there playing. Chase deliberately averted his eyes. *Fine. I'll ignore you ignorant bastards.*

To Chase's surprise he heard heavy footfalls and panting behind him. Terrified that the men had recognized him and it was time to beat up the homo, Chase peered over his shoulder in paranoia.

"Wait!"

Seeing it was only one man, Chase halted, reining in Mutley.

When the stranger approached, he gasped for breath, leaning over with both his hands on his knees to recover from his sprint.

Chase had the opportunity to check him out as the man seemed slightly incapacitated at the moment.

He was wearing a white loosely fitted muscle-t that barely covered his solid pecs and broad back. Green gym shorts showed off his long muscular legs and he was spattered with mud from head to toe.

His brown hair conservatively cut, he was clean-shaven, and if Chase had to guess, he would say he was in his late twenties. Finally the man recovered enough to make eye contact. Sparkling blue eyes found his. Chase melted right down to his running shoes.

The man had Mutley curious as well. After a moment to think about it, Mutley went for a crotch sniff.

Before the man uttered another word, Chase held up his hand. "Look. I'm new in town and I didn't mean anything by watching you guys, okay?"

"Huh?" The man petted Mutley's head and asked, "What do you mean, you didn't mean anything by watching us?"

Instantly frustrated, Chase crossed his arms over his chest and asked, "Why did you stop me?"

"I…we…wanted to know if you'd be interested in joining the game. We're a man down."

Stunned at the request, Chase watched the man lick his dry lips and couldn't be more pleased. "You ran me down to ask me to join you?"

"Sorry." The man appeared upset. "I thought it was a bad idea, but some of my friends egged me on. I didn't mean to bother you."

"No. No bother at all." Chase held out his hand in greeting. "I'm Chase Arlington."

"Gary Wilson." He shook Chase's hand. "Are you from the east coast?"

"New York." Chase smiled. "You can hear my accent?"

"I can. I like it."

A spark sizzled up Chase's back at the man's sexy smile. Could there be hope of a gay man living in Dayton, Ohio?

"And who is this fella?" Gary scratched Mutley behind the ears.

"That's Mutley. He'll be on his back for a belly rub if you keep that up."

It appeared Gary was biting his lip on a comment. His eyes crinkled as he smiled at Chase.

Chase looked back at Gary's group. "They're all staring at us."

Spinning around Gary replied, "Uh, I know. Look, can you play now? I don't want to interrupt your run…but we'd love it."

Love it? Chase was more intrigued. "Sure."

"Will Mutley mind?" Gary asked, grinning as they walked back to the group.

"Yes, but he'll deal with it." Chase wanted to touch Gary. Just a light touch on the small of his back, but resisted.

As they approached the crowd of eight men, Chase found very wry smiles on them all. Something was prickling his gaydar scanner at the moment. Could he seriously be this lucky?

Gary handled the introductions. There was no way Chase was going to remember all their names the first time he heard them. He just nodded as each man either waved or said hello.

Once he had finished, Gary even introduced Chase's dog. Mutley panted, wagging his tail happily.

"Let me tie him up. If I don't, he'll be after the ball."

"Okay." Gary gave Chase a big smile.

As Chase walked to the closest tree, he whispered to Mutley, "You behave. This may be my one chance to meet a nice man around here. So just chill and catch a nap, all right?" Chase looped his leash to a narrow sapling and gave Mutley a reassuring rub on the nose. "Lie down." Mutley obeyed. "Good boy."

When Chase spun around to look back at his dog while he approached the group, Mutley was sitting up, his pink tongue still hanging out from the heat of their run.

❧

"Son of a bitch, he's gorgeous," Dev whispered into Gary's ear.

"I'm dying." Gary shifted his weight as they all watched Chase approach. "Jesus, look at the package on him."

Kevin leaned against Gary. "I got dibs if he's gay."

"Fuck you. I saw him first," Gary said. "And I went after him."

"Guys," Sam warned, "Shut up, he's coming."

"He'll be coming all right," Kevin said.

Gary nudged Kevin in the ribs angrily.

"Right." Chase rubbed his hands together eagerly. "Who wants me?"

A show of playful hands annoyed Gary. "He's on our team. We're a man down."

Dev waved Chase over. "You're with me, Sam, Lewis and Gary."

"Okay." Chase joined their huddle.

"Just cover Jerry," Sam said.

"Which one's he again?" Chase looked back at the other side who currently had the ball.

Gary wanted to touch him so badly he ached. On the pretext of whispering, Gary put his arm around Chase's shoulder. "The guy in the Buckeye's shirt."

"Got it." Chase smiled at him.

From behind them came an insistent nag from Lewis, "Can we play?"

Dev waved his group away from their huddle. As they dispersed Gary and his teammates formed a defensive line. Chase was positioned next to him.

A 'woof' was heard in the distance. Mutley was standing, wagging, eager to join in.

Licking his lips, Gary was distracted by Chase's presence. The man was near six feet in height, lean, mean, with shaggy brown hair and deep chocolate brown eyes. His features were so angular, masculine and sharp, Gary was captivated by Chase instantly.

"Hep one! Hep two! Hike!" Chris held the ball and looked downfield. Gary tried to keep Barry under his control, but kept being distracted by Chase waving his arms over Jerry's head.

The ball went sailing through the air. There was a flurry of activity. It went into and out of Jerry's hands and down to the grass. Chase scooped it up and ran.

When Kevin tackled Chase, landing on Chase's legs and bottom, Gary grew jealous instantly. *Oh no, we need to be on different teams or I'll never get to land on him.*

Sam helped Chase to his feet. "Great fumble recovery. Have you played ball before?"

"In college. Ages ago." Chase handed Dev the ball and brushed the dirt off his legs.

"Ages ago?" Dev chuckled. "You look twenty-five. It can't be ages ago."

"I'm thirty. But thanks for the compliment."

Gary salivated over everything about Chase. His cool confidence, his athletic skill, his sex appeal. The effect on him was as bad as having a sudden onset of a schoolgirl's crush.

When Dev called them into a huddle, Gary wrapped his arm around Chase and squeezed him close, getting a good sniff of his sweat. Chase glanced at Gary quickly before being distracted by Dev.

"Let's let Chase catch the ball," Dev said, "Look, Chase, just try your best to get free. You're taller than Jerry so I'll pass it over his head."

"Okay."

"Fake right, then swing left sharply."

"Got it."

Gary patted Chase's bottom in encouragement. It must have seemed normal because Chase didn't react.

Dev reached between Sam's thighs for the ball. "Hep one, hep two…hike!"

Gary blocked Barry and tried to keep his eye on Chase at the same time. As directed, Chase faked right, jarring Jerry with his shoulder as he veered left, his hands high over Jerry's head.

Dev sent the ball like a missile through the crisp blue air and into Chase's outstretched hands. Chase began sprinting. He was so quick on his feet that the five men pursuing him struggled to catch up. When he was about to enter the end zone, Joe and Kevin nailed him around his shins, but Chase fell over the line and made the goal.

Hearing Sam, Lewis and Dev cheering in excitement, Gary noticed Kevin taking his time getting off Chase's body. Chase still had a hold of the football, laying on his front.

Storming over, Gary then grabbed Kevin and shoved him off roughly. "Let him up!"

"I was! Sheesh! Give me a second!" Kevin said.

Gary caught Chase looking back over his shoulder at him curiously. As Chase made it to his knees, tossing the ball at Dev, Gary reached out his hand to haul him up. "Nice play."

"Thanks." Chase smiled, whacking the caked dirt off his knees once he was standing. "Do we do the point after kick?"

"No one's good enough to kick the extra point." Gary smiled.

"No. Really? No goal kickers here?" Chase asked.

"Can you?"

"I'd love to try. It's been a while."

Thrilled at the prospect of seeing Chase punt, Gary shouted to Dev. "Hey! Chase wants to try for the point after."

The group of eight spun around in surprise.

"You can kick?" Sam asked in admiration.

Shaking his head and waving his hands in defense, Chase replied, "I was only suggesting it. I have no idea if I can still do it."

"Let him try." Gary reached for the ball in Dev's hands.

"Sure. Impress me!" Dev tossed Gary the ball.

"Uh oh. What have I gotten myself into?" Chase blushed hotly.

Gary loved it. He jogged back to the twenty-yard line and held the ball tip to tip on the grass. "Fire when ready."

Mutley let out another 'woof' in the background.

Seeing all the guys watching handsome Chase Arlington attempt a field goal, Gary grew hard in his pants. *Fuck you, Kev, I saw him first.*

"You ready, Gary?" Chase asked, positioned to fly when signaled.

"Go, baby!" Gary beamed at him.

Like poetry in motion, Gary watched this brawny handsome male approach. A few elongated leaps towards him, and Chase's foot made contact with the upright ball, sending it flying high into the air. Gary set back to watch it sail. No doubt, it was going directly between the uprights. *Son of a bitch!*

The men's roars echoed through the open air instantaneously. Gary stood to gape at Chase as everyone surrounded him, patting his back and picking him up off his feet.

You amazing man! Gary felt his throat go dry. *I want you!*

～≈

Chase was hysterical with laughter as he was congratulated. Kevin had picked him up off the ground and everyone else was patting either his back or butt in excitement. The touch of so many men was exhilarating. Chase was dizzy from it. "All right, guys. It's not that big a deal."

"Are you kidding?" Sam said, "None of us can do that!"

"Come on," Chase replied, "Sure you can."

"Let him go, Kevin." Gary whacked Kevin's shoulder.

Chase's gaydar went off again. *Jealousy? Over me? Could it be?*

"All right, Gary. Take a chill pill." Kevin set Chase back on his feet.

Trying to catch any subliminal messages between these men, Chase was close to deciding he was with his own ilk but not one hundred percent certain. "Someone else try. Come on."

"I will." Gary perked up.

"Good man." Chase reached for the ball. As Dev tossed it to him, Chase noticed Dev exchange a sly smile with the pretty one they called Sam. *Hmm. Something's going on around here. What could it be?*

Chase steadied the ball between the grass and his index finger. "Anytime, Gar."

"Just kick it?" Gary shifted nervously from leg to leg.

"Yes. Kick it. Aim up." Chase thought the guy was adorable. He couldn't get enough of those baby blues.

"I don't want to hit your hand."

"I'll pull back. Don't worry."

As the rest of the crowd watched, Gary worked up the courage.

Kevin taunted, "Jesus, Gary! It's not Lucy Van Pelt that's holding it. He won't pull it away."

"Shut up!" Gary snarled, obviously growing uptight.

"Nice one Staff Sergeant Wilson," Chris yelled, "ya chicken shit."

Hearing a military title, Chase perked up. Staff sergeant? Could he be lucky enough to be dealing with an air force dude from Wright Pat? His pulse quickened.

Gary approached like a locomotive engine. As Gary's foot aimed for the heavens, Chase released the ball and sat back. Gary's shoe made a loud smacking sound as the pigskin was booted. Watching the ball wobbling as it went, Chase knew it was close but not quite. It hit the upright and bounced back. A series of hisses and boos were heard.

"Hey," Chase said, "not bad for a first try. At least he had the balls."

Kevin leaned on Chase seductively. "He's not the only one with balls."

Sam said, "Cut it out, Kevin. Don't make Chase uncomfortable."

That clinched it for Chase. Gay men. He could just about hear the church choir singing *Hallelujah!*

"Am I making you uncomfortable, handsome?" Kevin purred.

Before Chase could answer, Gary pushed Kevin so hard he went stumbling off, trying to keep his footing.

"All right," Dev said in anger. "This is deteriorating fast. If we're done playing football, let's call it a fucking day."

Sam whispered into Chase's ear, "Sorry. No one is intending on offending you."

"No. You're not. Believe me." Chase laughed happily. "I'm thrilled.

"Yeah?" Sam asked, his brown eyes brightening. "Cool!"

Gary drew close enough to kiss. "You're gay?" He panted the sentence out in excitement.

"Yes. And very happy all of you are as well. Or at least I think you all are."

"We are," Lewis said as he began walking to the parking lot. "The only fucking queers in Montgomery County."

"Shut up!" Sam laughed. "You don't know that."

"Don't we?" Joe wiped the sweat off his face with his shirt.

"Gay huh?" Kevin flirted. "Single?"

"Yes." Chase caught Gary's irritation. In Chase's opinion, Gary was by far the more delightful of the two. But being fought after by a couple of gay guys was a hell of a lot better than sitting home alone stewing about being alone.

"Woof!"

Chase heard his dog's call for his attention. "I should go get Mutley." As he spun on his heels, Chase caught Gary shove Kevin backwards again. Soon Gary was walking beside Chase towards his dog.

Before Dev and Sam left, Dev said to the group, "Remember next week we play Saturday, not Sunday!"

The few men waved in acknowledgement.

"Are you busy later?" Gary asked.

"No." Chase smiled in invitation. "You?"

"No."

Chase knelt down by Mutley who was very excited to be with his master again.

"What a sweet dog." Gary cuddled Mutley as he was released from his small tree.

"He is. He's great. I have no complaints." Chase looped the leash around his wrist. "Did I hear right? You're a staff sergeant?"

His cheeks going crimson, Gary rose up from his crouching position near the dog and replied, "Yeah. Over at Wright Patterson."

"I work there."

The look of enthusiasm from Gary was palpable. "You do?"

"Yes. I'm a PT over at Occupational Therapy."

"Son of a bitch!" Gary smiled. "Perfect!"

"Perfect for?" Chase said as he began their stroll to the parking lot.

"Shit. Sorry. I'm being a bit forward." Gary lowered his head as they walked.

"Don't worry. I'm gobbling it up."

"Sure you are."

"I'm serious. I just moved here from New York three weeks ago. I was going nuts without any friends, particularly gay friends."

"Don't go nuts. You found nine of us." Gary smiled sweetly.

"How did you guys all connect up?" Chase paused at his car, opening the trunk to get Mutley water.

"Dev and Sam met at a motorcycle club, Lewis, Joe and Barry are clients of Sam, who hosts web sites, and the rest of us are friends of a friend. We just managed to get the game together this fall."

Once Chase had put the bowl of water on the ground, he leaned back against his car. "No kidding? This fall is the first time you guys all got together for football?"

"No kidding. We've only had three games so far." Gary leaned against the car next to Chase.

"Which guy do you know?"

After making a strained expression, Gary said, "Kevin."

"Ah." Chase smiled.

"He likes you. I guess that's more than obvious."

"Yeah. It's flattering." Chase watched Gary's expression darken. "But you're a lot nicer."

"Am I?" Gary brightened up.

"Staff Sergeant. Growl!"

Gary blushed. "You like men in uniform?"

"Who doesn't?" Chase checked on Mutley. He was finished drinking and sitting in the shade of the car, panting. "Are you still on active duty?"

"Reserves. But I expect a call up soon, actually."

Chase's heart sank. "No."

Gary shrugged. "Rumor has it we're going to Al Taji Air Base for some training of the Iraqi military."

Unprepared for how much of an impact it would have on him after just meeting Gary, Chase rubbed his face wearily.

"Don't worry." Gary brushed his shoulder against Chase's. "We have time."

"I'm sorry, Gary." Chase felt a lump in his throat. He had a very strong opinion about that war, but it didn't mean he wasn't patriotic and a staunch supporter of the US military.

"Sorry?"

"Yes. I'm not going to say anymore. I don't want to get political."

A sad smile washed over Gary's expression. "I get it." He faced Chase, touching his shoulder gently. "You want to wash up and go grab lunch later?"

"That would be terrific."

"I know you all of five minutes and I'm dying to kiss you."

That made Chase smile instantly. "Kiss? In public in Dayton? Are you insane?"

"I know. We'd be crucified."

"How about kissing at my place, after lunch?" Chase stared at Gary's full lips and wanted to taste them, very badly.

"You got it. I can pick you up. Where do you live?"

"Right off Alex Bell. Hang on. Let me get some paper. I'll write all my info down for you. Hold this." He handed Gary Mutley's leash.

As Chase rummaged in the glove compartment for a pen and something to write on, he heard Gary baby talking to Mutley. The idea Gary liked dogs as much as he did reassured him. *Love me, love my mutt.* Once he'd written his home info down, including all his phone numbers, he found Mutley with his paws on Gary's chest, getting a good ear scratching.

"You've made a permanent friend," Chase said. "He'll be expecting that from now on."

"And he'll get it. He's a good boy." Gary almost got nailed in the face with a big pink tongue. "What is he? Shepherd and what?"

"I don't know. Something big. Husky? Malamute? Heinz fifty-seven? I have no clue. I picked him up at the pound."

"Who would give you up?" Gary asked Mutley.

"He was a mess. I took him for obedience training. Now he's the perfect gentlemen. And the running gets his yayas out." Chase tugged on Mutley to get off Gary. "Here."

Gary took the piece of paper, reading it. "Cool. How much time you need?"

Chase checked his watch. "It's ten. How about noon."

"Be there noon."

They stared at each other, dying to connect mouths. It wasn't going to happen. Instead, Chase caressed Gary's upper arm lightly. "See you soon."

"Yes."

Chase smiled, as he watched Gary walk to his black Hummer. He couldn't wipe the grin off his face as he loaded Mutley into the car. Once he was behind the wheel with the engine started, Chase said, "Well? We did it, Mutley. We got ourselves a man! Yeeha!"

❧❧

Gary checked himself out in the mirror after he had showered and shaved. Decked out in a pair of faded jeans and a cotton shirt, his black Doc Martin boots on his feet, he shut off the bathroom light and tucked his keys, wallet and mobile phone into his pocket.

A quick look around his condo to make sure everything was shut off, Gary jogged out to his SUV in excitement and couldn't wait to see Chase again.

It'd been ages since he felt this way about a man. Over a year ago he and Kevin had dated. After it ended badly, they weren't on speaking terms for months. It was only since Sam intervened and got them both to play football together that Gary was even was able to look Kevin in the eye.

Kevin had both lied and cheated on him. Those were two very good reasons to hate him. And he did, though lately that anger was turning to apathy. But seeing Kevin flirting with Chase was infuriating. He wouldn't wish Kevin Baker on anyone. The guy was into sex, period, not relationships. Motivating Kevin to talk about his feelings was impossible.

Sitting behind the wheel of his Hummer, Gary tried to stop his thoughts from including Kevin. It put him into a terrible mood and that wasn't where he wanted to be for his first date with the remarkable Chase Arlington.

As he drove the short distance from his home in Kettering to Chase's house in Centerville, Gary debated on whether he should make a move on Chase for sex or let Chase make that decision.

Christ, I want you! I want all of you!

A year was a long time to go without a good fuck. And feeling pent up was an understatement. Gary was very choosey when it came to men. He was a snob. Looks and a nice body were paramount in his book, and unfortunately in Ohio, it was a rare combination. And on the base? No way. No sex at Wright Patterson Air Force Base. In his opinion that was strictly taboo. He knew men and women snuck around screwing when they could. It would land them in big trouble if they were caught, and the allegations of rape were rapidly increasing. Gary wanted no part of a relationship that could jeopardize his career. The 'don't ask, don't tell policy' scared him as well. He didn't need anyone knowing his private life. It was his business, period.

"Chase, you are perfect." He worked as a civilian on base so they would never cross paths, yet Chase was a sympathizer to the military. "And gorgeous." Gary moaned loudly, rubbing his crotch.

"How will I not jump on you?"

∽≈

Chase rushed around making the house neat. Vacuuming dog hair wasn't his idea of fun, but Mutley shed like mad.

The hound hated the sound of the Hoover. Chase gave him a chiding glance when he found Mutley cowering in a corner. "It's your fault. Look at all this fur."

Once that task was done, Chase checked his hair and face in the mirror in the bathroom, washing his hands. "Right." He dabbed on cologne and straightened his back. "Staff Sergeant Gary Wilson, come and get it!"

Shutting the bathroom light, Chase tried to imagine Gary in his army fatigues. "Argh!" He massaged his hard dick excitedly. "What is it about men in uniform? Jesus."

He stared at Mutley for a moment. "What do you want to do? Hang out inside or out while I'm gone?"

Mutley walked directly to the back door.

"Outside?" Chase asked again.

Mutley pawed at the door, wagging his tail.

"Okay. Just don't bark and piss anyone off." He opened the door and Mutley raced out encouraging a couple of birds that were lingering on the grass to take wing. Chase made sure Mutley had enough water and the gate was locked. Before he shut the back door he tossed a few milk bones down on the cement patio. Mutley was munching them before Chase even made it back into the house again.

As he washed his hands at the kitchen sink the doorbell rang. His heart pumped in excitement. Shaking off the water, he went to grab the towel. Once he dried his hands, Chase tossed the cloth on the counter and jogged to the front door. When he opened it he got his second glance at the adorable man he couldn't stop thinking about.

"Hey." Chase opened the door to allow him in.

"Hey." Gary smiled invitingly.

"Come in."

"Where's Mutley?"

"He's in the backyard. I think he'll be happier out there while I'm gone."

Gary nodded, rubbing his hands nervously on his jeans.

"You want to just head out?" Chase felt as anxious as Gary looked. First dates were awkward.

"Sure. Are you hungry?"

"Starved." Chase made sure he had his keys and wallet. "Any idea where you want to go?" As Chase moved them back to the front door, he paused for Gary's reply.

A pained expression washed over Gary's handsome face.

"You okay?" Chase was about to add another line about lunch, when Gary cupped his jaw. At the touch, he held his breath.

In a soft voice Gary said, "I'm very attracted to you."

Laughing nervously, Chase replied, "Ditto."

"Can I just kiss you once before we go?"

"Of course. You can kiss me twice," he teased.

Though Chase expected a snappy comeback, Gary didn't even smile. Slowly Gary reached with his other hand so both were holding Chase's face. As Gary leaned forward, his body began to meltdown. The first brush of their lips made his cock rock hard.

Gary's tongue entered his mouth. It wasn't overly aggressive, more tentative and sweet.

Chase wrapped his arms around Gary's body, drawing them together firmly. Tiny moans slipped out during their kisses.

At one point Gary drew back to catch his breath. "If I keep going, we'll skip lunch."

Smiling affectionately at him, Chase said, "Let's eat and come back here after."

"I'd like that." Gary released Chase reluctantly. "I'm not trying to rush you though, Chase. I'll go at your pace."

"I appreciate that, Gary, but I'm guessing our pace is the same." He caressed Gary's hair lightly.

Closing his eyes, Gary sighed. "You feel so nice."

"So do you."

Shaking himself out of his dream, Gary turned and opened the front door. "Food."

"Food," Chase agreed happily.

"Do you like Italian?"

"I do." Chase locked the door behind them and pocketed the key.

"Good."

Climbing into Gary's Hummer, Chase asked, "Is this machine killing you on gas?"

"Yes. I don't want to talk about it." Gary grinned impishly. "I love it, so I'm willing to make sacrifices."

"Really?" Chase fastened his seatbelt.

"Pretend it's my pet."

"I get it." Chase winked at him. As they began driving south, he tried to pay attention to the roads and directions. "I'm so new here, I'm still finding my way around."

"This restaurant is right by the Dayton Mall."

"I do know where that is." Chase felt Gary's fingers touch his hand. He clasped it firmly, holding tight.

"Bravo Cucina. Ever hear of it?"

"Yes, I have. They have them all over."

"Ohio is the land of the chain restaurant, get used to it."

"I noticed that. I'm so spoiled from the delights the Big Apple has to offer, I'm a terrible snob."

"I know. Even I get sick of the mediocre fare. And I don't consider myself a gourmet."

"Do you cook?" Chase enjoyed Gary's profile as he drove.

When he stopped at a traffic signal, Gary's light blue eyes met his. "I do. A little. Again, mostly home style recipes from my mom, nothing extravagant. But being a bachelor, I learned to feed myself. I hate eating out all the time."

Allowing Gary to shift gears as the light turned green, Chase gripped his hand again after. "I do as well. At least I try."

Chase had so many questions he wanted to ask Gary. But the last thing he wanted to do was make Gary feel like he was being interviewed.

They pulled up to a brick building with black and white striped awnings. Gary parked his beast in one of the perimeter parking spaces and they climbed out together to walk to the main entrance.

Not holding hands, but brushing shoulders as they went,

Chase knew if he were in Manhattan he would indeed hold Gary's hand. Not here. No way. Besides, he didn't know if Gary was 'out'. It was another unanswered question.

Gary opened the door politely, allowing Chase to enter first. There was a small line in the lobby. After making his way to the hostess, Gary gave her his name and backed up to stand with Chase near a wall, out of everyone's way.

"Smells good." Chase sniffed.

"That's the wood smoked pizza."

"My stomach is growling." Chase rubbed his belly. Seeing Gary staring at him, he asked, "Am I embarrassing you?"

"What? Are you kidding me?"

Out of the corner of his mouth, Chase asked, "Are you out?"

"No." The smile fell from Gary's lips.

Chase nodded in understanding. They kept silent as they waited. It was tightly packed in the small area and they could easily be overheard.

Ten minutes later they were led to a table near the window. Chase thanked the hostess for the menu and had a seat. "Looks good. What do you usually get?"

"I love the Sicilian pizza."

"Want to split it with a side salad?"

"Perfect." Gary set the menu down. "Do you want a beer?"

"Are you getting one?" Chase didn't usually have alcohol for lunch.

Gary leaned across the table and asked playfully, "Are you?"

"I will if you will." Chase enjoyed the game.

"And I will if you will." Gary licked his lips hungrily.

The waiter appeared at their table. "Can I get you anything to drink?"

Both Gary and Chase moved backwards, away from each other as if their posture alone would give away they were gay. "I'd like a Peroni, please." Chase made the choice for them, ordering Italian beer.

"The same." Gary grinned.

"Do you need extra time to decide on the food?" the waiter asked.

"Nope. We've got that as well." Chase pointed to the item on the menu. "We'll split the Sicilian pizza. And I'll have a side Caesar."

"Side Caesar," Gary echoed, handing off his menu to the man.

"Very good." The waiter took both menus and left.

When they were alone, Chase wanted to grab Gary's hands, look deeply into his baby blues and croon, "I adore you." *Silly me!*

"I have so many things I want to know about you," Chase said shyly, "but I don't want to hammer you with questions and make you feel like you're on a job interview."

"Hammer away." Gary grinned demonically.

"Augh!" Chase shifted in his seat. "Don't say things like that."

After a chuckle at the comment, Gary shrugged. "Ask me anything you want. I'm flattered you're interested."

"I'm interested," Chase said, "very interested."

"Good." Gary's leg met his under the table.

Before Chase could begin, their two beers were set in front of them. "Thank you." Chase smiled.

"You're welcome." The waiter poured each into the tall glass.

Once he vanished, Chase sipped the refreshing ale. "Nice."

"It should complement the pepperoni and sausage on the pizza."

"Definitely."

"Where were we?" Gary licked the foamy beer off his lip distracting Chase.

"Uh…"

"You were going to ask me something?"

"I forgot. I got lost on your tongue."

Gary blushed and laughed.

"Never mind. Just tell me about yourself." Chase relaxed in his seat.

After another sip of beer, Gary replied, "There's not too much to tell. I was born and raised in Vale, Oregon. My dad owns a roofing company and he decided to move here after the economy over in Vale dried up in the nineties. Of course it has here now as well. But he's doing all right at the moment. I have traveled quite a lot with the military reserves. I work on the base in between tours."

Drinking his beer as he listened, Chase nodded for Gary to continue.

"I have one brother, Lyle, who is younger. He lives out in California…I enjoy being physically fit. I workout a lot." Gary sipped more beer. "That's really it. Your turn?"

Chase set his glass down, tipping the remainder from the bottle into it. "I was born and bred in New York. Everyone in my family is still there. I have two sisters, both younger. And I left Manhattan because my private practice dried up with the lousy payment policies of HMO's. A friend of mine found the job listing on the net for Wright Pat base. I suppose the idea of helping out the military was my motivation for taking it."

"Good man."

"I want to believe I am. But I worry about everyone in Iraq. Please tell me I heard wrong and you aren't getting called up to go there."

Gary finished his beer, placing the glass down carefully on the small table. "I wish I weren't, but I will be going."

"For how long?"

"Anywhere from three to six months." Gary leaned his elbows on the table.

Chase felt a lump in his throat. *Okay, I only know you a few hours, but I can't lose you. Not yet.* "Gary…" Chase made a tentative move to reach out his hand.

Shaking his head, Gary whispered, "Chase, don't."

Chase retreated, but didn't know if it was the physical action Gary was reproaching or the sentiment, or both.

The waiter appeared with their salads. Once he set them down he asked, "Ground pepper?" holding up a grinder.

Chase shook his head no, losing his appetite.

"No, thank you," Gary replied, smiling. The minute the waiter left, Gary's smile dropped. "Chase."

Chase met his eyes.

"Don't end this before it begins."

"It's the furthest thing from my mind."

"Good. Look. I'm not gone yet."

Hating how his mind began to think of Gary 'gone' as in 'killed in action', Chase actually felt emotional.

"Let's just have fun and take it a day at a time. Okay?"

"Yes. Okay, Gary. I'm sorry."

"I'm not." Gary grinned sensually. "If you're upset about me leaving, you must feel something for me."

"I do. I feel very strongly for you already."

"Great!" Gary ate a bite of his food. "The salad is excellent. Try it."

Remembering he had a meal to eat, Chase tasted a romaine leaf and nodded. "Very good."

Another silent moment passed while they ate. Gary finally broke the quiet by saying, "The feeling is very mutual, Chase. I can't believe how attracted I am to you."

Chase set his fork down and struggled not to reach for him. His hands ended up clenching in frustration. "If this was New York I'd already have leaned over the table and kissed you."

"It ain't New York." Gary laughed.

"I want us to take advantage of the time you have. If you're agreeable to that."

"I am." Gary ate another bite of his salad.

"But I don't want to smother you. You know."

"Smother me, baby."

Seeing that impish twinkle in Gary's blue eyes, Chase had to laugh. "Man, am I going to enjoy you."

"Same here."

"So…uh…you won't think I'm too forward when we get back to my place and I attack you?"

"Nope." Gary wiped his lip with his cloth napkin. "Can't wait."

Chase shifted in his chair as his cock stiffened. He couldn't remember the last time he fell this hard for someone, and was having tiny panic attacks he had managed to do it with a staff sergeant who was about to go to Iraq.

Keeping his fears inside, Chase had to have faith. Though he wasn't religious, he had to believe in something now. Because if anything happened to Gary Wilson, he'd be devastated.

CHAPTER 5

Before the door even closed, Gary attached himself to Chase's lips. Kicking the door to shut it with his foot, Chase embraced Gary and moaned at the intense passion burning between them.

A 'woof!' was heard from the backyard as Mutley realized daddy was home. As far as Chase was concerned, the dog had water and his dinner could wait.

With their mouths pressed together, Gary asked, "You got to go get Mutley?"

"Later." Chase yanked Gary's shirt from his jeans to feel his skin. He kept them moving towards his bedroom as they sucked at each other's tongues. By the time they reached the stairs to the second floor, both men had removed their shirts.

Stumbling awkwardly one step at a time, Chase wanted to lick Gary's nipples but Gary's mouth was too enticing to move away from. When they hit the top landing, Gary had Chase's jeans open and halfway yanked down his hip.

"Oh God." Chase whimpered as the craving to rub cocks overwhelmed him.

"Where's the bedroom?" Gary panted, his hands digging into Chase's blue jeans.

"That way. There." Chase kept them going in the right direction. The minute the bed came into view, Gary yanked Chase's pants down his thighs. "Augh! Son of a bitch, look at you."

Chase kicked off his shoes and felt a frantic need to be naked. His socks were tossed aside, his jeans and briefs disappeared and now it was Gary's turn.

Spreading wide the material of Gary's jeans, seeing his washboard abs and that delicious treasure trail of hair leading to his pubic patch, Chase was ready to combust.

Lowering Gary's pants, Chase fell to his knees with them, helping Gary step out of everything on his lower half. The minute Gary was nude, Chase took a moment to sit back on his heels and admire him. "Baby, baby…" he sighed filling his sights with Gary's long straight cock and dark brown curling hair. His balls were heavy and hanging wonderfully low between his thighs. "Where do I start?"

Gary combed his fingers through Chase's hair. "Dig in. Call it dessert."

"Better than dessert." Chase rubbed his face into Gary's crotch, inhaling his scent and cologne. After nuzzling his balls, he glanced up at Gary. "Would you rather lie down?"

"Up to you."

"Lie down." Chase stood, waiting for Gary to recline on his bed. He looked nice there. Like he belonged.

Another frustrated 'woof' came from the yard below his window. *Sorry, Mutley. You'll have to wait. Daddy's very busy.*

Chase knelt on the bed and smoothed his fingertips from Gary's neck, down his chest to his belly button. Massaging his lower abdomen affectionately, Chase began kissing where he had touched, making a path downwards to his prize.

Gary shifted on the bed, caressing Chase's hair and whimpering softly as he was attended.

When Chase made it to Gary's erection, he paused, raising it upwards to admire before he consumed it. "Nice dick."

"Thanks."

Closing his eyes, Chase lapped at the head leisurely. Gary let out a low breathy groan. Chase dug his tongue into his slit, yearning that tangy pre-cum. Repositioning so he was relaxing between Gary's thighs, Chase sucked on his balls gently, surprised at just how much he was enjoying Gary and the physical contact between them. It was glorious.

"Chase…wow…"

Chase was glad he was pleasing Gary. It meant something to him on so many levels. Gary was serving his country and should be rewarded. It may not be a medal, but it was important to Chase to give to this man.

Urging Gary's legs apart, Chase lapped at his sack and tickled his tongue towards Gary's rim. Gary released another delightful moan. "Baby, baby...wow!"

Hmm, maybe New Yorkers are better at giving head than mid-westerners. The thought made Chase smile and certainly wouldn't surprise him. After all, New York had Greenwich Village. What the hell did Dayton have? Xenia?

Gary reached to tug on his own cock. It was Chase's sign to get back up and get sucking. Taking that delightful organ out of Gary's hands and into his own, Chase allowed it all the way into his mouth to the base.

Gary howled in pleasure and his hips raised off the bed.

Chase decided he would make Gary come in hopes Gary would let him screw him. They hadn't discussed tops or bottoms. Chase went either way, but he knew some men were one or the other exclusively.

Leaning up so Gary's cock was at a better angle for devouring, Chase held the base in his fingertips and began lapping along the underside of his cock, feeling the ripples and veins of Gary's length as he did.

Gary began vocalizing his pleasure and his body responded with lovely shivers and jerking hips in reflex. "Nice. Very nice."

Good. Come for me, soldier boy.

In the silence of the house, but for the occasional 'woof' of Mutley to remind them he was there, Gary's panting breaths began to quicken, his body started pumping in time with Chase's sucking mouth.

"Yeah. Yeah..." Gary's fists clenched the bedspread under them.

Finally Chase tasted a tiny blast of his pre-cum. He sucked faster and stronger, massaging Gary's balls as he did.

A deep guttural moan accompanied Gary thrusting his hips as he moved upwards more aggressively. Chase knew Gary was there and pushed the tip of his finger into Gary's ass to make sure he got a good one.

Gary's cock began throbbing like mad and Chase tasted his thick spunk on his tongue. *That's it, Staff Sergeant Gary Wilson. Come for me.*

Chase ground his cock into the bed, dying for a good screw. He massaged Gary to prolong his pleasure while he fucked Chase's mouth.

Slowing down, lapping gently at the tip, Chase felt Gary's body relax as he recuperated.

Once Gary's breathing softened, Chase crawled up his body, his own cock dragging along Gary's skin, until Chase was face to face with this military hunk. "Hey, soldier. Come here often?"

After a tired chuckle, Gary replied, "I'm hoping to 'come' here constantly."

Purring loudly, Chase chewed and licked at Gary's coarse jaw, humping Gary's crotch under him.

"What do you want, baby?" Gary caressed Chase's cheek. "Tell me. Anything."

"Can I make love to you?" Chase kissed his lips.

"Yes."

At the affirmation, Chase deepened his kiss, dropping down on top of Gary to embrace him tightly. *Why do I like you so much? This is insane.* The sense that it was mutual gave Chase goose bumps. Did he believe in soul mates? No. Not until today.

Parting from their kiss, Gary whispered, "Where do you want me?"

"Face up. Please." Chase ran kisses all over Gary's chin, cheeks, forehead, eyelids.

"Okay, baby." Gary spread his legs.

Before he went for the lube and condoms, Chase paused to kiss Gary for a long delirious moment. The kissing was top notch in his book. Gary knew how. Many men didn't. They thought they had to swallow another man's face whole and shove their thick tongues down a throat to be passionate. No. Gary's technique was flawless. Soft and assertive without being over-dominating: from just lips mashing to twirling tongues, to combining everything at once. Chase's head was spinning with the connection and he could hardly wait until they were connected somewhere else.

After a breathy gasp at parting from Gary's luscious lips, Chase leaned up to reach inside his nightstand. Yes, he had prepared for this event. Always the optimist, Chase kept things handy, just in case. He just began losing hope of it happening here in Ohio.

It was happening. Yes, indeed.

Kneeling between Gary's knees, Chase rolled the rubber on his cock and when he squeezed some gel into his hand he found Gary smiling at him. "Hello."

"Hello," Gary echoed dreamily.

"How are you feeling, hot stuff?" Chase used two fingers to circle around Gary's rim.

"Good. About to be very good." Gary wriggled and closed his eyes.

Chase dipped in gently. A hiss of air was released through Gary's clenched teeth. "Still good?"

"Mr. Arlington, you just go for it and don't worry."

"That's very kind of you. I've always heard the mid-west had the nicest people."

"Shut up, New Yorker, and fuck me." Gary laughed.

Chase urged his fingers in deeper, relaxing Gary's body. Gary groaned and his legs splayed open limply.

"Lovely. What can I say?" Chase admired him. He withdrew his fingers and pushed Gary's legs backwards so he had access inside that slick hole. Penetrating Gary's body, Chase shivered and closed his eyes. "Yes," he hissed softly, edging deeper.

"That's it, baby," Gary encouraged.

Making his way as far as he could go, until their bodies were pressing tightly, Chase had to control the shivers rushing over him. Not only was the sex fantastic, but Gary was so wonderful, Chase knew this act meant something to both of them. He could tell Gary was the sincere type. The honesty in Gary was broadcasted every time he spoke or touched him.

Chase wasn't the type for casual sex anyway, and sex on a first date was rare for him. Though he had to admit he made the mistake once or twice.

But with the situation he and Gary were in, and Gary possibly called up for action, they had agreed to accelerate the time frame.

Now, deep inside Gary's body, Chase was very glad they did. Chase opened his eyes and began thrusting his hips. Watching Gary's expression, seeing his rising bliss, he felt more confident to quicken his pace. When Gary reached for his own cock, jerking it, Chase felt his body surge. "Ah! Yes! Gary…ahhhfuckinghell!" Chase jammed his cock in hard and deep, feeling his balls tighten up with the climax. Below him Gary was fisting himself frantically and cum spurted out of the tip, spraying Gary's chest.

As he watched Gary milking his cock, Chase continued to jam his hips up and in, licking his lips at the desire he had to continue a long-lasting relationship with this god. He had to have him.

Gently pulling out, Chase caught his breath and waited for Gary to open his eyes, coming back from his own swoon. When they gazed at each other, Chase had a sudden overwhelming sensation to tell Gary he loved him.

Am I insane? Slow the fuck down, Arlington!

"That was fantastic." Gary touched Chase's arm.

"It was." Chase bit his lip on saying more.

"I'm really enjoying you, Chase."

"Same here, Gary."

Gary sat up and cupped Chase's jaw, kissing him tenderly. It was so affectionate it brought tears to his eyes.

"Woof!"

They parted to laugh at each other.

"I think someone wants his dinner," Chase said.

"He has been very patient." Gary's eyes twinkled impishly.

Chase climbed off the bed and held out his hand, hauling Gary up with him so they could clean up in the bathroom.

❧

Once he and Chase were in their jeans and t-shirts, Gary followed Chase down the stairs to the kitchen. Another 'woof' sounded at their progress.

Chase opened the back door and Mutley bounded in excitedly. "I take it someone is starving." Chase opened a closet revealing an enormous bag of Iams lamb and rice dog food.

"Hey, big fella!" Gary roughed up the happy animal while

his master filled a large metal dog bowl. Mutley wriggled around in excitement making yipping sounds of joy, his tail a wagging flurry of fur.

Hearing Chase laugh, Gary peeked up at him. "Yes?"

"Nothing," Chase replied, his back still facing Gary.

When Chase opened the refrigerator and removed an egg, Gary watched curiously. Chase cracked it over the kibble, stirring it around. "Wow, spoil him much?"

"It's good for his coat." Chase picked up the bowl and Mutley went crazy until he set it down for him.

They both stood staring as Mutley wolfed down his meal.

When Gary glanced up, he caught Chase's eyes. The sensuality of his gaze lit Gary on fire instantly. "So, uh…you're a physical therapist?"

"I am."

"You like it?"

"I do."

Gary imagined Chase had the opportunity to touch a lot of men in his career. "How are they treating you on base?"

"Good. I have no complaints."

The dish Mutley was eating out of clanged against the baseboard as he licked it clean.

Smiling as he watched, Gary said, "That didn't take long."

"No. He doesn't mess around when it comes to food."

Gary noticed Chase check the clock on the wall. It was nearing three. "Am I keeping you from something?"

"Hell no. Am I keeping you?"

Grinning, closing the gap between them, Gary wrapped his arm around Chase's narrow waist. "I hope so."

Chase drew Gary to his mouth. As they kissed they rocked side to side. A noise of disapproval made Gary open his eyes. Mutley was sitting up, still licking his chops from his meal, staring at them.

"Jealous?" Chase asked the dog.

Mutley squeaked again, tilting his head.

"I should take him out once more before it gets dark." Chase still had his arms surrounding Gary's hips.

"Does he like to catch a Frisbee or anything?" Gary asked.

"Loves it."

"Let's take him to a park."

Chase met Gary's eyes. "You don't have to do this."

"Why not? I want to."

"You have nothing else you'd rather do on a Sunday afternoon than throw a Frisbee with my dog?"

Squeezing Chase tighter, Gary replied, "No."

After Chase inspected Gary's expression for what Gary interpreted as any sign of a lie, Chase shrugged. "Okay."

Gary pecked Chase's lips lightly and waited as Chase located a leash and the Frisbee.

"Here."

Gary opened his palm up to receive what Chase was trying to hand him. He realized it was a plastic bag. "What's this for?"

"Shit patrol." Chase grinned wickedly.

"That's cruel." Gary tried giving the bag back.

Chase dodged out of his reach, laughing as he and Mutley raced through the house to the front door.

When Gary caught up to them, Chase was still laughing at him. Shaking his head at his antics, he waited as Chase locked up.

"Take my car. No use in getting dog hair all over your pretty Hummer." Chase used a key fob to unlock the doors of his Hyundai. Opening the back, Chase instructed Mutley to get in and sit. The dog did.

"You really have him well trained." Gary reclined on the passenger's seat.

"Took forever to get him to listen." Chase stuck the keys into the ignition after he closed his door and fastened his seatbelt. "He was a stubborn motherfucker until he decided I was boss."

Gary smiled sweetly as Chase started the car and lowered the window for the dog.

"I had to take him to obedience class twice. He failed all the tests the first time. I changed tactics."

"What worked?"

"Food." Chase backed out of his driveway. "The first class was dead set against bargaining with treats. That failed miserably.

Believe me, the way to a dog's brain is through his stomach."

"I suppose they're a lot like men," Gary said.

"They are." Chase reached for Gary's hand.

"Is he neutered?"

"Yes. The pound did it. I prefer it. I don't need him humping everything in sight."

Gary spun around in the seat. Mutley had his face out of the window, his nose twitching, and his tongue eating up the cool breeze. "I had a dog as a kid. My parents always had one. I just thought with being in the air force, I'd be gone too much."

"I hear ya." Chase wrapped his fingers around Gary's thigh and squeezed.

Gary rested his own hand on top of Chase's. He wanted to ask him about what they were doing for dinner, but was that too forward? How much time did he expect Chase to spend with him on their 'first date'? If Gary could make that decision, he'd stay overnight.

"I found a school with a fenced in playfield." Chase drove into a vacant parking lot.

"Would Mutley run away?"

"I just don't want to take the chance around cars. He listens when I call him, but if he sees a squirrel? He's gone." Chase pulled into a space and shut off the car. Mutley was going nuts in the back seat.

"He knows." Gary smiled as he unfastened his seatbelt.

"He's been here before. He's no dummy."

Gary waited while Chase held Mutley's leash. They walked to the playfield together. The minute they were inside the chain linked fence, Chase unleashed the dog. Mutley sprinted off excitedly, looking backwards as he did.

As if it were a well-practiced routine, Chase flung the Frisbee and Mutley caught it while leaping five feet in the air.

"Wow!" Gary was impressed. "He's as athletic as you are."

"Toss it for him."

Seeing the dog bounding back, Gary took the Frisbee out of Mutley's jaws and whipped it as hard as he could. The disk sailed across the finely trimmed lawn and the dog caught up to it, showing off with another spectacular jump into the air.

I'm sunk. I love them both. Gary felt his heart brimming with warmth. Thinking back to early morning and making his own leap of faith, Gary recalled running Chase down to meet him and invite him to play football. He was so glad he did, he couldn't believe his luck. As Mutley alternated between them, handing off the chewed up glow-in-the-dark Frisbee, Gary hoped Chase felt as strongly for him, suspecting he did. But time would tell. Who knew what would happen when he left the country and Chase had the opportunity to play without him.

❦

After an hour, even Mutley seemed too tired to keep going. He lay down on the grass, his tongue hanging out, dripping.

Both Chase and Gary had taken off their t-shirts as they heated up. Yes it was October but it was the warmest one he could recall. It had to be nearing eighty. Insane.

"Is it hot or is it just me?" Chase asked, using his shirt to wipe his sweat.

"It's hot." Gary approached him. "You're hot."

In the vacant schoolyard, Gary touched Chase's exposed nipple.

"Careful. You're liable to get me excited," Chase said.

"Wouldn't that be a shame?" Gary pinched Chase's hard bud teasingly.

"I'll suck your cock right here in the field." Chase growled.

It made Gary laugh.

Chase gave their surroundings a good look before he swung Gary into his arms.

"Uh oh." Gary searched around in paranoia.

"No?"

"No. Sorry." Gary gently backed up.

"Okay." Chase felt hurt but tried to respect Gary's feelings. "I'm sorry."

"I started it. I couldn't resist your damn nips."

Chase checked his watch. "Am I keeping you from anything? I'm starting to feel as if I'm monopolizing your time."

The sweet expression fell from Gary's face. "I can go any time you need me to."

After clenching his fists in frustration, Chase replied, "I don't want you to go anywhere but into my arms again."

The light instantly returned to Gary's eyes.

"You'd tell me if I was being too possessive of your time, wouldn't you, Gary?" It was hell not touching him.

"I would. I consider myself brutally honest, Chase. Believe me. I'd say if I had to go."

"Good." Chase liked that in a man. He wanted to know where he stood. No games. "In that case, come back to my place, let's shower, have some fun, and I'll make us dinner."

"Excellent."

Chase called to his dog, "Let's go, Mutt."

Mutley approached Chase, allowing him to clip on his leash again.

They walked back to Chase's car quietly. Chase wanted Gary to spend the night. *What the heck is going on? We just met this morning? I can't keep him from leaving.*

As he instructed Mutley to get in the back seat, Chase realized why he was being so clingy. Gary was leaving for Iraq. Maybe not tomorrow, maybe not the next day, but he was.

The sense of urgency to get what he could share with him was gnawing at Chase. He'd never been in this position before. It was agony. He felt complete empathy for the wives, husbands, and families of the troops all across the world.

The pain at the idea of separation was bad enough, but the sense that something catastrophic could happen to a loved one was pure torture.

So he had gone from lonely, to anguish in ten seconds flat.

"You okay?" Gary asked once they were seated side by side in the front seat.

Unaware he was showing his emotions, Chase smiled to cover his aching heart. "Yes. I'm fine."

Gary rubbed Chase's thigh in reassurance. Chase had a feeling Gary knew exactly what was inside his head. The guy was way too smart not to.

And who knew? Perhaps Gary had been in this exact place before, leaving a lover behind in the States. What did Chase know about Gary's previous love life? Nothing. He wasn't sure he wanted that information.

The idea of examining his own past failures wasn't pleasant. Leave it alone. The past is past.

"Should we stop for some beer?" Gary asked. "There's a Kroger's on the way."

"Sure. Good idea."

After a few minutes, Chase pulled into the lot of the Kroger's grocery store off Whipp Road.

"Let me run in." Gary released his seatbelt.

Chase tried to hand Gary money, but it was nudged aside.

Watching Gary walk away, Chase felt so sick inside he almost wished he'd never met him.

No. Who am I kidding? I'm crazy about him.

A nose snuffled at his ear. Chase absently reached behind him and pet Mutley's muzzle.

As he lost himself in his daydreams, Gary returned with a grocery bag. Mutley grew excited at his return. A wry smile on Chase's face, Chase knew he wasn't the only one growing attached to this wonderful man. His dog was as well.

After Gary settled into the seat and they were on their way back to Chase's house, Gary held up a package of dog snacks.

"Couldn't resist?" Chase loved it.

"Fake bacon. My family dogs went crazy for this stuff."

"If you don't put it back in the bag, you'll have Mutley on your lap."

The dog was leaning as far over the seat as he could, sniffing.

Gary wrapped his arm around Mutley's neck and laughed at him. "You'll get it. Soon."

And so will you, my handsome friend. Chase gripped Gary's leg and shook it affectionately. "I don't want this day to end."

"Me neither." Gary covered his hand over Chase's.

"Where you been all my life, sergeant?"

"Here. Waiting for you to get sick of the Big Apple and come out to corn country."

Clasping Gary's hand in a death hold, Chase said, "And I am so glad I did."

⁓⁓

They entered the house through the front door. Mutley charged for his water dish and lapped at it thirstily. Chase followed him into the kitchen, tossed his keys down on the table and loaded the beer into the fridge. "You mind if I brush him out? He's a mess from all the leaves in the park."

"Let me."

As Chase set the dog treats Gary had purchased on the table, crushing up the plastic bag, he asked, "You want to brush my dog?"

"Well," Gary drew closer, "I want to make love to his owner, but I would enjoy giving Mutley a good brushing as well."

Chase didn't know how to respond. There was such an intense feeling of devotion between them already, he was mute. He reached into the same closet that Mutley's dog food was in, and handed Gary his grooming brush. "I usually do it on the back patio."

"Yes. I think that's smart." Gary smiled.

The minute Mutley noticed Gary had his brush, he did little circle dances at Gary's feet.

"I take it he likes it."

"Loves it." Chase opened the back door.

"I'll be back."

Watching Mutley bolt out and Gary following, Chase's throat drew tight with emotion. When the phone rang he was so deep inside himself, it scared him. Seeing who it was on the caller ID, Chase said, "Hi, Mom," after he picked it up.

"Hi, sweetie. How's your day going?"

"Great." Chase leaned on the doorframe to see Mutley sitting like a statue as Gary ran the brush through his thick coat. "I met the most amazing man."

Silence followed, and his mother said tentatively, "Does that mean you're not moving home?"

"I don't know what it means. I met him early this morning in the park where Mutley and I run. And he's still with me now. He's out back brushing Mutley. We just played Frisbee."

"What's his name?"

"Gary Wilson. Or should I say, Staff Sergeant Gary Wilson," he boasted.

"A military man?"

"Air Force. He works at the base." Chase watched Gary pulling the hair off the brush before continuing to stroke Mutley's dense fur. "Mom, he's unbelievable."

"I'm happy for you, Chase, and upset at the same time."

"I know. You had your hopes up I'd come back. And believe me, I thought I would."

"But you just met him. It still may not work out."

"Gee, thanks, Mom." He laughed sarcastically.

"You know what I mean."

"I do. But the connection between us is almost scary. I've never fell this hard and this fast before in my life."

"Yes you did. For Brock Hart, remember? That handsome stockbroker?"

Cringing, Chase snarled. "Brock Hart was a self-centered bastard who never returned my calls."

"You mooned over him for weeks."

"I'm going to hang up if you keep talking about him." Chase hated that man. They had a one night sex fling at a club. That was it. He sucked Brock's cock, got his jerked off, and they exchanged cell phone numbers. He always wondered why Brock bothered to give him his info. Brock never answered when he called. "Let me go. I want to cook dinner for Gary."

"Just don't get your hopes up. You just met this man. And if that other fellow, Brock, hurt your feelings, be careful."

"Gary is not Brock Hart. Not even close." Chase was furious his mother had brought that man up.

"I'm just saying—"

"I have to go. Talk to you soon." Chase hung up. He was so enraged he ground his teeth. To rid that horrible memory, Chase made a move to sit with Gary on the patio. At the last minute he remembered he was going to put two of the beers and mugs into the freezer to chill them. Once he had, he opened the back door and felt the evening air finally cooling off the unseasonably warm day.

Mutley wagged but didn't move. Chase could tell he was in heaven.

"Look at all that." Gary gestured to a large pile of fur blowing in the breeze.

"I know. Gets all over the house. It's the one pitfall of owning a dog like him." Chase ran his hand over Mutley's silky black coat.

"Is everything okay?"

"Yes. Why?"

"I heard the phone ring."

"It was my mom."

Gary nodded, continuing to brush Mutley.

"Remind me I stuck two beers into the freezer."

"Okay."

Echoes of his mother's warning still ringing in his ear, Chase scooted closer to Gary so they were attached.

Gary glanced back at him and smiled. "Yes? Horny?"

"More than horny. I mean. This connection I feel for you. It isn't just sex, Gary."

At the comment, Gary's smile dropped. "I know. At least I hoped that it was more."

"I'm not the type for going out every night to pick up men and not call them back."

Once he had knocked the hair out of the brush, Gary turned to face him head on. Mutley lay down at their feet. "What's brought this on? Are you trying to warn me or something? Or asking me if I'm one of those?"

"No." Chase shook his head feeling stupid. "Just something my mother said. Never mind."

"Beware of mothers," Gary replied, "they can put evil thoughts into the hearts of their sons."

That made Chase chuckle. "She means well."

"Don't they all?"

Feeling he owed Gary an explanation since he had made such an odd statement, Chase inhaled deeply and said, "I once had a fling on this cute guy."

After Gary set the brush aside, he gave Chase his undivided

attention.

"It was ages ago. I met him at a go-go bar in Manhattan and he sort of swept me off my feet." He peeked at Gary wondering if this story would completely turn him off. "He was this stunning playboy. You know the type. Gorgeous, rich, snazzy dresser…we had a little casual sex in the men's toilet. I thought it meant something. It didn't mean squat to him. I found out later he was notorious for getting his cock sucked by a different man every night."

Gary let out a blast of air as if the story were annoying him.

Chase almost didn't continue but he had come this far and couldn't leave it as it was. "I did get my hopes up, but of course he never called. I hate guys like that."

"And you think I'm like that?"

"No. Not even close. I just wanted you to know why I had a strange attitude when I got off the phone. My mother decided to remind me about, Mr. Brock Hart."

"Ah." Gary nodded. After a moment to contemplate, he replied, "I had my own version of Mr. Hart."

"Did you?"

"Yes." Gary picked up the tip of Mutley's tail and fluffed up the furry end. Mutley didn't flinch. "I dated an asshole about a year ago. Fucker was going out on me constantly. Lied, cheated…I hate the bastard."

"Christ." Chase rubbed Gary's back in sympathy. "That's worse than what I went through. At least Brock never gave me the impression he wanted anything from me."

"Believe me. Kevin wanted something from me. Just not my heart."

"Kevin?" Chase gestured behind him, as if the Schoolhouse Park was there. "That Kevin?"

His cheeks blushing crimson, Gary whispered, "Yes."

Considering the implications, Chase asked, "Are you over him?"

"Completely."

"You sure? You sound angry."

"And you sound angry about Brock Hart. Are you over him?" Gary asked.

Chase held up his hands in surrender. "Yes. I get it." He rose to his feet. "Let me get us those iced brews."

"Sounds perfect."

When Chase opened the door, Mutley scurried in to lie down again at the threshold between the living room and kitchen.

Gary stood behind Chase as he washed his hands, taking his turn next. Once he had dried them, Chase took the two beers and frosty mugs out of the freezer. "Ice cold."

At Gary's pensive mood, Chase felt badly. Once he poured them both their beers, he sat down next to Gary at the kitchen table. "I'm sorry. I'm nervous about how fast I want our relationship to progress and anxious it won't progress at the same time. I've never felt like this before."

After sipping his beer, Gary met Chase's eye. "I know. I know exactly what you mean as well as why it's happening."

And Chase knew he did. "I can't lose you." Chase bit his lip, not wanting to say what he was saying but unable to stop himself. "I can't let you go before we even get to know each other."

Abruptly Gary set his beer mug down and wrapped his arms around Chase's neck.

Chase crushed him in his embrace. "Why do I feel so strongly about you already, Gary? I feel like I'm sixteen and have a crush."

As Gary feathered kisses along Chase's neck, he said, "Me too. I adore you. You feel so right."

Chase felt like wailing, "Don't go," but he knew Gary had no choice.

"Please," Gary begged, "don't let me leaving bring us down. I don't even have a date to go yet."

"I'm sorry. I'm really sorry." Chase found Gary's lips and kissed them, running his hands through his thick brown hair. "It's just scaring the hell out of me."

"Don't let it. There's nothing to be afraid of."

"Nothing? Over four thousand soldiers have lost—"

Gary put his hand over Chase's mouth. "Please."

Biting his lip on real tears of worry, Chase clung to Gary tightly. "Don't let anything happen to you."

"It won't. It's not the front lines, Chase. It's a military training camp."

Closing his eyes, tasting the skin on Gary's neck, his salty sweat from the earlier game, Chase wasn't comforted. He knew fatalities occurred all over Iraq's 'safe' zones. "Baby…"

As if trying to break the somber mood, Gary leaned back to smile. "Do I get fed dinner or what? I'm famished."

Pulling himself together, Chase nodded. "You do. You relax, sip your beer, and let me get some pasta cooking."

"Perfect." Gary winked at him.

CHAPTER 6

The meal of spaghetti and tomato sauce consumed, the dishes washed and in the drain board, Gary held Chase's hand as he led them up the stairs once more.

"We should shower. The Frisbee throwing left me feeling grimy." Chase drew his shirt over his head.

Gary lost himself on Chase's naked torso for a moment. "Yes." He began to feel as if their time together was some strange dream. From ten this morning to the present, eight hours later, Gary was staring at Chase as he undressed wondering how and why they grew so close so quickly.

Once Chase was nude, he gazed at Gary solemnly.

Gary felt odd, as if he had too many beers and was tipsy. He had two. Hardly enough to give him a head buzz.

"Come here, babe." Chase reached out to him.

Taking the few steps to close the gap between them, Chase helped him remove his clothing. It was as if Chase sensed him feeling helpless when confronted with a desire that was so strong it scared him to death.

With delicate care, Chase assisted Gary in undressing. When they were both naked, Chase held his hand and escorted him to the shower.

Behind them, Mutley settled down on his cozy pillow at the foot of Chase's bed.

In silence Gary waited, oddly detached from his body yet too needy for his liking. Chase urged Gary under the hot spray. It felt delightful to rinse off his salty skin and the dry dusty dirt from the schoolyard. Once he had doused himself, he relinquished the showerhead to Chase.

His senses still feeling somewhat dulled, maybe from a long physical and emotional day, Gary groaned in pleasure as Chase began scrubbing him with a loofa from top to bottom.

"I don't deserve you." He moaned, allowing Chase to control his every move. Gary closed his eyes and his head drooped forward as he was washed front, back, sides, from his face to his feet. Even his hair was shampooed and his genitals were given special attention. It was so relaxing he almost dozed standing up. When the touching ceased, Gary blinked drowsily. Chase was giving himself a quick scrub. Opening his lips, Gary was about to ask if he could return the favor, when Chase shut the taps and stood dripping, smiling adoringly at him.

"You're so good to me." Gary felt his throat tighten.

Chase reached out, wrapped his arms around him and sealed their wet bodies together. Closing his eyes at the flood of sensations, Gary ran his lips over Chase's wet neck, sucking his clean skin gently.

"Come to bed."

Though he was reluctant to release Chase, Gary did. Pausing as if waiting for directions, he allowed Chase once again to take control. He took the towel he was handed and rubbed it over his hair and back. After drying off, Chase reached once more for Gary's hand and brought him to his bed.

As they reclined side by side, Chase stared into his eyes, caressing Gary's wet hair with the tips of his fingers.

With his head resting on his arm across the pillows, Gary stroked Chase's neck to his shoulder, down his arm and hip. He couldn't recall ever sharing a tender moment like this with anyone else.

Like they had an eternity to spend together, they took their time exploring. Gary ran his hand over Chase's semi-erect cock, making it move as he did. When he glanced back at Chase's warm brown eyes, they both leaned forward to meet lips. At the first brush of Chase's mouth, Gary's cock responded. Chase's hand dug behind Gary's head, drawing him deeper, closer.

Gary rolled them to Chase's back, crawling over Chase's body to feel his flesh under him. The kissing accelerated in passion until they were groaning at the longing they felt.

Their clean skin stuck together until slightly sweaty dew began to form between them as they both heated up to flames.

The scent of musky soap, the feel of Chase's large muscular build flexing beneath him was bringing Gary up quickly. He shifted off Chase's hips just so he could get a touch of Chase's dick. It was stiff and pre-cum was pooling at the tip.

Running his thumb over the slick drop on Chase's smooth head, Gary began to squirm with desire. Through their succulent kisses, Gary asked, "Can I make love to you?"

Instantly Chase whimpered, crushing Gary tighter to his body, and spreading his legs.

At the tacit approval Gary went wild for him. He pinned Chase down to the bed by his shoulders and sucked at his mouth, fucking it with his tongue. His legs tensed up between Chase's, Gary humped him hotly, their two cocks rubbing with delightful friction.

Unable to contain his breathing, Gary broke for air, panting, "God! Chase…"

Chase grabbed Gary's jaw strongly, making Gary meet his eyes. "I want you in me."

Gary shivered from the power of that sentence. It made him mute from emotion. When Chase's eyes darted to the night table, Gary noticed the items from earlier still within reach. The attraction he had for Chase was overwhelming him. Before Gary went for the condom, he gripped Chase's face in the same way as Chase had gripped his and kissed him again, growling sensually with his craving and growing love.

Chase wrapped his legs around Gary's hips, locking his ankles together. They rocked on the bed, going mad for each other, touching everywhere, sucking at each other's mouths.

Gary was ready to burst. He was so keyed up from Chase's feel, taste, scent…

Breaking out of Chase's grip roughly, Gary grabbed a condom and tore it open with his teeth.

At the act, Chase's legs dropped to the bed in a wide straddle, his knees bent tightly to his body.

Shaking from the yearning and fatigue from the long physical day, Gary squeezed some gel on his fingers and stared directly into Chase's brown eyes as he went for his rim.

Chase inhaled sharply and his hips jerked in reflex.

As Gary drove his fingers inside that tight hole, he was grinding his jaw, dying to get them connected this way. Massaging Chase's prostate from inside, Gary felt him tense up and Chase's eyes sealed shut as he groaned, "Ahhh."

Chase's reaction almost made Gary spurt. Quickly he replaced his fingers with his prick. He was so hard he knew it would take nothing to make him come. Without hesitation he burrowed balls deep. Once he was up to the hilt, Gary moaned in soul-wrenching pleasure. "Chase…God…Chase!"

"Gar—" Chase couldn't even manage to finish his word when he began thrusting upwards, his cock spurting cum all over his chest in creamy white blobs.

The wicked, sexy surge of pleasure that shot through Gary almost made him pass out. At the sight of Chase's orgasm, knowing it must have been intense, Gary let go. Jamming his hips as far as he could into Chase's body, Gary felt his balls squirm with the pleasure and his cock throb madly inside the tight heat. All he could manage to do was grunt and choke at the sensation it was so strong.

In what felt like suspended animation Gary and Chase stayed completely still. Deep inside Chase, Gary's cock gave a few last pulsating blasts, but his hips weren't moving any longer. A drop of sweat rolled down Gary's nose. When he opened his eyes he noticed it had hit Chase's washboard belly. Raising his gaze to Chase's face, he melted at the sight.

Chase's head was thrust back into the pillows, his eyes sealed shut and he was biting his top lip. The image of pure bliss.

Slowly coming back to life, Gary began backing out of Chase's body. Holding the lip of the condom, Gary sat on his heels and caught his breath, gazing at this muscular god on the bed beneath him.

When Chase didn't open his eyes, but instead covered his face with both his hands, Gary grew concerned. "Chase? What's wrong?"

His expression still concealed, Chase only shook his head in reply.

Dragging the rubber off his limp cock, dropping it on top of the wrapper on the nightstand, Gary dove on top of Chase and gripped him as tightly as he could. "We'll be okay. Please. You have to stop worrying."

Chase finally revealed his face only to hold onto Gary just as tightly as Gary was holding him. Gary could see two rivers of tears running down Chase's cheeks and died inside.

"Baby, don't." Gary had no idea how they had become so attached so quickly. It was madness.

"I'm sorry," Chase cried, "I don't know what's come over me. I'm never like this."

Gary knew exactly what it was. And there was nothing he could do about it.

≈≈≈

Once they had washed up and made sure all the lights were off and the doors were locked, Chase set the alarm and cuddled with Gary under the covers. Chase caressed Gary's hair soothingly as he rested his head on the nook between Chase's shoulder and chest. Kissing Gary's forehead, Chase nestled against him loving the warmth of his body and the sense of being completely sated and exhausted.

They hadn't spoken any more about their feelings. What was there to say? More words would bring more discomfort and pain. Chase had to stop feeling dread. Gary would be fine. He'd do his time in Iraq, come home and resume his duties at the airbase. Nothing to worry about.

Feeling Gary's breath deepen as sleep finally caught up to him, Chase was both thrilled and petrified he had fallen so hard and so fast for this amazing man. He had to stop dreading the unknown. It wasn't helping either of them.

"Goodnight, lover," Chase whispered, knowing Gary was already asleep. "I will watch over you while you sleep."

Drawing Gary closer, Chase closed his eyes and tried to drift off.

CHAPTER 7

The next morning over coffee, they were quiet. Gary didn't know what to say. Though perhaps Chase needed more reassurance, when one was in the military, even constant mutterings about how things will be all right, sounded slightly trite after a while, even condescending.

Chase cleared the table of the remnants of toast and jam. Mutley was outside in the yard, ready for his long day on his own.

Sipping his coffee, Gary felt Chase's caress on the nape of his neck. He raised his eyes to meet Chase's, giving him a smile.

"What time do you get out of work?" Chase asked, setting the plates and silverware in the sink.

"Five."

"The clinic closes at four-thirty, but I leave around five as well." Chase leaned back against the counter.

"Do you want to get together later?" Gary felt nervous to ask. Was that clingy?

"I do if you do."

Seeing Chase's wry smile, Gary teased, "I do if you do."

"I do! I do!" Chase leaned over to hug Gary around the neck from behind.

"Good. I should stop home for clean clothing and to check the mail."

"Of course." Chase kissed his hair and moved around the table so they could catch eyes. "Are we crazy?"

"I hope so." Gary finished his coffee.

"No. I mean—"

"I know what you mean, Chase." Gary rose up to set his mug

in the sink. He ran the water and began washing the few items that were collected there. Feeling Chase's warm hands surround him and the bulging crotch press into his ass, Gary smiled contentedly.

"You'd make a good wife." Chase purred playfully.

"I thought that last night about you after the nice dinner." Gary balanced a wet plate on the drain board. As Chase began chewing on his neck behind his ear, Gary covered in chills. "You're giving me a hard-on."

Laughing, Chase rubbed his along Gary's ass.

"I know." Gary shut the water and reached for the dishtowel. "You think I can't feel that big dick knocking at my back door?"

Chase smoothed his hands down to Gary's crotch and rubbed it hotly. "Wish we had time."

"We will later. Promise." Gary made a move to spin around. When he did, Gary kissed him, knowing the time was getting tight. Gary parted from the kiss and whispered, "I'll come by later, after I stop home."

"Okay." Chase stepped back, allowing Gary the freedom to move.

Gary gave Chase's bulge a good squeeze before he headed to the door.

"See you later?"

"See ya." Gary pecked his lips and left. Looking back, seeing Chase waving, he waved and climbed into his Hummer.

Too bad they'd never see one another on base. He'd have no reason to go to the occupational therapy unit unless he was injured, and Chase didn't have any reason to mix with military personnel. But just knowing Chase was nearby was enough to put a smile on Gary's face.

❧❧

Once Gary had left, Chase rushed around making sure everything was secure and off so he could go. He peeked out at Mutley and found him chewing an enormous rawhide bone he had just given him. Grabbing his keys, Chase left for work, the memory of Gary's body and scent washing over him like lightning.

❧❧

Chase helped an older gentleman off the examination table. "I suggest you use the cane until you feel completely confident about putting pressure on that leg." Chase handed him the cane that had been propped up beside him.

"Yes. I do feel I need it. Just for a little more time."

"Don't push yourself anymore than necessary. Are you in pain?" Chase felt his phone vibrate in his pocket and ignored it for the moment.

"Not too much. Only if I put too much pressure on it for long periods of time."

With his hand on the man's arm, Chase escorted him to the door of the clinic. "Take it slow, Mr. Jenson. There's no reason to get anxious and end up hurting yourself more than you already have."

"I agree, young man."

Chase watched Mr. Jenson walk out of the room for a moment before he took his phone out of his trouser pocket. Checking the missed message he found a text from Gary in delight.

"Miss me?"

Their first love note. Chase felt a flush of boiling heat wash over him. Texting back, Chase replied, *"Like mad. Counting the hours."* He hit send, his heart pounding in excitement.

"Mr. Arlington?"

Chase looked up at the receptionist.

"Your next appointment is here." She gestured to another patient staring at him as he sat in the waiting area.

Dropping his phone back into his pocket, Chase smiled and waved at the gentleman as Chase walked to the receptionist for the man's file. Reading his name, Chase greeted him, "Mr. Smith. Come on back. I'm ready for you."

≈≈

Gary read the reply and chuckled in excitement. He was on a break between meetings and leaning against the wall in the hall in his army fatigues. After glancing up and down the empty corridor, Gary held out the camera lens of the phone and took a photo of himself. Checking it out before he sent it, he knew Chase would get a kick out of seeing him in his uniform. Laughing wickedly under his breath, he sent it, adding another text with it, "*Into erotic fantasies?*"

"That'll get you going," Gary muttered.

A colleague patted him on the back in greeting. "Hello, Staff Sergeant Wilson."

"Sir," Gary replied, slipping the phone back into his pocket.

"You look well. Things going good with you?"

"Very good, Jim."

"I hear the orders are coming down soon."

Gary tried not to express his regret. "Yes. I heard the same. Any idea of a time frame?"

"Only a vague reference to November through February."

"Christmas." Gary bit his lip in annoyance.

"Someone's got to go."

"Yes, sir." Gary tried to smile as the man walked into the meeting room. Watching Jim take his seat at the oblong table, Gary wished his timing could be a little more favorable to his social life. But it never was a concern of the armed forces. The military came first, period.

∽∾

A response to his text vibrating in his pocket, Chase forced himself to concentrate on his patient and behave in a professional manner.

Inside he felt like a little kid wanting to giggle and dash off to a corner to read his mail.

"It says here in your chart that you pulled your back out doing some lifting." Chase waited for a response.

"Yes."

"Fine. Can you describe to me what you did and where it hurts?" Biting his lip, trying to listen, Chase nodded politely and pretended he had all the time in the world.

A half hour later, the patient finally gone, Chase anxiously took his phone out of his pocket and pushed the tiny keys to get what he had missed. "Ah!" Seeing his new lover in his army fatigues sent his cock upright. "Erotic fantasies?" Chase peered around the area before he dashed to the staff men's room. Dialing as he went, he paused to check it was vacant and took one last look at the photo before he put the phone to his ear.

Gary's voicemail picked up. After the robotic voice, Chase left his own sensual message. "You hot motherfucker. Bring that set of army fatigues home. You want an erotic fantasy? I'll give you one. You're already mine."

He hung up, panting as he stood near the sink. "Fuck!" he stared at the photo again. The expression of seduction on Gary's face was too much to bear. "I need to fricken jack off." But there was no way Chase was going to do it.

Forcing himself to stop gawking at that amazing picture, he returned the phone to his pocket, feeling as if it were a hot coal and burning his skin through the material.

Before he headed back to his patients, he stood at the sink and splashed his face, trying to get under control. *I cannot believe how much I adore you, Gary. My God. I'm going insane. Absolutely insane thinking about you.*

Chase had to force himself to get through the day. The image of Gary waiting for him near his bed in his army uniform was going to keep him on edge for the next six long hours.

Drying his hands on paper towels, making sure he looked presentable, Chase exited the men's room and made his way to the reception desk. He took the new folder and read the name. Seeing a young man in the same outfit his lover had just teased him with, Chase forced himself to keep his features straight. "Ron? Right this way."

"Thank you, sir." Ron had his hat in his hand.

As Ron walked by him and into the rehab clinic, Chase tried not to imagine his lover in those camouflage trousers or he'd have an irrepressible urge to grab this soldier's ass.

❧

Sitting in his Hummer after an exasperating day apart from his partner, Gary caught up on the messages and texts he'd missed. Switching from listening to the voicemail, to reading the typed words, he was roaring with laughter. They had successfully teased each other all day.

More than willing to fulfill Chase's request, Gary was still in his ABU's, Airman Battle Uniform. "You're so easy to please, Arlington." He started the Hummer and headed home to check on his mail and get clean clothing.

Chuckling to himself as he did, he kept remembering Chase's suggestive text messages about wanting to be dominated. "You will play submissive, babe. Yes, you will."

Parking in his condo space, Gary stopped at the mailboxes and opened his with his key. Taking out the stack of bills and fliers, he tucked it under his arm and headed up one flight to his unit. Once inside, he tossed the mail on a counter and walked directly to his answering machine, hitting play.

"Hello, Gary, it's Mom. Just calling to say hello. Any plans to stop by and see us over the weekend? Call me."

He waited for the next message. It was from Sam Rhodes. *"Hey, Gar, any luck with Chase? Did you guys hang out at all? Dev and I were wondering if he was going to show up next weekend for our game. That's it. Hope things are good on the base. See ya."*

One unheard message was left.

"Gar."

Gary stiffened at the voice.

"It's me. Look…uh, I know after the bad time we had you most likely don't want to see me. But after hanging around with you playing football—"

Gary deleted it before Kevin had even finished talking. "Fuck you, dipshit." He picked up the phone as he found his backpack. "Sam?"

"Gary!"

"Hey, I got your message. Yes, things are going well with Chase."

"Excellent!"

"We spent all day and night together. What a guy, Sam, what a guy." Gary tucked fresh clothing into the pack.

"He seemed like it. You know. Really genuine."

"He is. I can't believe how well we've hit it off."

"I'm really happy for you, Gar. Honest."

"I'm heading over to his place now. I just stopped home to

get a few things."

"Nice! Well, he's adorable."

"Don't I know!" Gary laughed, poking his head into the bathroom to see what he needed to bring to Chase's place.

"Uh, Gar?"

"Hm?" Gary stuffed his toothbrush into the front zipper part of his backpack.

"Kevin was going a little crazy after you walked off the playfield with Chase."

Instantly Gary was boiling mad. "He just left a fucking message on my machine, Sam. I don't want anything to do with the guy."

"He's insanely jealous."

"Tough. You know what he did to me. I don't even need him calling me." Gary paused, too angry to continue packing at the moment.

"I know. I told Kevin that. He messed you up pretty bad. He said he was sorry. But to be honest Gar, you're better off with Chase."

Choking at the absurdity, Gary replied, "Even if I didn't have Chase in my life I'd never go back to Kevin again."

"No. I think he knows that."

"Then he shouldn't be calling here." Gary checked the time. "Look, Sam, let me go. I have to get to Chase's place."

"Okay. Have fun! Oh, call me and Dev if you two can pry yourselves out of the bedroom long enough to grab a beer."

His good mood returning, Gary laughed. "You got it."

"Bye, Gar."

"See ya." He hung up and finished what he was doing. As he closed and locked the front door, tossing his pack into the back seat of his Hummer, he took out his mobile phone.

"Hello?"

"Mom?"

"Hello, Gary."

"I just got your message. I'm not sure about this weekend. Can I let you know?" He backed out of his driveway.

"Yes. Of course. Did you meet someone? Or just going out

with the boys?"

Biting his lip, wishing he had the guts to come out to his parents, Gary lied, "Just hanging with the guys."

"Okay, sweetie. If you change your mind and want to stop by for dinner, let us know."

"Okay, Mom. See ya." He hung up, tossed the phone on the seat beside him and tried to get back on track for his evening with Chase.

≈≈

Rushing to get everything done before Gary arrived, Chase had breaded chicken cutlets, roasted potatoes in the oven and asparagus ready to steam on the stovetop.

He lit two tapered candles and blew out the match while adjusting the place settings to perfect symmetry. It was a little anal but he liked to impress his men. Tossing out the burnt matchstick, Chase spotted Mutley on his haunches watching him, his nose twitching at all the cooking smells. "I assume you'll be on your best behavior." He pointed at the dog. "One of us has to be."

When the doorbell rang, Chase went running only to be beaten in the race by Mutley.

Pausing, smoothing back his hair nervously, Chase made his face a mask of calm and opened the door. When he found Gary in his army fatigues he almost fell over. "No!"

"Yes!" Gary laughed.

Mutley whimpered and pawed at the screen door.

"Are you going to let me in? Or do I stand on your porch all night while you gawk at me?"

Chase woke up from his daydream and fumbled to open the door.

"Hello, big boy!" Gary fed Mutley a milk bone he had brought for him from the pocket of his camouflage trousers.

Chase stepped backwards to give Gary space to enter the living room.

"It smells good in here. Did you cook again?"

Seeing Gary in all his staff sergeant glory, the patch on his sleeve of a five-point star in a circle with four black, and three white stripes extended on either side like wings, Chase was in awe.

Once Gary had greeted Mutley, he focused back on Chase. Chuckling, Gary asked, "You're really that smitten with my ABU's?"

"Huh?" Chase didn't hear a word he said. In his fantasies, he was already playing submissive to this powerful sergeant.

"Hello? Chase to Earth?" Gary waved his hand in front of Chase's face.

Blinking, Chase sighed. "I think I love you." It was half a joke, and half not.

Gary just laughed nervously. "Wow. If I'd have known you would have that reaction, I'd have worn them for you all day yesterday."

Chase rushed to embrace him, squeezing him tight. Yes, the uniform was sexy, but it was also a grim reminder.

"All right." Gary patted Chase's back. "Don't get mushy on me."

Leaning back to stare into Gary's beautiful baby blues, Chase smiled sweetly. "You're my ultimate fantasy."

"I know! Those text and voicemail messages…geez, Chase, I was going crazy."

"You? All right. Enough sex talk. We have a dinner to consume." Chase held his hand and brought him to the kitchen. "Beer or wine?"

"What kind of wine do you have?" Gary took off his hat and stuffed it into his pocket.

Chase reached into the fridge and pulled out a bottle. "This."

"Okay."

"Sit. Relax."

Pouring them both a glass of rose', Chase handed one to Gary and placed a second one near his own plate. "Mutley, sit and leave Gary alone."

"It's okay." Gary sipped the wine.

"No. Go." Chase pointed. Mutley looked dejected and dropped down in his spot between rooms.

"What did you make?" Gary balanced the stemmed glass on the table.

"Chicken cutlets, potatoes and asparagus." He started the burner under the asparagus to get it steaming. "Is that okay?"

"More than okay," Gary replied, rubbing his hands together.

Chase could not get over the power that uniform gave to an already forceful man. It was an aura of the most alluring kind. "You really are a gay man's fantasy."

Gary blushed, smiling modestly.

The urge to get on his knees between Staff Sergeant Wilson's legs and yank down the zipper of his 'ABUs' was slightly overwhelming. Instead, Chase reached for his wine and downed it in one gulp.

Avoiding Gary's intense stare, Chase busied himself with dinner. Using a potholder he removed the chicken and potatoes, setting them on the stove top, then poked the asparagus to see if it was tender.

"You okay?"

Deflating as he stood over the meal, Chase said, "Stop being so smart."

"I thought it would turn you on. I'm getting the feeling its upsetting you." Gary shifted to get to his feet. "Let me change."

"Don't you dare," Chase warned him, pointing his oven mitt his way. "Sit!"

Mutley made a noise as if he thought he was being yelled at.

"Not you. Him," Chase clarified.

Gary just started laughing.

After portioning out the food, Chase placed the plate before his heartthrob, sitting across from him, refilling both their wine glasses.

"You're spoiling me." Gary gave Chase a sexually smoldering glance that sent his pulse racing.

"Good. I want to spoil you." Chase cut a piece of his chicken waiting for Gary to taste it before he ate his.

"Delicious." Gary smiled as he chewed.

"Enjoy."

"I will. Believe me." Gary crooned wickedly.

"I meant the meal."

"I didn't."

Chase grinned back in invitation.

"Did you mean what you said in your text and voicemail messages?"

"I did." Chase took another sip of wine.

"You dirty dog."

"Me?" Chase feigned innocence.

"Yeah, you." Gary continued eating, making short work of the meal and wine.

"There's only one dirty dog in this house." Chase chuckled.

"That's where you're wrong."

Pausing mid-bite, Chase caught one of the most sensuous expressions he'd ever seen on a man, particularly one in uniform. His cock was so hard, it was pressing painfully against his zipper and needed to be adjusted. He just wasn't sure he wanted to show Gary how excited he was. And groping your own cock during dinner seemed a tad crude. He continued to eat calmly while it appeared as if he and Gary were having a staring contest.

Gary finished his last bite, last sip of wine and tossed his napkin down as if it was a signal. The red cape to a bull.

Chase gobbled his final mouthfuls, gulped his wine and imitated the throwing down of the napkin.

Like a dare, Gary rose up, leaning on the table with both hands. Chase heard himself gulp audibly.

After cupping each wick, Gary blew out the candles. "Leave the dishes."

"Mutley will climb on the table after them." Chase wanted to leave the dishes as well.

Quickly stacking the plates and silverware, Gary set everything 'lick-worthy' into the stainless steel basin. "Get over here now."

A direct order from a sergeant was not to be ignored. Chase scrambled to his feet to obey. Clutching Gary's outstretched hand, Chase was guided to climb the stairs first, both of Gary's hands on his shoulders from behind. Chase's breathing began to escalate and his excitement was piqued as they drew closer to the bedroom.

Out of the corner of his eye, Chase noticed Mutley curl up on his dog bed. Regarding it only for a moment, Chase's attention returned instantly to the soldier in the room. Gary began opening the buttons of Chase's shirt. There was no way to stop his chest from heaving like he'd just run cross-country. Chase was in serious heat.

His shirt was tossed onto a chair. Gary leaned down to remove Chase's shoes and socks. All Chase could do was pant and watch, as if he were the voyeur and not a participant.

Next, Chase's slacks were slid down his thighs with his briefs. Standing stark naked next to this American soldier was making Chase weak in the knees. The tough New Yorker wasn't so tough anymore.

"Get on your hands and knees on the bed."

The urge to salute and scream, 'Yes sir!' was overwhelming. He resisted the temptation. Chase crawled from the foot of the bed up, pausing in the middle. When those rough warm palms circled around the globes of his ass cheeks, Chase melted to a puddle on the bed. His bottom was spread and Gary's tongue began lapping at his ring. He couldn't prevent the shivers of excitement. His entire body was shaking.

One of Gary's hands tugged on Chase's balls as they hung heavily between his thighs. Chase peered down at himself. His cock was so engorged it was nearly purple. "I need a fucking mirror," he said quietly.

"What?"

"I said," Chase enunciated, "I wish I had a mirror so I could see you."

Gary grabbed Chase's knees and flipped him over to his back. The movement surprised Chase. He stared at Gary in awe.

"Can you see me now?" Gary grinned wickedly.

"Yes. Thank you."

"You're welcome." Gary pressed Chase's thighs wider, pinning his legs to the bed, making his cock stand out like a pole from his crotch.

The bed shifted with Gary's weight as he knelt between Chase's feet. When Gary began running kisses inside his thighs, it sent Chase into a tailspin.

Using his teeth, Gary chewed his way towards Chase's balls enveloping them into his mouth when he arrived. A long sticky drop began running from the tip of his dick, hovering over his low abdomen like a thread of silk.

Chase spread his arms out, reaching for the edges of the bed, giving total submission to this military hunk.

Gary forced Chase's leg backwards, getting another chance to lap at his ass. It was pushing Chase very close to a climax. Closing his eyes for a moment to calm himself, when he opened them to see this uniformed staff sergeant going down on him, Chase decided he couldn't be calm. No way. Finally after a long moment of silence, he whimpered. "Gary…"

Gary perked up, his face appearing from between Chase's legs.

Chase didn't want him to stop, maybe he was just warning him he was about to pop.

It was then Gary seemed to notice the thread of pre-cum that connected a sticky line of liquid from Chase's slit to his treasure trail. Immediately Gary raised Chase's dick to his mouth to suck on it, next, licking the spot on his stomach where it had pooled.

"Jesus!" Chase squirmed in agony.

Wiping his mouth with a masculine swipe, Gary unzipped his fatigues and exposed his dick. Just the sight of that big cock hanging out of those air force clothes was enough. Chase pinched the base of his prick to stop the cum from shooting out.

Trembling, as if he too was near the edge of exploding, Gary rolled on a condom and applied lube liberally to his cock.

"If you stick your finger up my ass, Gary, I'm a goner." Chase breathed in gasps.

"Okay, babe. I'm ready. Let's find our way to heaven."

Nodding, releasing his cock, Chase felt the head of Gary's dick knocking at his back door. As it made its way deeper, he raised his hips to meet it. The pressure on his prostate was making him dizzy. After one deep quick thrust of Gary's hips, Chase moaned, "Ahhfuck…" and came, blowing spunk all over his own chest.

One, two, three more quick pelvic thrusts, and Gary joined him, choking out a deep grunting sound and grinding hard against Chase's body as he came.

Catching their breaths, dewy with sweat, Chase heard Gary chuckle softly, so he opened his weary eyes.

With his big brown lashes blinking innocently, Mutley had his head resting on the bed beside them.

"You watching us, ya perve?" Chase scolded him.

Gary rolled off Chase, holding his gut as he roared with amusement.

"Go lay down." Chase pointed to Mutley's pillow on the floor. "Or you'll be locked outside the room next time."

Mutley slunk back to his bed, dropping down with a groan of annoyance.

Leaning up on his arms to see Gary's reaction, Chase smiled as Gary struggled to contain his laughter.

All Chase could do was shake his head in wonder.

Once Gary calmed down, he stood looking at down himself as he pulled off the spent condom.

"You're amazing," Chase whispered, joining him in the bathroom to get cleaned up.

After he tossed the condom in the trash, Gary wrapped around Chase with his uniform-covered sleeves and kissed him. As they rocked together in an embrace, Chase knew he loved this man. *Who cares if I only know him a day? Fuck everyone if they can't take a joke.*

Naked under the blankets, Gary tucked his arm behind Chase's neck and cuddled him close. It wasn't late, barely eight o'clock, but the idea of not being naked and in bed wasn't appealing. There was a dim streetlight outside the house that lit the ceiling with an elongated rectangular pattern. He gazed at it lazily. The days had begun shortening and soon clocks would change making the evenings even more dreary and dark.

"You up?"

Gary perked up to Chase's voice. "Yes." As Chase shifted to face him, Gary tilted his head on the pillow to meet his gaze.

"Penny for your thoughts?"

Gary smiled. "I'm thinking of you."

Obviously pleased with the reply, Chase kissed Gary's chest. "Are you happy with this arrangement?"

"I am." Gary caressed Chase's hair back from his forehead. "Will you be hanging out here after work all week?"

"Is that what you want?"

"Yes."

The conviction with which Chase answered made Gary tingle. "Good."

"Am I being a possessive girlfriend?" Chase smiled wryly.

To tease him, Gary said, "Yes, a regular bimbo. So lay off."

Getting the jibe, Chase roughed him up, shaking him playfully. "I'm serious, Gary. Am I asking too much of you too soon?"

"No. Like I've told you. If I was uncomfortable with it, I'd tell you."

"I respect that in a man."

"So do I. And I expect the same from you. If this is too heavy, we can slow down."

"No."

Gary stared critically into Chase's eyes. "You feel that sure?"

"Yes. Not even a doubt in my mind."

His eyes were drawn back to the pattern on the ceiling as he thought about it.

Chase climbed on top of Gary, leaning up on his elbows so they could still chat. "What about you?"

Shaking his head, Gary echoed, "Not a doubt in my mind."

"How could that be? Why are we so sure about each other?"

"I wish I could answer that question."

"Have you felt this way about anyone before?"

Instantly Gary thought of Kevin.

In the pause, Chase whispered, "You don't have to answer that."

"No. It's okay. I'm just thinking about it." Gary smoothed his hands along both of Chase's shoulders. "I've really liked someone before, but I've never felt confident it was requited. Does that make sense?"

"Perfect." Chase pecked his lips, setting back to stare again. "Are you close with your family?"

"Yes."

"Do they—"

"No." Gary cut off the obvious next question.

"None of them? Not even your younger brother?"

"No." A slight uneasiness slipped into Gary's gut.

"My whole family knows." Chase put his weight on one arm so he could caress Gary's cheek. "I just told them during a family dinner a few years ago. I couldn't take it, sneaking around, making excuses all the time as to why I never brought a woman to meet them."

Gary's mouth tightened across his teeth. *No way. Not with my parents. That's not going to happen.*

"Do you ever think about it?"

"No." Gary averted his gaze. "They're not the type to accept it."

"Why? Right wing? Religious?"

"Both."

Chase nodded.

"Change the subject." Gary nudged Chase to lie next to him.

"Wow. That sore of a topic?"

"Yes. Seriously, Chase, there's no point discussing it."

"What do they think about you serving in Iraq?"

"They couldn't be prouder."

"So, it's okay if their son comes home in a box, but not if he loves a man."

"Chase!" Gary jerked back from his touch.

"Sorry, Gary, that was way out of line. Please. I'm sorry." Chase gripped onto Gary tightly.

After a moment to calm down, Gary relaxed onto the pillows again. "Believe me. My mom worries about me coming home 'in a box'. But she respects my decision and doesn't nag me about it."

"Like I am?"

Gary connected to Chase's dark eyes. "Like you're beginning to." Instantly Chase's expression appeared conflicted. He was obviously anxious about their separation. Gary stroked Chase's face gently. "Do you regret meeting me now?"

Shaking his head emphatically, Chase said, "No. No way."

Gary stared at Chase's expression, struggling to read it in the bad lighting. He heard Mutley shifting on his pillow-bed, letting out a long exhale.

"Gary…"

"What, babe?" Gary dug his fingers into Chase's hair behind his ear.

Another silent moment past. Gary tried to be patient.

"I'm falling in love with you."

A flash of fire ignited inside Gary's body. Cupping Chase's jaw he drew him to his mouth. At the feel and taste of Chase's lips, Gary knew he was in love too. Why? Why did it happen this way? So quickly? Were they both that lonely and desperate that they latched onto the nearest warm body? Or was this truly as it seemed–a match made in heaven? He had no idea and wondered if it mattered.

Their soft kisses became superheated magma. Gary's body began to stir awake after its soft relaxed state. Chase's hand found Gary's crotch and kneaded his genitals causing Gary's cock to harden. Loving Chase's tongue, Gary whimpered and deepened their kiss, urging Chase's head closer to his with his hand still burrowed in Chase's thick brown waves.

Parting from their kiss, Chase pecked Gary's nose, chin, neck, and licked his way to his chest. "I love you. I love you."

Those words spun in Gary's head making him dizzy. "We're crazy. Chase…"

"I know. I don't care." Chase lapped his way down Gary's skin to his belly button.

Chase's hot mouth approaching his cock, Gary tensed up and his heart rate soared.

As his cock was enveloped in wet boiling heat, Gary cried out and arched his back, massaging Chase's scalp, encouraging him to work his magic.

And Chase sucked him, deep, strong and hard.

From a state of total relaxation in the dark, Gary had become a writhing, moaning sex whore, willing to beg his lover to make him come again. If he could form words, Gary would moan, 'More! Deeper! Harder!' But he didn't have to. Chase was already doing exactly that to him.

His balls were squeezed, his root and ass massaged powerfully, and his dick devoured to the base. Add to all that stimulation was Chase's tongue drawing patterns underneath Gary's length.

"Fuck!" Gary's legs tensed and he drew his feet closer to his hips to be able to pump upwards. Pleasure began in his nuts and burst out through his dick, making his ass and spine tingle. His grip tightened in Chase's hair as intensity overpowered him. After another choking guttural gasp, Gary came, arching his back off the mattress and digging his head backwards into the pillows. His whole body trembled from the surge as Chase sucked him down, milking it, stroking between his legs as his cock throbbed.

Still spinning, releasing tiny sounds of ecstasy, Gary heard Chase's breath accelerate and felt hot spatters hitting his abs and chest. Forcing his eyes to open, Gary found Chase kneeling, fisting himself, spraying spunk all over him.

The image of Chase's expression of euphoria, his hand working himself and his torso gleaming with the moonbeams and streetlight, Gary knew he'd never seen a more beautiful sight in his life.

That picture would be forever burned in his brain as inspiration to get him through the nights during his long lonely tour in Iraq.

CHAPTER 8

"You sure you don't mind getting up early on a Saturday?"

"Mind? For you and Mutley? Why would I mind?"

"Because it's a fricken Saturday!" Chase laughed, crouching down and tying his running shoe. "Not to mention, we're playing football right after. How good a shape are you in, Staff Sergeant Wilson?"

"You think this compares to boot camp?" Gary slanted his eyes at him. "Give me a break, Chase. Nothing you got is harder than what I've been through."

"No. I suppose not." Chase stood, sliding his hand from Mutley's collar to the end of his leash. "Ready?"

"I am." Gary opened the front door.

Once they were outside, Chase locked up his house and used his key fob to open the Hyundai.

"Hang on," Chase said.

At the comment, Gary turned to look.

"Nature calls." Chase gestured to Mutley as he raised his leg.

"I love you guys." Gary chuckled opening the passenger's door.

"Good! We love you too." Chase led Mutley to the back seat after tossing three water bottles into the trunk. Mutley climbed in excitedly, obviously aware of where they were headed.

Once he was behind the wheel, Chase lowered the rear window for the dog and backed out of his driveway. "You think the guys will be surprised to see us getting into the same car after the game?"

"Sam and Dev know about us. I spoke to Sam earlier this week and told him we were seeing each other. I assume he told Dev."

"Oh." Chase had no idea about that conversation and decided it was unimportant. "What about Kevin?"

Gary screwed up his expression. "Who gives a shit about that dickhead?"

Chase shut up, trying not to say anything controversial. He was notorious for it. Weren't all New Yorkers? Too willing to speak their minds? Lacked filters? He was beginning to believe he fit the stereotype.

"Where do you run?" Gary asked, massaging Chase's bare knee that was exposed from his shorts.

"I found a trail that I believe is around six miles or so. Is that okay?"

"Yup. No problem."

"Stud." Chase winked at him, placing his hand over Gary's.

After a quiet drive, Chase parked near his usual spot in the lot of the park and shut off the car. Tucking his key into the tiny pocket of his gym shorts, he made sure he had Mutley seated obediently before he climbed out and opened the back door.

Gary stretched his legs, showing off his lovely derriere. The urge Chase had to either stroke it, nip it or at the very least, sniff it like a hound, made him tear his gaze away before he molested the man.

Not one for long warm ups, Chase lunged a few time, waiting for Gary.

"Okay." Gary nodded.

"This way." Chase directed Mutley on the opposite side of Gary so his leash didn't trip them up. Chase didn't say a word about changing his usual pace, just assumed assertive, outspoken Gary would most certainly mention if it was too slow or too fast.

"I love the fall." Gary smiled up at the changing leaves.

Inhaling the nice cool air, Chase agreed. "Beats sweating your ass off in the summer."

"Definitely."

Feeling closer to Gary every day they spent together, and now sharing his routine with him, Chase was content to simply enjoy the run: him, his dog, and the new love of his life.

❦

As far as Gary was concerned, the run was the perfect length. Not too far as to kill him, and not too short as to feel worthless. As they stood at Chase's car, cooling down, getting water for Mutley and for them, Gary noticed two Kawasakis already in the parking lot. "Dev and Sam are here."

Chase spun around to where Gary was pointing. "Cool. Nice bikes."

"You like to ride?"

"No." Chase laughed. "A motorcycle in Manhattan? Are you nuts?"

"You're not in Manhattan anymore." Gary nudged him playfully.

"I'd still not own one. Too lethal."

Gary narrowed his eyes at another car parking near the motorcycles. Gary realized Chase had noticed it also.

"Well," Chase said, "we did expect him to show up."

At the sight of Kevin getting out of his car, Gary couldn't prevent his snarl.

"Just ignore him," Chase said.

"That's the problem. He won't stand for being ignored."

And sure enough, Kevin spotted them, strutting over.

Kevin was handsome, Gary hated to admit that. He was big, brawny, and adorable. But that didn't make him any less of a dickhead.

"Well, well…" Kevin gave each man a sensual once over. "Aren't we getting cozy? Came in one car? What'd ya do, Gar," Kevin opened his hands in a questioning gesture, "already move in?"

"Fuck off." Gary sneered.

"Cut it out, guys," Chase said.

When Mutley went to give Kevin a sniff, Kevin backed off in annoyance.

Chase tugged on Mutley's leash. "Sit." Mutley plopped down on his haunches obediently.

In amusement, Kevin asked, "Does Chase have you that well trained, Gar?"

Gary tensed up, wishing he could just have it out. Fight. Get all this crap out with a good physical scrap. He'd had so much pent up anger about the treatment he received from Kevin, he was dying to belt him in the mouth.

"Let's go." Chase touched Gary's elbow.

Allowing Chase to draw him away from Kevin, Gary grumbled as they went. "He'll just keep it up during the game."

"Don't let it upset you. Forget it. If he sees it bothers you, he'll get off on it."

"No. He'll get off on tackling you." Gary peered behind him and noticed Kevin watching them.

Once Chase had secured Mutley to the same small tree and made him lay down, Gary and Chase walked to the group of men.

"Good to see you again, Chase," Sam greeted him excitedly. "I hear you're keeping Gary busy."

"I try." Chase smiled.

"Same sides?" Lewis asked, tossing the football into the air, spinning it.

Gary knew if Chase and Kevin were on opposing teams, Kevin would use every chance he got to touch him. "I want Kevin on our side."

All nine men gaped at him in surprise. It wasn't a secret they had a bad break up.

"Why?" Dev asked.

"Yeah, Gar, why?" Kevin taunted.

Chase touched Gary's arm. "Just let it go."

"Come on, same sides as last week," Joe said in annoyance.

Avoiding Kevin's smirk, Gary grabbed Dev to tell him, "I'm guarding Kevin."

Sam shook his head. "That's not a good idea."

"You think I want Kevin all over Chase?" Gary replied, then peered back at the other team who were conferring in a group.

Lewis said in annoyance, "Can't you guys just get over it? It's football. Not a soap opera."

"All right." Dev held up his hands for calm. "Did we even flip a coin to see who's got the ball first?"

"No." Sam appeared upset.

Dev marched to the other men. "Who's got a quarter?"

Jerry held one up. "Heads or tails?"

"Tails."

Jerry flipped it into the air. "Tails."

"You receive."

"Fine." Jerry pocketed his quarter, tossing Dev the ball.

Through his fury, Gary noticed Chase's expression of worry. "Hey." Gary touched Chase's arm.

After a blast of frustrated air from his lips, Chase said, "I'm fucking this game up."

"You're not," Gary replied, "Kevin's the one who's fucking it up."

"Please." Sam held up both his hands, pleading. "It's just a game of tackle football in a park. That's all. Okay?"

Dev gestured for them all to come closer. "Kick the fucking thing hard." He handed Chase the ball.

Chase grinned. "Sure."

"Wait," Lewis said, "We don't usually kick the ball. We throw it."

"Not this time." Gary showed his teeth as he snarled.

"Hang on," Lewis said. "We all know how hard Gary can kick a ball. What's the point, guys?"

"Dev," Sam replied.

"Fine." Dev stood tall and yelled, "We'll receive first." He threw the ball at Chris.

"Make up your fucking mind!" Kevin said.

"Fuck you, asshole!" Gary yelled.

Chase gripped Gary's shirt and tugged him back to their huddle. "Behave."

Gary was not happy. Shifting his weight anxiously side to side, he said, "Give Kevin five minutes and he'll have you on the ground with his face in your crack."

Sam and Dev chuckled before they covered their mouths.

Lewis whined, "Can we just play?"

"Gary," Chase tightened his grip on Gary's arm, "it doesn't matter what he does. Okay?"

"Are you morons going to take all day?" Kevin shouted rudely.

"I'll block Kevin," Sam said.

In irritation, Dev replied, "Fine. Lewis you take Joe. Gary, Barry, and Chase, you handle Chris."

Gary had to be content with that. They jogged back to the goal line waiting for Chris to throw the ball towards them downfield.

It sailed high into the air. Gary knew it was heading towards Sam and Chase. Chase caught it.

They ran as a group until they met up with the other team. When Chris guarded Gary, he realized it didn't matter who Dev had allocated in his master plan, Kevin had gotten his way.

Gary watched helplessly as Kevin wrapped around Chase like a boa constrictor, pulling Chase to the soggy wet grass. He went crazy as Kevin took full advantage of Chase's vulnerable position. With Chris holding him firm, all Gary could do was roar in anger.

"All right," Chase scolded Kevin, "let me up and stop tormenting Gary."

"Damn you smell good." Kevin pushed his nose into Chase's armpit.

"I said let me up." Chase tossed the ball to Dev.

By the time Gary made his way over, he was seething. He gripped Kevin by the scruff of his neck and warned, "Touch him again and you die."

"Get off me!" Kevin twisted away from Gary's hands.

Geared up for another pounce, everyone clung to his back preventing it.

"This ain't gonna work." Chase held Gary tight.

"Come on, guys!" Dev said. "Now we can't play a stupid game of football?"

"Hang on." Chase held Gary and walked a few feet away from the rest. "Babe."

"What?" Gary was still furious.

"I don't love that asshole. I love you."

Instantly Gary met Chase's eyes.

"Don't allow him to get to you. Please. I really enjoy this game with everyone. I want to play."

"Me too." Gary could see them all talking behind his and

Chase's backs.

"So?" Chase shrugged. "He thinks he's smart. And by you letting him know he's upset you, you're making him look good."

"Chase…" Gary shook his head in frustration.

"If the jerk goes for my ass or balls, I'll deck him. Believe me. But as long as he plays by the rules…" Chase raised his hand as if he wanted to touch Gary's hair, lowering it again.

"Okay." Gary nodded, his gaze on the grass.

Gary heard a 'woof'! He looked up to see Mutley sitting up, staring at them. That made him laugh.

"I'm yours," Chase said.

"I know. Let's play."

With an affectionate pat to Gary's bottom, they then jogged back to Dev.

"Ready, QB." Gary grinned at Devlin.

"Good. Okay," Dev said, "Gar, fake left, go right, as deep as you can."

"Got it." Peeking over at Chase, Gary gave him a wink and an adoring smile. Chase threw him a kiss.

Dev reached between Sam's legs for the ball. "Hep, one, hep, two…hike!"

Gary avoided Chris, dodged Barry and broke free. Spinning around, he looked for the ball as it sailed through the air and caught it. As he sprinted to the end zone, Joe tripped him up around the ankles and Gary came down with a thud.

Getting back to his feet quickly, Gary spun around and couldn't believe Kevin had tackled Chase even though he didn't have the ball. "Son of a bitch!"

As Gary stormed over he could hear Chase's annoyance at the obvious attempt to make him jealous.

"Look, Kevin, cut it out. I'm not interested and I want you to stop hounding me." Chase tried to nudge Kevin off his legs. Kevin appeared reluctant to relinquish his hold as they both lay on the ground.

"Come on, Kev!" Dev said.

Gary didn't wait for Kevin to take his sweet time climbing off Chase. He seized Kevin's shirt, hauled him to his feet, and punched him in the face.

An all out melee started between the two men. Gary grabbed Kevin in a headlock violently as he took a few shots at Gary's chest and stomach.

The rest of the men were shouting and pulling the two combatants apart.

Suddenly a very large furry mass intervened.

Mutley had broken free and was on Kevin so quick he shocked everyone. The passive mutt had turned defensive, growling and snapping his menacing jaws at Kevin.

"Holy shit!" Kevin immediately backed off Gary, petrified of the large canines being exposed near his face.

Chase got a grip on Mutley's collar and drew him back, calming him down.

Gary was in awe at Mutley's sense of loyalty to him. It was blatantly obvious Mutley was there to defend him in the fight. The dog's actions had stunned Gary and everyone appeared shaken up.

"Okay, baby, calm down," Chase cooed to the agitated dog as he crouched next to him.

Mutley was visibly upset, shifting his weight and making high pitched noises.

Gary sat on the grass next to Mutley. Immediately Mutley leapt on him, licking his face almost as if he were making sure he wasn't hurt.

"Okay, big boy. Calm down." Gary held onto Mutley tightly.

"Wow," Sam said, gaping at them.

"Nice." Kevin sneered. "A trained attack dog?"

"Hardly!" Chase laughed. "I've never seen him do that before. He just loves Gary and thought you were hurting him."

"Serves you fucking right." Barry pointed at Kevin. "What the hell were you doing tackling Chase when Gary had the ball?" When Kevin didn't answer, Barry added, "Give it a rest, Kev, k?"

"Let's play. Come on." Dev tried to motivate the group.

Gary walked with Chase to another tree to secure Mutley. The one he was originally tied to was bent in half.

"That was amazing," Gary said, "I can't believe Mutley did that for me."

Smiling at Gary as he looped Mutley's leash around a bigger trunk, Chase replied, "He adores you, babe."

Kneeling in front of Mutley, Gary gave the dog a good ear scratching. "Thanks, big guy."

Mutley yipped at him in excitement, wriggling his back end and wagging his tail in a flurry.

"I have a feeling it put Kevin in his place," Chase said, standing up and reaching for Gary.

Gary took Chase's hand, giving it a squeeze before releasing it. "I bet it did. He looked terrified." Gary laughed.

"Wouldn't you be? Christ, Gary, Mutley weighs over a hundred pounds. He's a big beast."

"Nah, he's a pussy cat." Gary brushed against Chase as they returned to the group.

"Just like you," Chase whispered.

Gary gave him a loving smile.

When they came through the door to Chase's home, they were laughing, caked in mud and exhausted. Chase unhooked Mutley's leash and followed him to the kitchen. While Mutley lapped at his water bowl, Chase handed Gary a bottle of water from the fridge.

"And when you nailed Kevin in the face with your elbow?" Chase shook his head, "I thought he was going to cry."

Gary held up his hand after taking a long drink of the water. "I swear it was accidental."

"I thought you broke his nose." Chase leaned back against the counter.

"So did he."

Chase shook his head, calming down. "Look at you, Mutt. You're a mess."

"Him?" Gary gestured to the two of them.

"Yeah, well. Us taking a bath is easy, him? Christ. What an ordeal."

"Does he hate baths?"

"Yup."

"He could use a good scrub." Gary tossed his empty water

bottle into the trash.

Mutley looked from one man to the other suspiciously.

"He knows what we're talking about," Chase said. "He heard the word B-A-T-H."

"Do you do it in the tub?" Gary chuckled at Mutley's odd expression.

"Yes. Unless it's summer. It's too cool outside now to use the hose."

"Come on. I'll help."

"Wait until you see his face when he's soaking wet. He gets very depressed."

"Huh. I thought most dogs like water."

"Not him." Chase set his bottle on the counter and crossed his arms over his chest. "Well," he addressed Mutley, "is this going to be the hard way or the easy way?"

Mutley tried to make his escape out of the kitchen.

Gary roared with laughter at the scene the two made.

The big dog caught around his four legs, Chase hoisted him into the air and said, "Go. Get the water running."

Gary sprinted in front of them as Mutley moaned in annoyance.

Once the three of them were closed into the bathroom, Gary knelt on the floor and turned on the taps in the tub. Chase set the big dog down on the porcelain and immediately Mutley tried to get out.

Crouching next to Gary, both he and Chase blocked the way.

"You have dog shampoo?" Gary asked, holding Mutley's collar as he became agitated.

"Yes. Flea shampoo." Chase dug under the sink cabinet, keeping his hand up in case the dog got any ideas.

Water filling the tub around him, Mutley fidgeted and tried to get his paws on the rim. Gary nudged him back. "Behave."

Chase removed a bucket from the cabinet and began scooping the water from the bottom of the tub to douse the dog. Mutley's ears went flat and his eyes drooped. When he tried to shake off, Chase held him tight, stopping him, pouring another bucket on him. "Start shampooing him."

Gary grabbed the bottle and poured a palm full. Once the dog was soaked, both men worked on getting him clean. Gary kept laughing in bursts as Mutley managed to shake off a few times, spraying them with soapy water.

"Mutt! Cut it out!" Chase shouted, wiping the suds off his face.

Once the dog had a good washing, Chase began using the bucket to rinse him off.

"We should have just gotten in with him. I'm soaked." Gary used his shoulder to wipe at his face.

"It's easier this way. Believe me, I've tried everything."

Gary shut the water, holding Mutley by his collar to keep him still. "Look out. Here comes another one."

They both winced as Mutley gave another good shake to dry off his body. Again Gary laughed in hilarity as the entire room was now dripping.

"What an ordeal." Chase moaned. "Hang on to him. I have some crappy towels I use to dry him off with."

"Okay."

Chase sprinted to the cupboard and collected a few old beach towels. When he returned, Mutley was spraying Gary with more water from another shake of his body. "Jesus, Mutt. Give us a minute and we'll get you dry." He handed Gary one of the towels. "This part he loves," Chase said, rubbing the towel along Mutley's back half as Gary dried Mutley's face and chest.

Instantly Mutley was wriggling at the rubdown.

"Ahh," Gary chuckled, "see, Mutt, it's worth the wait for a good scratching."

"Let him out of the tub. It'll be easier." Chase used his upper arm to push his wet hair back from his forehead.

The minute they backed up, Mutley leapt out, shaking again. They dove on him, both of them laughing at the noises Mutley was making as he seemed to be in heaven getting a rub down with the towels.

"Enough!" In exhaustion Chase dropped to his bottom on the tile floor. "Go!" He opened the bathroom door and Mutley dashed out. Panting as he smiled at Gary, Gary was sprawled out on the floor, the soggy towel in a heap next to him.

"Man."

"I know. Crazy huh?"

"That was more work than the run or the football."

Chase gave a soft chuckle. "Do you have the energy for our own shower?"

"Yes. I stink like flea shampoo and wet dog." Gary struggled to get to his feet.

Chase reached out for help in getting hauled up. When they were both upright, Chase said, "Thanks for being such a good sport."

"Are you kidding me? That dog was my backup today in a fight. I owed him."

Chase imagined Gary in a real battle. A war, not a playground tussle.

"Chase."

Feeling his eyes burn as they filled, Chase avoided Gary's intelligent gaze. "Right. Our turn." Chase nudged aside the wet dog towels and stripped off his clothing.

"Babe."

Deflating at Gary's tone, Chase looked over his shoulder at him. The adoration in Gary's expression overwhelmed him. Chase fell into his embrace. Gary's warm hands ran down his back to his naked bottom. Chase closed his eyes and savored Gary's strong arms holding him. He had to stop torturing them. Chase knew that. He'd just never been in this situation before and was struggling with how to deal with it.

"You stink like dog shampoo."

Chase smiled and backed up so he could see Gary's blue eyes. "Not an aphrodisiac?"

"Afraid not." Gary reached into the tub and turned on the shower. "Get in." He whacked Chase's bottom with a loud smack.

Chase climbed in and soaked beneath the hot spray, moaning at how good it felt after so much sweat and exertion. A second later Gary joined him. Giving Gary the showerhead to stand under, Chase admired his solid build as the water ran down Gary's tanned skin. Grabbing the soap, Chase lathered up his hands, instantly going for Gary's cock. At the touch, Gary straddled his legs and reached back for the wall.

"Do you want to come now, or inside me?"

Gary said, "Both."

Fire scorched Chase's skin at the sensual reply. He moved closer, tighter, holding their cocks together in his slippery hands. Gary's groan echoed off the wet tiles.

Seeing Gary's erotic posture, his pelvis thrust forward, his shoulders leaning against the wall, his thighs spread wide, and his expression smoldering hot, Chase's body responded, throbbing with pleasure.

While both Chase's hands worked their erections at once, Gary gently smoothed his palms up Chase's arms to his shoulders. Gary squeezed his muscles tighter, and Chase knew he was close. He quickened his pace until his hands were a blur.

Gary grunted and his body jerked in a pre-climax spasm. It sent Chase reeling. Chase came, continuing to work their bodies in tandem until he heard Gary's moan and felt his cock pulsating in his fingers.

Opening his eyes, Chase first gazed down at their two dicks nestled together, raising his lashes to see those fabulous baby blues. The moment their eyes connected, Gary wrapped around Chase and hugged him, meeting his lips. Chase reciprocated, tightening his hold on Gary to seal their wet skin from chest to thighs.

The kiss made Chase delirious. He was so happy he forgot New York, the family he had left behind, and the rest of the universe. All that mattered was he had found his perfect match. Let all else be damned.

❧❧

They lounged in Chase's den with the lights out. Mutley was asleep at their feet. Gary was sprawled out on the couch, his head on Chase's lap while Chase combed his fingers through Gary's hair gently as they watched the television. The old Hitchcock movie, *Psycho* was playing on cable. Chase imagined with Halloween approaching it wouldn't be the last scary movie to appear in the listing. They had eaten another homemade meal he had cooked, and now, as ten approached they were both weary from a long physical day.

Chase smiled contentedly as he gazed at Gary's handsome profile highlighted by the glow of the TV, petting his soft brown hair, very happy he was with him.

They didn't talk much since they made themselves cozy in the den. They didn't have to. Chase liked just hanging around with the man.

Running his hand down the nape of Gary's neck to his broad shoulder, Chase massaged him, adored touching him, craving him.

Gary adjusted his head on Chase's lap and stared up at him.

At the contact of Gary's light eyes, Chase's cock moved in his jeans.

"Hi," Gary's voice was hoarse and deep from his exhaustion.

"Hi." Chase cupped his rough jaw.

"If you want to go to sleep, just let me know."

"Not unless you want to. I'm loving this." Chase caressed Gary's face and dug his fingers into his short hair again.

Gary smiled sweetly at him.

When Gary reached up around Chase's neck, Chase was drawn down to Gary's lips. As Gary met him halfway, they kissed. Immediately Chase draped his arms around Gary's head to hold him close. The feel of Gary's tongue in his mouth began to motivate Chase for bed, but not for sleep.

Gary parted from him, staring up at him.

Cupping Gary's jaw, Chase accepted that powerful stare.

In the background Anthony Perkins lurked, wearing a wig and a dress as the music grew more intense. For some reason the melodramatic movie scene made their contact seem surreal to Chase. It was as if Gary was an image on a screen, and soon that image would vanish and all Chase would have is the memory of it.

Unable to stop the coming anguish, Chase broke down again. He released his hold on Gary and twisted his face aside to bite it back.

Immediately Gary sat up and held him, kissing his hair.

That wail welled up in Chase again. *Don't go! Please. Don't go!*

"Come on. Let's get in bed." Gary stood and reached for Chase's hand.

Gaining a hold on his emotions, Chase knew his weakness was not going to make it easy on Gary when he had to go.

Chase shut off the television, reaching in the dimness to turn on the light. Mutley stood up with them.

"Do you have to go out, Mutt?" Chase asked him quietly.

Mutley's tail gave a slight wag and he headed out of the room.

"Let me let him outside for a last pit stop." Chase rubbed his tired eyes.

"I'll be upstairs."

Nodding, Chase allowed Gary's peck on the lips before they went separate ways.

Following Mutley to the back door, Chase opened it and Mutley scampered out. Yawning, leaning on the doorframe, Chase chided himself over his lack of strength when it came to Gary's imminent departure. *What are you, a baby? Christ, the man's in the air force, he doesn't need a wimp nagging and crying every five minutes. Pull yourself together, Chase!*

"I'm an idiot." Chase noticed Mutley at the back screen door and opened it for him. Shutting off lights as he went, they headed up the staircase to the bedroom.

As Chase entered he could see into the master bathroom. Gary was naked, leaning over the sink, brushing his teeth. Undressing as he stared at him, Chase couldn't believe his luck.

Thinking back to his frustration at being alone here in Ohio, to the day Gary had the gonads to run and catch him before he left the park, Chase couldn't get over how fate had brought them to where they were. The question Chase had was, "What did fate have in store for them in the future?" This arrangement was just too perfect. Chase wanted Gary to move in. Now. Today. Yesterday.

When Gary finished up in the bathroom, he noticed Chase watching him. Smiling devilishly, Gary struck a macho pose, leaning on the doorframe, one hand propped up over his head, the other touching his balls.

"Damn. Staff Sergeant Wilson." Chase shook his head in admiration as he took his last article of clothing off.

Gary sauntered over proudly. When they kissed Chase tasted mint on his tongue. "Let me wash up. Get in bed."

Giving Chase's cock a nice squeeze first, Gary made his way to the bed. Chase got lost on Gary's back view for a moment until he was lying prone. Snapping out of his dream, Chase hurried to the bathroom to get ready for bed.

∽≈

Gary stroked his cock as he waited. Peering behind him, seeing the rubbers and the lube still sitting on the nightstand, he smiled warmly. His attention back on the bathroom door, Gary massaged his dick in anticipation. He heard Mutley sigh loudly as he curled on his pillow on the floor.

I could so easily live here. Sleep in Chase's bed every night, work out with him, share everything together.

A slight feeling of apprehension passed over Gary at the thought of his parents wondering why he was cohabitating with another man. It would be too obvious to deny at that point.

Could he claim it was economical? That they both worked at the base and were saving money?

"Christ." Thinking about his father's reaction, Gary lost his erection.

Chase appeared in the doorway, attempting the same seduction Gary had treated him to. Locking his vision on Chase's fantastic form, Gary soon forgot his negative thoughts.

As Chase licked his lips slowly, he pinched his nipples in a tease.

Gary's gaze lowered to Chase's dick, it was erect and bobbing enticingly. "Get over here." Gary purred.

Moving slowly, his hips swaying making his cock swing, Chase stood next to Gary by the bed. Gary rolled to his side, taking Chase's cock into his mouth.

The taste of Chase's body, the tiny drop of pre-cum that oozed out, sent Gary reeling. Reaching out to grip Chase's ass, a cheek in each hand, Gary sucked him deeper.

Chase's hands dug into Gary's hair and Chase let loose a sensuous moan.

Gary sat up, urged Chase down on the bed, and pinned his body to the mattress under him. Finding Chase's lips, Gary fucked his mouth with his tongue hungrily.

In response, Chase opened his legs in invitation.

Yes! Gary preferred topping and it seemed they were falling into the roles he craved the most. He was a willing bottom, but loved being the aggressor.

Cupping his hand over Chase's entire package, Gary used the tips of his fingers to explore Chase's balls and the tight hard root of the base of his dick. Chase broke their kiss and let out a breathy moan.

"I want to make love to you." Gary used his index finger to penetrate Chase's hole.

"Take anything you want, babe." Chase panted, smoothing his hands over Gary's skin.

Before he went for the lube, Gary raised Chase's legs off the bed, bending them backwards against Chase's body. He smothered his face in Chase's balls, licking his sack and rim aggressively.

Chase went crazy, writhing and whimpering.

Chewing lightly on Chase's skin as he made his way from his ass to the head of his dick, Gary was so hot he was going to combust. Inhaling Chase's masculine scent, lapping his clean, fresh-from-the-shower flesh, Gary released an animalistic roar he was so keyed up.

"Baby!" Chase reacted to the sound. "Take it!"

Coming around from a swoon at the delight he was taking in eating his partner's body, Gary sat on his heels and pumped his own cock a few times.

Chase handed him a condom.

Tearing it open with his teeth, Gary slid it on. Exchanging the empty condom package for the lube, Gary coated his own dick and was about to go for Chase's ass when he noticed Chase's slit oozing with pre-cum. Smiling wickedly, Gary slid one finger inside Chase's butt.

Chase inhaled sharply and arched his back. "Ffffuck!"

After dropping the lube bottle on the nightstand, Gary pushed his cock into Chase's tight ring. Instantly a rush of chills washed over Gary's spine. Under him Chase's body had tensed up in anticipation of the rocket launch. Gary thrust in deep and hard, staring at Chase's tightly packed abs, then moving up to see his face with his lips parted and his eyes sealed tight.

Chase's arms spread out wide on the mattress, his fingers gripping the blankets underneath. He bucked upwards, fucking Gary from below.

Gary cupped Chase's balls, rolling them in his fingers as he humped Chase, jamming Chase's body back against the headboard.

"Aah!" Chase huffed and his body jerked in a spasm as he came. "Ffuck! Ahhshitt…"

Gary went wild watching cum shoot out of Chase's cock. Braced on both his hands, he thrust deeper, pulling almost all the way out and ramming back inside Chase's hot hole again. When it hit, his climax was so strong Gary felt his entire body clench. He choked out a breath of air and felt his balls churning. Releasing his cum into the condom in Chase's tight ass, Gary could feel the veins in his neck pumping blood, no doubt, to his cock.

Prolonging the pleasure, smoothing his length in and out slowly, Gary felt his skin coat with sweat and couldn't catch his breath. When he finally stopped moving his hips, he opened his eyes.

Chase was gazing up at him with so much affection it was Gary's turn to choke up. He pulled out, dropping down on top of Chase. Digging his arms under Chase's back, Gary gripped him in a strangle hold, burrowing his face into Chase's neck.

"It's okay, baby," Chase cooed, rubbing Gary's back.

It's killing us. And I'm not even gone yet. Gary wiped his wet eyes on the pillow under Chase's head. He let go of his tightly wound muscles and allowed all his weight to settle on Chase's body. As they recuperated, Chase gently tickled Gary's back with the tips of his fingers.

Forcing himself to get under control, Gary knew the day they parted would be so painful it would kill them both. He had no idea when he ran Chase down in the park that morning that it would bring them to where they were now. Petrified of losing each other.

CHAPTER 9

Sunday morning a cold wet nose startled Gary. He opened his eyes to a large snuffling muzzle and big brown eyes with long eyelashes gazing at him. "Yes?" Gary asked the dog.

Mutley danced in a circle.

"He has to go out," Chase said tiredly from the other side of the bed.

"You have to go out?" Gary repeated, smiling.

Mutley did another dance and uttered a yipping noise.

As Gary made a move to sit upright, Chase moaned. "I'll go."

"No. I got it." Gary stood, scuffing his way to the doorway as Mutley darted down the stairs. He yawned and rubbed his head, still waking up. After opening the back door to let Mutley out, Gary filled the coffeemaker with water and started it dripping. Once it was, Gary leaned against the wall near the back door to watch Mutley sniff around the yard. It was a decent sized patch of land surrounded by a wood fence, a tool shed sat in the far right corner. The sight was domestic and serene, just the kind of thing Gary was craving. The condo was a place to sleep, period.

Scratching his balls and stifling another yawn, he heard a noise behind him and found Chase wearing a pair of gym shorts admiring him.

"I got the coffee going."

"You're awesome." Chase draped his arms around Gary's neck and kissed him.

"I didn't brush yet." Gary chuckled, tasting the mint on Chase's tongue.

"The mutt got us out of bed too early. I wanted to snuggle."

As Chase lapped at his chin stubble, Gary said, "Let's get back to bed."

"Good idea." Chase held Gary's hand and led him up the stairs.

"Let me take a piss." Gary gestured to the bathroom.

Chase released his hand and dropped his shorts, crawling back into bed.

Once Gary had relieved himself and washed up, he found Chase waiting for him, patting the spot next to him.

They cuddled together under the sheets, wriggling on each other's naked skin and hairy legs.

"You feel so good." Gary hummed happily.

"You too."

They groaned and stayed still, enjoying the close, knotted contact of their limbs. Gary could feel Chase's chest rumbling with his voice.

"Let's stay like this all day," Chase said, kissing Gary's rough jaw.

"Woof!"

Gary met Chase's eyes. They both cracked up.

"It's like having a spoiled child." Chase smiled.

"He's jealous," Gary said, finding Chase's tongue and wrapping his own around it.

"Woof!" came a louder plea from the backyard.

"He won't shut up until we let him in," Chase warned.

"Let me." Gary tossed off the blankets.

"No. Why? He's my problem." Chase sat upright.

"Problem? That dog is not a problem, he's a saint." Gary made for the hall.

"Saint?" Chase followed him. "Saint Mutley? You have no idea how wrong you are."

Gary smiled as he descended the stairs. "That animal came to my aid in a fight. Enough said."

"That meant a lot to you, didn't it?" Chase met Gary at the back door along with a waiting dog.

"Yes. It did." Gary opened the door and Mutley rushed in excitedly.

"Huh."

He closed the door and looked up at Chase's expression. "Back to bed? Or breakfast?"

"You hungry?"

Gary sniffed the coffee. "Yes. But I cook for you this time."

"Yeah?" Chase started heading up the stairs again.

"Yeah." Gary pinched Chase's bottom as they ascended. Mutley brushed by them both, sprinting up to the top landing.

Once they were standing in the bedroom, naked, Gary paused. It was as if Chase had the same idea. They grinned at each other and did a nosedive back into the bed. When a one hundred pound canine joined them, Gary cracked up with laughter as Chase pushed Mutley off the bed. "Go lay down!"

Gary dabbed at a tear and said, "I love you guys!"

"I have a gay dog." Chase shook his head, as Mutley gave a grumbling sound and dropped to his own pillow on the floor. "Where were we?" Chase scooped Gary around his waist and drew him on top of him.

"We were about to have a three-way." Gary kept laughing, wiping his eyes.

"I draw the line at animals! You're the only mammal I want. Now get over here and kiss me."

Calming down, Gary gazed into Chase's chocolate brown eyes and sighed sensually. When he met Chase's mouth, he knew he was hooked. Completely and utterly in love.

∽∼

After breakfast they stopped at Gary's condo so he could replenish his clothing supply. It was Chase's first visit. He tried not to be nosy but while Gary was doing what he needed to do, Chase snooped around. He spotted a few family photos and inspected them.

Gary in his uniform, his parents on either side of him smiling broadly. A different photo was with a younger, very good looking man, Chase suspected was Gary's brother, holding Chase around the waist. It appeared the backdrop was the base, or somewhere outdoors.

Another one piqued Chase's interest; Gary in his ABUs with an F15 aircraft in the background. "Wow." Chase set it back in its place.

Standing at the doorway of Gary's bedroom, Chase noticed Gary peering down at his answering machine. "You want me to leave?"

"No." Gary pushed the button. A woman's voice was heard.

"Gary, it's Mom. Where are you? I've been calling both your mobile phone and home and I'm trying not to get worried. Call me."

The next two were similar in content, one was from Gary's dad, the next his brother calling long distance telling him to call his parents because they were getting upset.

"You mind?" Gary asked, setting his backpack down on the bed.

"No! Do I mind? Come on, Gary. Call them." Chase pointed over his shoulder. "I'll wait in the living room."

Gary nodded, picking up the phone and dialing.

Sitting on the couch, staring into space, Chase could over-hear the conversation in the other room too easily and felt as if he should wait in the hall. Instead, he rested his head on the back of the couch and closed his eyes.

"Hi, Mom…I know. No. Nothing's wrong. I've just been busy…I didn't even realize my cell phone was off. Hang on." After a pause, Gary said, "It needs a charge. That's why. What's so urgent anyway?"

Chase exhaled a deep stressful sigh.

"So?" Gary responded to the phone conversation. "No, but I expect to hear any day now."

Cringing, Chase felt his skin crawl.

"Yes, I'll most likely be gone over Christmas. Sorry, Mom… Over at Al Taji again…it's no big deal. Yes…I'll probably find out next week. One of the other staff sergeants said it's coming down the pipe within a few days. Yes. I will. I don't know. We could just have dinner before I go."

Chase choked up and rubbed his face in agony.

"You can see me off. Yes. I'm not sure yet. When I know I'll give you all the details…okay. Bye, Mom."

Struggling with every ounce of strength he had, Chase bit back his emotions. Through his blurry vision, he kept catching the sight of Gary in his uniform with his family and him with the jet airplane in the background.

A few minutes later Gary appeared, holding his backpack and looking around the room. Chase didn't look at him for fear of Gary seeing his red watery eyes.

It didn't matter. Gary knew.

After he dropped the pack off at the door, he sat next to Chase on the sofa and embraced him, bringing their bodies to connect.

A sob escaped Chase's throat and he cursed himself angrily.

"It's okay." Gary rubbed his back.

"I'm sorry I'm being such a baby, Gary. I'm embarrassing myself."

"I'm not sorry. It shows me how much you care." Gary sat back to kiss Chase lightly.

"I care a lot, Gary. A hell of a lot."

"Good." Gary brushed a tear that slipped down Chase's cheek.

"I've lived in Manhattan my whole life and I can't say I've been around men from the military," Chase began, "but I have very strong opinions of the war in Iraq. The first one in the Gulf I understood. But this one?"

"Shh. I know." Gary touched Chase's lips.

"What's your opinion of it? How do you feel about what that asshole Bush did while he was in the White House—"

"Chase." Gary cupped his hand over Chase's mouth. "I'm in the air force. I go where they tell me to go. It makes no difference what I think."

In denial, Chase shook his head, his eyes filling again.

"Please."

Chase urged Gary's hand off his mouth. "You told your mother you were expecting orders next week. You didn't tell me that."

A sad smile appeared on Gary's lips. "She's used to it. You're not."

"That fast? Gary, that fast you'll go?"

Gary sighed. "Yes, Chase. I'm sorry."

Chase's lips formed the word 'no', but it was just mouthed and not spoken.

"I can't stand hurting you this way," Gary whispered, petting Chase's hair.

"Hurting me?" Chase choked at the absurdity. "I'm going to be safe and sound in a fucking clinic in Ohio."

"Chase, please."

"What do we have left, Gary? A week? A few days?" Chase's chest was so tight he was in pain.

As if Gary knew it would be devastating, he didn't answer right away.

"Gary." Chase gripped his hands.

"My guess is less than a week." Gary didn't make eye contact.

Chase's lip began to quiver. "I haven't had enough of you yet, babe. I'm not ready."

"I'm sorry. Chase, don't worry. The time will pass quickly. I'll have you on e-mail—"

Chase lunged at him, pushing Gary back on the cushions and held onto him, dying, literally dying inside. Hot tears ran down his face and onto Gary's t-shirt.

When Gary felt his tears with his fingertips, he begged, "Chase, don't. You'll get me going."

"I can't help it. I'm about to die." Biting his lip, Chase knew that was a horrible choice of words. If anything, Gary was the one risking his life. "I love you. Gary, I love you. I'm not ready for you to go."

"Chase…please."

Hearing Gary choked up, stabbed Chase with guilt. He gazed down at Gary as he lay there and spied tears running down the sides of his face. Chase crawled his way up Gary's body and rested his cheek against Gary's.

"Everything will be fine." It felt as if Gary fought hard with his emotions. "I promise. I've been through this drill before. Don't make it sound worse than it is. It's a base, babe. A training camp for the Iraq military."

"Yes." Chase tried to find comfort in that.

"I'm not hunting guerillas in the mountains of Afghanistan."

"Right."

"So? A few months. That's it. I'll be back and we can laugh about us acting like a couple of babies."

Chase tried to laugh, but it erupted in another sob. He sat up and stared down at Gary. Gary's tears had dried and he had gained complete control.

"Right. Yeah, Gary. I'm being silly. I'm sorry."

Gary moved upright and kissed Chase's cheek. "Nothing to worry about. We can send hot e-mails."

Giving Gary his bravest smile, Chase nodded. "Perfect."

"Good. I've got everything we need. What's the plan for the day?"

"Up to you." Chase stood, waiting for Gary to finish shutting lights and gather his things.

"Frisbee in the park?"

Seeing Gary's blue eyes light up, he laughed. "And you think I spoil Mutley?"

"Aw, come on. He loves it."

Chase patted Gary's back as he exited through his front door waiting in the stairwell as Gary locked up. "He does." *And he loves you.* "Fine. Back to get the mutt."

Gary winked at him as they climbed into his Hummer.

He had to think positive thoughts. If he didn't, he'd go insane.

Instead of cooking, Gary offered to take Chase out for dinner. He felt guilty that Chase slaved over the stove for him every evening and he wanted to treat him.

Showered and dressed in casual slacks and cotton shirts, they headed out to Beavercreek.

While they sat together at Brio's at the Greene, a handsome fair-haired waiter with a finely trimmed beard greeted them. "My name is John, and I'll be your server. Would you like something to drink?"

Gary smiled at Chase. "Have a beer."

Giving Gary a sweet wink, Chase said, "I'll take a bottle of the Sam Adams."

"The same." Gary nodded.

"I'll be right back with your drink order." The waiter left.

Gary became distracted by Chase's good looks as he perused the menu. Gary had been to this restaurant before. One of his parents' favorite spots, he already knew what he wanted. He and Chase were sitting next to each other as opposed to across the tiny white tablecloth-covered table. The arrangement felt more intimate to Gary. From here Gary was able to reach under cover and rub Chase's thigh through his black slacks.

At the caress, Chase's brown eyes raised from the menu to send a sensual message, which instantly made Gary hard. "Have you decided?" Gary asked quietly.

"Yes. You topping me again."

Gary laughed softly. "I meant for dinner."

Seeing Chase trying to focus on the food, Gary brought his hand back to rest on the table.

"What are you having?"

"My usual. I like the roasted chicken risotto."

"Where's that one?" Chase searched the menu. Gary pointed to its place. "Mm. I'm torn between that and the lobster risotto."

"Get the lobster and we'll share."

"Perfect." Chase grinned. "Appetizer?"

"How about the field greens salad?"

Setting his menu down, Chase said, "I do adore you."

"Behave," Gary replied playfully.

"I hate to behave. If we were in Manhattan…" Chase rubbed his hand up Gary's thigh hotly.

Laughing seductively at Chase's tease, Gary was about to add something delicious to the conversation when he heard his name.

"Gary!"

When his parents appeared at their table, he blinked at them in shock as they smiled back at him. "Mom! Dad!"

Chase's hand instantly retracted to his own lap and he stood up to greet them.

Assuming his cheeks were blushing red, Gary gestured to

Chase. "This is a friend of mine, Chase Arlington. Chase, this is my mom and dad."

"Nice to meet you, Mr. and Mrs. Wilson." Chase shook both their hands.

Gary's father replied, "I'm Bill, and my wife's name is Mary."

"May we join you?" Mary asked, after an awkward pause.

Gary knew they had to or he'd never hear the end of it. "Yes. Of course." He shot Chase a nervous glance.

Chase gave a very discreet shake of his head, meaning, don't worry.

Mary and Bill draped their jackets on the backs of their chairs and relaxed at the table.

The waiter was just bringing over the men's beers when he noticed the two new guests. He introduced himself as he placed the beers down in front of Chase and Gary. "Can I get either of you a drink, or do you need a minute to decide?"

"Yes," Mary replied, "I'll have the lemonade, please."

"Iced tea," Bill said.

"Very good. I'll be right back."

Gary took a moment to recover. Did it seem odd? He and Chase in their dress slacks and cotton shirts seated together for a romantic dinner…alone…without women? Gary knew what he would think under the circumstances.

Mary set her napkin on her lap. "So, how do you two know each other?"

"Chase works at the base." Gary sipped his beer, but imagined sucking it down in one gulp, thanks to his anxiety.

"Are you in the air force?" Bill asked, his elbows resting on the table, his hands clasped together near his chin.

"No. I'm a physical therapist."

"I hear an accent." Mary smiled. "East coast?"

Smiling shyly, Chase replied, "New York."

"This must be a big change for you," Bill said.

Gary was in pain. What on earth were his parents thinking? Does this look like two guy pals or two gay guys? They couldn't suspect him. He'd never given them any hint. None whatsoever. So what if Chase was stunning-looking, and dripped with class and charm? That didn't mean Chase was gay. Or that he and Chase were lovers, did it? *No. I'm panicking for no reason. Calm the fuck down!*

"Yes." Chase chuckled. "I hate to admit, Dayton isn't anything like Manhattan."

"No. Not by a long shot." Mary laughed. "We're originally from Vale, Oregon, so it isn't as much as a culture shock for us."

Bill said, "And we've been out here for ten years now. So we're well acclimated to the area."

The waiter appeared. "Here you go. One lemonade, one iced tea."

Gary was a wreck and couldn't seem to relax. Though he was driving, he asked, "Could I get another beer?"

"Of course. And you, sir?" the waiter addressed Chase.

"I'm good." Chase glanced over at Gary curiously.

"Do you need another minute to decide on dinner?" the waiter asked.

"Do you boys know what you're ordering?" Mary looked at them from over her menu. "Bill and I usually order the same thing every time we come."

"We're ready." Gary nodded mechanically, wishing he had gone to a restaurant in another county.

The attentive waiter took their orders while they each told him what they would like. Once he had left with the menus, Gary waited for the next battery of questions. Unfortunately their relaxing dinner had turned into the inquisition.

Mary touched Chase's sleeve. "That lobster risotto is my favorite. You'll enjoy it."

"Yes. I noticed you ordered the same thing." Chase gave Mary a charming smile.

"So," Bill's expression turned serious as he addressed his son, "I heard you'll be leaving next week for your tour?"

Gary stuck his finger into his collar to loosen it, hoping Chase didn't tear up and get emotional at the topic. "Yes."

"Have the orders shown up yet?" Mary sipped her lemonade.

"No. But I expect them first thing Monday." Gary glanced at Chase who was attempting a poker face and failing miserably.

"I can't believe you'll miss Christmas." Mary shook her head angrily. "You do realize Lyle is coming in from California. Or at least he promised he was."

"Your brother?" Chase asked.

"Yes." Gary felt overheated and began rolling up his cuffs.

"Here's your beer," the waiter said as he set down the new one, taking the empty. "Everyone doing okay?"

"Yes, thank you." Mary smiled sweetly at him.

Once he left, Gary suppressed the urge to chug down beer number two.

As if resuming where they left off, Mary again rested her hand on Chase's forearm. "Lyle is a model in LA. He grew tired of a career in the roofing business with Bill and decided on a change. Of course he ended up working in construction because it was all he knew. He didn't have a college degree or anything. Then! He was 'discovered' by an agent. Isn't that wonderful?"

Chase's eyes brightened up. "It is. You rarely hear about those stories anymore. It seems the only way to make it in acting or modeling is to have a parent that is one."

"Nepotism is rife in Hollywood," Bill sneered. "I get tired of seeing the same offspring of the same bad actors and actresses. The whole industry has become a total bore."

"I agree completely." Chase nodded. He glanced at Gary.

Gary had no idea what to say. He was afraid if he spoke, he'd give away his attraction for Chase. It was absurd. He knew that. *But look at the way my mother is acting. She can't keep her hands off him. She knows he's a doll.*

In the strange gap in conversation, everyone was staring at Gary. Gary cleared his throat and sipped his beer.

"Is," Chase tried to fill the silence, "is Lyle a big name in modeling?"

"I don't know. Gary, would you say that Lyle is a 'big name' in the industry?"

"I don't really keep up on his career, Mom." Gary was still boiling hot. His nerves were shot. He dabbed discreetly at a drop of sweat running down his temple.

"He does ads in magazines mostly," Mary spoke softly, rubbing Chase's sleeve with her fingers. "I don't think he has any aspirations to act, does he, Bill?"

"Not that he's mentioned." Bill sipped his iced tea through a straw. "I'm just happy he's out of construction. The whole economy has taken a nosedive. I'm just eking out a living here in Dayton as it is. And Lyle had a terrible incident while he was living with one of his co-workers."

Gary caught Chase giving him a curious glance. *It's not my fault we never speak about family. Why are you looking at me like that?*

"His roommate hung himself on the scaffolding at a work-site," Mary whispered. "Terrible."

Chase leaned closer to Mary to ask, "Why? Why did he hang himself?"

"Lyle never said. I suppose the boy was unstable." Mary sat upright in the chair as the waiter brought out their salads.

Once they were served their first course, Chase continued where they had left off. "That must have been harsh. How did Lyle take it?"

"He's a strong boy. He was upset of course," Mary answered calmly, "but it came right before his big break. I think the timing was perfect. It got his mind off of it and he was able to move out and into a nicer place."

"Have you visited him in LA?" Chase asked, while digging into his salad.

"No. He says he's too busy." Mary addressed her husband, "We should insist, Bill. I mean, how busy can he be that he only comes here and we never go there?"

"What does it matter, Mary? Lyle comes home every Christmas or Thanksgiving. Don't nag the boy."

"Yes. You're right. We have Gary." She reached for her son across the table.

Gary gave her a weak smile, wishing he had moved to LA. Who knew what Lyle was up to? He kept his social life so vague he could be doing anything and they wouldn't know. *Lucky Lyle. Here I am, under scrutiny constantly. Can't even hold my boyfriend's hand.*

The waiter appeared with a tray and began setting out their meals.

"Looks good," Chase said, leaning over for a sniff.

Gary noticed his mother seemed lost on Chase for a moment. Trying to read his mother's expression, Gary didn't have to when she announced, "Chase, I have a friend who has a beautiful single daughter—"

"Ma!" Gary cut her off.

"What?" She reacted defensively. "Chase is a very handsome man, Gary, and you remember me telling you about Susan? The daughter of our good friends, Tom and Cheryl? Well, you have no interest in her so I just thought—"

Before Gary blew his fuse, Chase reached for Mary's arm and touched her lightly. "I appreciate the sentiment. But I'm already involved with someone."

"Oh." Mary deflated slightly. "Well. That's certainly understandable. Is she still back in New York?"

"No. She's right here." Chase smiled wickedly at Gary.

Gary felt his cheeks go crimson.

"That's very nice, Chase." Mary began eating. "Mm. This is delightful."

When Gary caught Chase's eye, Chase gave him a sweet smile. It melted Gary's heart instantly.

❧❧

Chase was too full for dessert. He sipped a cup of coffee as Mary once again brought up Gary's imminent departure.

"The night before you go I want you to come over for dinner like we did last time."

Trying not to flinch, Chase wanted Gary to spend as much time with him as he could before he left. He hadn't anticipated competition. And one in which he could not join.

"Uh," Gary's response was full of apprehension, "maybe an early dinner. You know. I have to pack."

"All right." Bill raised his cup to his lips. "As long as we get to say goodbye."

"You will. Promise."

Chase touched the corner of his eye to stop a tear from rolling down. Gary's knee pressed against his under the table offering support.

"Is there anything else I can get for you?" the waiter asked upon his return.

Bill responded, "Just the check, please."

The moment Chase reached for his wallet Bill stopped him. "Our treat, Chase."

"No. Don't be silly."

"Chase," Gary said, "I was getting the meal for us anyway."

"That was awfully nice of you!" Mary smiled. "Was there an occasion?"

"I got the last one," Chase said, seeing Gary grow tongue-tied. It seemed to suffice.

"How long have you two known one another?" Mary dabbed her lip with the cloth napkin.

"We met at a football game, we play in the park."

Gary jabbed him abruptly under the table.

"What football game?" Bill asked.

Chase went mute, having no idea the gathering of men on a Saturday or Sunday morning for tackle football was a secret.

"Gary? You get together with friends for football? Really?" The waiter handing him the check distracted Bill momentarily. After he gave the man his credit card, Bill continued, "Which park?"

Gary didn't reply.

"Do you play an organized game?" Bill pursued it like a wolf on an injured caribou. "Gary? I'd love to come watch you."

"Gary?" Mary asked in a serious tone.

"Ah…we just did it a couple of times. No big deal. I don't think we'll be doing it again." Gary set his napkin on the table.

Chase could see his hands tremble slightly. The amount Gary was hiding his sexuality was painful to witness.

"That's a shame." Bill actually sounded accusing, like he had been deceived. "If you have another game, can you let me know?"

"We won't. I'll be gone before next Saturday."

Just as Gary said it, Gary's eyes darted to his in panic.

Chase died. *Gone before next Saturday? Oh, God, no.*

The waiter reappeared. Bill signed the credit card slip, giving him the pen and paperwork while taking his card back.

"Thank you all," the waiter smiled. "Have a good night."

"Uh…" Gary appeared completely ruffled at his place between a rock and a hard spot. "We have to go." Gary moved his chair back.

"It's early. Would you like to come back to our place for a little while?" Mary slid her coat on.

"No. Thanks, Mom." Gary pushed in his chair.

Chase felt all the food in his stomach turn into a cold ball. *Gone by next Saturday? No!*

"Both Chase and I have to get up early for work tomorrow." Gary tucked in his shirt nervously. "Thanks for picking up the tab, Dad."

"My pleasure, son." Bill had a very strange expression on his face.

Chase tried not to catch the man's eye. Could he sense something? Finally see through the charade to the attachment that Chase knew was very hard to conceal. "Thank you, Bill. It was very generous of you." Chase reached out his hand and forced a smile through his breaking heart.

"My pleasure, Chase."

"See ya soon, Mom." Gary walked around the table to kiss her cheek.

"Goodbye, dear."

Chase waited. When Gary parted from their embrace, he reached his hand out to her. "Mary…"

"Chase, so good to have met you." She ignored his outstretched hand and hugged him. In his ear she whispered, "We'll miss him too, Chase."

It stunned him. Chase clamped down on the hysteria building inside of him as he bit his lip painfully and nodded.

They walked to the door as a group.

Outside the temperature had cooled to the fifties. A few people were strolling around the fountain and grassy square for either dinner or late shopping.

"Where are you parked?" Bill asked.

"By Mimi's café," Gary replied.

Nodding, Bill waved. "See you soon."

"Bye." Gary waved back.

Both he and Chase stood still as Mr. and Mrs. Wilson walked off, holding each other arm in arm.

Chase was about to implode. And as if Gary sensed it, he grabbed Chase by the elbow and dragged him to a bench facing the restaurant they had just exited, on the opposite side of the spouting water fountain.

Gary nudged him to sit.

Once they were side by side, he managed to squeak out, "You'll be gone before next Saturday?"

"Chase…" Gary appeared to want to hold his hand but didn't.

"You seem to know more than you're telling me and it's killing me, Gary. So please. Let me know everything so I can prepare myself."

"Prepare yourself?" Gary peered around the area. "Chase, there is no way we can prepare ourselves for this."

As if he were punched in the gut, Chase doubled over and covered his face with both his hands. He heard Gary release a long sigh, but Gary did not touch him in comfort.

Rubbing his face, Chase groaned and forced himself to pull himself together. He slouched on the bench and stared at the spouting water as it jutted out of holes in the cement at random intervals.

After a long silent moment, Gary said, "Look, this is all I know or can predict. I'll get my orders tomorrow morning and have a few days to get ready. My guess is that I'll be leaving by Thursday morning. That means Wednesday night I'll have to have dinner with Mom and Dad."

Numb, nodding, Chase said nothing.

"I'll come to your place after, but I have to get up very early the next morning."

Chase gave him another slight nod.

"That's it, babe. Now you know everything I know."

Waiting for a couple to pass by, Chase whispered, "Okay." He felt ill.

"The minute I get the orders on Monday, I'll call your cell phone and tell you."

Biting his lip, Chase nodded. It was all he could manage at

the moment.

"I'm sorry."

"Don't be. I'm a big boy." Chase corrected the last statement, "A big boy behaving like a blubbering idiot."

After a soft laugh, Gary replied, "I love the fact that you're so attached to me, but I'm in agony over the pain I'm causing you."

Chase grabbed Gary's hand. "You aren't to blame and believe me, I can deal with this. It's you I'm worried sick over."

Gary, less than subtly, untangled his hand from Chase's fingers.

"If I can't touch you, I can't discuss this here." Chase rose up off the bench. "Let's go."

They walked in the twilight to Gary's Hummer. Trying to be patient, Chase wanted to be home before they spoke again.

As Gary drove them back home via Interstate 675, Chase fell into a deep contemplative silence. He'd deal with it. Gary and he would e-mail, write letters. He'd send Gary care packages with homemade cookies in it. It'd be fun.

Yeah. A regular circus.

Once Gary had parked in Chase's driveway, and Chase had his key in the slot of his front door, the sound of a 'woof!' coming from the backyard made him smile. He had Mutley. Mutley would help him get through it.

"Darn."

"What?" Chase looked to see Gary after taking off his shoes.

"No doggie bag." Gary removed his shoes as well, giving Chase a sly smile.

"I think lobster risotto is too highbrow for my mutt."

"Nothing is too good for that hound." Gary walked through the house to the back door.

Chase was enamored by the fact that Gary had taken so well to his animal. "He'll cover your slacks in hair. Be forewarned."

"I know." Gary pushed back the screen door. "Hiya, big boy!"

Mutley did his happy dance, spinning around and making yipping noises.

"Give him a milkbone or some rawhide." Chase opened the cupboard.

"Which does he like best?" Gary petted Mutley's muzzle affectionately.

"Here. Let him choose." Chase handed him one of each.

Playing with Mutley, Gary cupped one in each hand and hid them behind his back. "Which one, Mutt?"

Mutley sat down, raising his paw to Gary's right arm.

Gary opened his fingers. Mutley devoured the milkbone in a few quick chomps.

"He's really smart," Gary said.

"I know. He knows he'll get both. He can spot a softie a mile away."

Mutley tilted his head at Gary. His long pointed ears twitched.

"At least ask him to do something." Chase began unbuttoning his shirt.

"Okay." Gary reached out. "Shake?" Mutley raised his paw. Gary shook it. "Lay down." Mutley did. "Can he roll over?" Gary asked. Before Chase answered, Mutley was on his back. "Hey! You're good!" Gary scratched Mutley's chest and belly, handing him the rawhide treat.

After Gary stood, Chase shook his head. "Covered in hair."

Looking down at his legs, Gary brushed fur off. "So what?"

"What do you feel like doing? TV? Or?"

"Or…" Gary grinned wickedly.

"Good." Chase headed to the staircase after shutting off all the lights and making sure the door was locked. While he ascended, Mutley, the chew still in his jaw, scooted passed them.

Chase turned on the bedroom light and took off his shirt, hanging it on a hanger in the closet. When he glanced back, Gary was already down to his briefs, draping his things over a chair near the dresser.

They entered the bathroom together. Chase relieved himself while Gary washed up. Chase could hear Mutley working on the tough rawhide chew, gnawing loudly.

He and Gary swapped placed. As Chase scrubbed up, he watched Gary pee in the toilet behind him in the mirror's reflection.

Once they were both finished, Chase left the bathroom and set the alarm clock.

"What time are you setting it for?" Gary emerged, shutting the bathroom light behind him.

"Six? Same as last week?" The atmosphere felt strained and Chase thought he was to blame. Poor Gary, putting up with his whimpering, not to mention being in the closet, going to Iraq, how much more could the poor man take?

"Yes. That's fine." Gary crawled under the blankets after tossing his briefs onto the same chair as the rest of his clothing.

Chase shimmied out of his own pair, meeting Gary under the sheets. They faced each other, heads propped up in hands. "I like your mom and dad."

"They're okay."

"You never mentioned your brother Lyle is a model in LA."

Gary shrugged. "He keeps to himself."

"Hmm." Chase smiled mischievously. "Hiding a gay lover?"

At first Gary's expression screwed up in disbelief, then he paused to think about it. "Huh."

"Possible?"

"I don't know. I swear it never occurred to me. But he's only given us his mobile phone number and is very vague about his social life."

Chase was grinning knowingly. "He's gay, babe."

"No! Lyle? Macho construction worker, Lyle?"

Imitating Gary's inflection, Chase echoed, "Gary? Macho Staff Sergeant Gary Wilson is gay?"

Gary shoved him back playfully. "Two gay sons? My parents would keel over."

"I'm telling you, Gary. Lyle may be covering up just like you are."

"Give me that fucking phone." Gary reached across Chase's body to the nightstand. "It's long distance, you mind?" Gary checked the time.

"No. I'm dying to know. You think you can worm it out of him?" As Gary stretched over him, Chase held Gary closer, keeping his body overlapping his under the blankets.

"I'll find out. Hang on." Gary leaned up on his elbow and dialed. When he finished, he lay back on the pillow with the cordless phone positioned so he and Chase could listen to Lyle's side of the conversation.

"Hello?"

"Lyle? Gary."

"Hey! How's life in the air force, macho man?"

Chase gave Gary an impish smile. "That is so gay!" Chase mouthed.

"Good. Lyle. Are you gay?"

Chase choked. "How subtle of you!"

"Shh!" Gary chided Chase.

"What," Lyle answered flatly.

Chase cuddled closer to hear.

"Look, Lyle, it's okay if you are. Just tell me. Are you living with a guy?"

"Why the hell did you call me the middle of a Sunday afternoon to ask me that? What made you do it?"

"You are." Gary rubbed his forehead.

"Gar' don't tell Mom and Dad. Please."

"Son of a bitch!" Chase laughed.

"I won't. What's your lover's name, Lyle?"

"David Thornton."

"Unreal." Gary scrubbed at his eyes.

"Do I sicken you? Gar?"

"No. How did you meet him?"

Chase massaged Gary's chest and belly as he eavesdropped.

"I helped remodel the building he worked in here in LA. He was a very high-powered partner at a law firm."

"Uh huh." Gary peeked at Chase who smiled wickedly at him.

"He's divorced, has a couple of kids. Nice kids. They've totally accepted me."

"Where do you live?"

"He's got this amazing penthouse."

"Is he loaded?"

"Yeah, but I don't give a shit about it."

"Sure, Lyle." Gary laughed sadly.

"I mean it, Gar. He's amazing. I love him."

The conversation died suddenly.

"Gar?"

"Yeah, Lyle?"

"You hate me?"

"No. It's hard to hate you when I'm in bed at the moment with a naked man." Gary glanced over at Chase.

Chase was so proud of him he could bust.

"What? No! You're gay?"

"Calm down, Lyle." Gary shook his head in disbelief.

"Does Mom know?"

"No. Are you kidding me?" Gary choked in irritation. "You've been hiding your lover for, what? How many years, Lyle?"

"Only one."

"Motherfucker." Gary sighed.

"I'm sorry. How could I tell any of you?"

"I'm sorry too, Lyle. I wish you didn't have to be ashamed."

"So?" Lyle asked, "Who's your man?"

Gary peeked over at Chase. "He's a PT that works at the base."

"Older guy?"

"Nope. Young and hot. Very hot." Gary winked at Chase.

"Nice!"

"Say hi." Gary turned the phone towards Chase.

"Hi, Lyle."

Chase heard Lyle crack up with laughter. "Hi!"

"His name is Chase Arlington." Gary spoke with the phone between them.

"This is too funny." Lyle kept laughing. "Come out! Hang out on the beach with me and David."

"I can't. I'm being called up for duty in Iraq next week."

Chase's good mood vanished.

"Shit. That sucks, Gar."

"Life in the air force reserves." Gary shrugged.

"When you get back. Take a vacation."

"I will. Count on it."

"I'm so glad you called. What tipped you off?"

"We bumped into Mom and Dad at dinner. When Chase and I got back to the house, we started discussing you. It occurred to me how vague your answers were about your life. Not to mention,

Chase and I are doing the same thing to them at the moment."

"Ah. Makes sense."

"Yes. I just wonder how long it'll take for Mom and Dad to figure it out."

"Hopefully never."

"Ditto. Okay, Lyle. I just wanted to touch base with you."

"Cool. Listen, good luck over there. Just be careful and keep your head down."

"I will."

"Call when you get back. How long will you be gone for?"

"I don't know. January, February?"

"Damn. I'm coming home for Christmas. You won't be there."

"No, sorry."

Chase cringed.

"You can meet Chase while you're here," Gary said.

"Awesome. What's his number?"

Before he rattled it off, Gary asked, "Is that okay?"

"Yes!" Chase nodded.

They heard Lyle laugh at hearing Chase's answer.

Gary gave Lyle Chase's phone number. "Don't make a pass at him, Lyle, or I'll kick the crap out of you."

"I'm loyal to David. Don't worry. Err…how good looking is Chase anyway?"

"Goodbye, Lyle!" Gary said.

"Bye. Take care, big brother."

"I will. You too." Gary disconnected the call and reached over Chase to set the phone back into the cradle. "Son of a gun." Gary flopped back on the pillows.

"How about that?" Chase cuddled up with him. "Lyle is gay."

"I'm stunned. Really. He was always a very masculine construction worker."

"He's still masculine, Gary. How could you stereotype him?"

"That's not what I mean…never mind. My poor parents."

"Forget them. They'll survive." Chase wanted to say, 'It isn't like you're dead.' But kept remembering where Gary was going and bit his lip on stupid comments like that. "Get over here. Why are you so far away?"

"Far away? We're overlapping."

"Not good enough." Chase shifted Gary so he was laying on top of his body between his straddled legs. "Better. Kiss me."

Seeing Gary soften up his expression considerably at the request, Chase closed his eyes as Gary pressed their lips together.

Chase opened his mouth to receive Gary's teasing tongue as his hands skimmed down his broad back until he squeezed his ass.

"Mm." Gary pushed his pelvis into Chase's.

Between kisses, Chase said, "Make love to me."

Gary kept their lips together, raising his lower half so he could reach down and touch Chase's cock.

At the grip of Gary's hand, Chase's dick throbbed and hardened. "Yes…" Chase pumped into Gary's palm. With both hands, he made for Gary's crotch. Finding his organ solid and eager, Chase ran his fingers over it teasingly, making Gary groan.

Blindly reaching backwards, Chase located a condom on the nightstand. Still kissing Gary, he ripped the package open. Feeling his way downwards again, he rolled the condom on Gary's cock. One more grab toward the nightstand and he had the lube in hand. It took but a moment to slick up the rubber. Once he knew Gary was ready, Chase slid down on the bed with his knees held backwards and wide open.

"Baby," Gary purred as he stared down at Chase's exposed body.

"Balls deep, baby. Balls deep," Chase said sensually.

"Grr…" Gary pushed his dickhead into Chase's ass.

Chase inhaled sharply at the penetration. "So nice." As he was filled, taking it to the hilt, Chase sealed his eyes shut and shivered at the pressure on his prostate. "Christ, I love your dick."

A low seductive chuckle reached Chase's ears.

Gary settled between Chase's spread thighs and began thrusting. Chase shivered down to his curling toes. "Yes…that's it…"

While Gary pumped deeply inside Chase, he nibbled at Chase's legs as they bent underneath his weight. "Jack off," Gary requested.

He reached between his own legs and realized his cock was

already dripping with pre-cum. With one hand he fisted it, with the other he toyed with his own balls.

"Ahh yes…" Gary whimpered as he watched.

Chase felt Gary's cock throb inside him and tensed up his ass muscles.

Gary began riding Chase harder, faster. At the friction inside and out, Chase was ready. "I'm there! Gary, I'm there."

"Aaggh!" Gary grunted, jamming his pelvis as tightly to Chase as he could.

Chase could feel Gary's cock pulsating, giving up its load. It was all Chase needed. He shot out cum, his head spinning with the intensity of the climax.

As they rocked gently, the sensations taking time to subside, Chase opened his eyes. Gary was staring down at the spatters on Chase's chest as Chase continued to milk his dick gently.

When it seemed Gary had recovered slightly, Chase felt him pull out only to drop down and begin licking the cum off Chase's skin.

Straightening his curled legs, Chase relaxed on the mattress as Gary lapped at his sticky fingers and the matted hair on his low abdomen.

Hearing snuffling, Chase tilted his head to the side of the bed. "Mutley!"

Mutley had rested his long muzzle on the blankets next to them. Gary roared with laughter again.

"Go. Lay. Down!" Chase pointed to Mutley's dog bed.

Mutley grumbled and dropped to his pillow in a huff.

"Oh, Christ, he is so fucking funny!" Gary held his gut as he rolled to his back.

"He's completely demented." Chase shook his head at him.

"He's a voyeur!" Gary dabbed at his eyes.

"I keep forgetting he's in here." Chase sat up, looking down at his limp cock.

"It's harmless, Chase." Gary climbed off the bed, heading to the bathroom.

"It's weird." Chase followed Gary to wash up. "He's never taken an interest before."

"Oh? Made love with other men while he was in the room?"

"Never mind." Chase gave Gary a sly look as he wiped himself with a wet washcloth.

They climbed back under the blankets and cuddled. Chase savored Gary's heat and scent beside him. Compelled to think about every detail of their sexual encounters, Chase knew it was going to be hell without him.

CHAPTER 10

Monday morning arrived whether they liked it or not.

Gary dressed in his uniform looking well groomed and delicious as any poster boy for the military. Chase ogled him as he sipped his coffee, fighting the impending gloom that was lurking.

Gary finished eating his toast, glancing briefly at the morning newspaper that showed up on their front stoop. After a moment, Gary rose up. "Right. Gotta go."

Chase watched him stand at the sink and rinse his mug quickly. Gary paused on his way out, kissing his lips. "I'll call you."

"K." Chase froze, staring at Gary as he put his cap on his head, picked up his backpack, and gave him a playful wink and salute as he left.

He managed a smile in response.

The sound of a car door shutting, the Hummer's engine igniting, and then silence, left Chase feeling as if he was dropped into a void. Forcing himself to function, he placed his coffee mug in the sink, made sure everything was off and locked, and gave Mutley one last peek through the back door before he left. On his drive to the base Chase listened to NPR on the radio, which included stock market reports and war updates. The icy chill in his veins would only get worse.

He had to find a way to cope.

❧❧

Chase was just escorting a patient out of the door when his mobile phone vibrated. Checking the time, seeing it was nearing ten, Chase dreaded this call. Reluctantly he took the phone out of his pocket, trying to find some privacy in the hallway. "Hey, babe."

"Hey. I got my orders."

Chase held his breath.

"I leave Thursday morning."

A stabbing pain seared through Chase's chest. "Okay."

"I can't talk long. I just wanted to let you know."

Nodding and biting his lip, Chase knew he had to verbalize something because Gary obviously couldn't see him. "K."

"So, I'll see you at your place after work?"

"Yes." Chase was collapsing inside.

"Good. See ya then."

"Bye." Chase hung up.

His co-worker Thomas passed him on his way to the reception desk. "You all right, Chase?"

Dropping his phone back into his pocket, Chase put on a brave face. "Yes. Fine."

Thomas nodded and continued on his way.

Needing a minute to recover, Chase did an about face and made his way to the staff men's room. He stood at the sink and washed his hands, dabbing the cool water on his face. When he met his eyes in the mirror he found them red-rimmed and filled with pain. "Stop."

He had to continue functioning normally. *You idiot. You're not the one going to Iraq! What the hell are you crying about!*

Chase was so angry at himself for his weakness regarding Gary leaving, he was becoming infuriated. Allowing the anger to obliterate the fear, Chase stood tall, resigned. *Take it like a man! For Christ sake! Gary is!*

❧❧

On his drive to Chase's house, Gary called his parents.

"Hello?"

"Hi, Mom."

"Hello, Gary."

"I got my orders. I leave first thing Thursday."

"Okay. Then we can expect you Wednesday evening?"

"Yes. Early. Like five? Okay?"

"No problem, dear. We'll see you then."

He disconnected the phone and stuffed it into his ABU's shirt pocket. In a place in his heart, Gary wished Chase could seek solace from his parents. His mom and dad had been through this routine before. They would be so much comfort to Chase. But that wasn't going to happen.

Thinking about Lyle seeing Chase over the Christmas holiday made Gary smile. "Unreal, Lyle. You son of a gun. Gay. How about that. Christ, if I'd have known I would have gone out to LA and hung out with you guys ages ago." Gary was dying to know what David Thornton was like. Judging by his description, Gary assumed he was an older man. But how much older? Gary didn't ask. He couldn't wait to come back and make plans for that trip. He and Chase could hang out in West Hollywood, play on the beach in Malibu. "Yes!" Gary grew excited. "Three or four months, Chase. It's nothing. It'll fly by."

∽≈

Chase was cutting up a salad for their dinner when he heard noise in the living room. Even before Gary had arrived at the door, Mutley made a mad dash to it. The dog already recognized the sound of Gary's Hummer when he pulled into the drive.

"Hey, big fella!"

Chase smiled at Gary's enthusiastic greeting and could picture Mutley's happy dance.

"Chase?"

"I'm here!" Chase wiped his hands on a towel and spun around. When that handsome soldier appeared Chase melted.

"Hey, babe." Gary pecked his lips.

"Hey." Chase gave him a loving smile.

"Smells great. What has the chef prepared?"

"Chicken enchiladas."

"Mm! I'm a lucky fucker." Gary chewed on Chase's neck and ear. "Let me change and wash up."

Nodding, chills covering his body, Chase said, "I'll have a beer for you when you get back."

"Perfect."

Watching him go, Mutley following him out, Chase took two iced mugs out of the freezer and filled them with Corona beer. After he set them on the table, he went back to his salad. *Act normal. Don't break down. Behave!*

Ten minutes later Gary returned in his faded jeans and t-shirt. He reclined on one of the kitchen chairs and picked up his beer. "Anything I can do to help?"

"Nope. I'm done. I was just waiting for you to show up before I took it out of the oven." Chase used a potholder to remove a casserole dish and set it on the stovetop.

"Boy oh boy!" Gary said, "I love Mexican food. What a treat."

"Here ya go." Chase brought two plates over, adding, "That's guacamole, and that's sour cream."

"Mm!" Gary rubbed his hands together greedily.

"Sit," Chase told Mutley.

Mutley scuffed to his spot between rooms and lay down.

"You have everything you need?" Chase asked, sipping his beer.

"And more." Gary's blue eyes were luminous.

"Good." Chase passed him his homemade guacamole after he took a dollop. His nerves were shot and he wasn't even feeling hungry, but Chase promised himself to act calm and normal right up to Thursday morning.

After his first bite, Gary moaned. "Good!"

"You like it?" Chase asked.

"Fantastic."

Chase wasn't sure why Gary was so enthusiastic. Maybe Gary had made a vow to himself to keep a good attitude about his departure as well. No use pining over it, making each other cry. What good would it do?

They ate in silence, except for an occasional moan from Gary and a smile or a wink in affection. Chase played the game, pushing the food down his throat.

⁘

The dishes washed and stacked in the drain board, Gary had settled down on Chase's lap as they watched TV in the den.

What was becoming their routine and felt normal and extremely comfortable. Chase caressed Gary's soft hair the way he had done several times before. Another old black and white movie was on AMC. *Dracula*. The one with Bela Lugosi. Yes, Halloween was definitely in the air.

Gary had wrapped his hands around Chase's thigh, his head resting on Chase's crotch warmly. Mutley was asleep on the floor in front of them. The lights were off in the room and just the television lent its glow to the familiar surroundings.

It was domestic bliss as far as Chase was concerned. This was all he wanted out of life–a fantastic partner who was content to be at home. Chase had done the club scene to death, had met the likes of Brock Hart and his many counterparts in Manhattan. He'd had enough. He wanted to be settled. Settled with one man.

Staff Sergeant Gary Wilson.

Chase smiled adoringly at him. Gary's eyes were glued to the set as the chilling music announced another attack of Dracula's bite.

It didn't take long for Chase to feel amorous. Once the meal had digested and they were cuddling, Gary's cheek against Chase's zipper flap was all Chase needed to get horny.

He moved his gentle caresses down Gary's shoulder to his waist. From there Chase dipped into the back of Gary's faded blue jeans to his fantastic ass. Under Gary's briefs Chase felt the taut skin of Gary's gluts. When his cock throbbed, Chase knew Gary could feel it. Gary was playing coy tonight. Chase could see his smile.

Sculpting Gary's ass in his palm, Chase then moved to the crack between those two luscious cheeks, and ran his fingertips up and down it. There wasn't much room in Gary's jeans to play, but Chase made do.

He easily read that wicked grin on Gary's lips. Chase's cock pulsated again, growing hard while Gary was still playing hard to get.

Showing more aggression, Chase found Gary's rim, touching it, nothing more.

He finally got a reaction out of his man. Gary bent his knee, resting his foot on the sofa, opening up access for Chase's probing fingers.

From his new vantage point, Chase made his way between Gary's thighs making contact with his balls. Finding the root of Gary's cock hard, Chase smiled. He rubbed it deeply, tunneling his way between Gary's legs as far as he could reach.

Gary flipped open the button of his jeans. Chase heard the zipper next. The material of Gary's denims loosened nicely. Slowly Chase sank down on the sofa so he could grope Gary's cock, worming his way from behind. He located it tucked on one side of Gary's briefs, already sticky with pre-cum. Chase massaged Gary's length where it was, running his hand from that bent organ back through his legs to his rim, teasing it.

Another peek at Gary's face and Chase noticed a very passionate expression. Gary's eyebrows had furrowed and his lips parted.

"You gorgeous man," Chase breathed.

Instantly Gary rolled over, trapping Chase's hand and gripping Chase's jaw. When their lips met, Chase felt his crotch throb and knew he'd spurted out a drop of pre-cum.

Once Chase managed to wriggle his hand free, Gary spun completely around to face him. A sensuous kiss later where Gary sucked Chase's tongue hotly, Gary paused, panting, to open Chase's slacks. The minute Chase's cock was exposed, Gary enveloped it into his mouth.

The boiling wet heat set Chase's skin on fire. In reaction, he moaned and tensed his thighs.

Gary's head moved up and down on Chase's lap quickly. The enthusiasm and technique were overwhelming him. From the base to the head, the suction was tight and strong. Gary's tongue was possessed, going wild as he drew designs on the underside of Chase's cock.

"Gary…" Chase gulped down a dry throat, unable to catch his breath.

Gary repositioned himself to kneel, getting a grip on Chase's dick at the base and digging his free hand under Chase's balls.

"Aahhfuckkk!" Chase jerked his hips upwards, deeper into Gary's mouth and came. The pleasure was so intense Chase felt his eyelids flutter and his ass pucker.

Gary kept sucking hard for another few draws, slowing down gradually, as if he didn't want to stop. When he finally did, he gazed at Chase.

"Baby…" Chase couldn't manage to slow down his pulse or respirations.

Gary stood, reaching for him.

With an effort, Chase rose to his feet, holding Gary's hand. Once Gary had shut the television with the remote, he escorted Chase up the stairs.

The sight of Gary's hips mesmerized Chase as his open jeans slung low on them.

Once inside their bedroom, Gary began to undress Chase.

So sated from the blowjob, Chase felt positively pliable. Stripped naked, Gary urged him to the bed.

Gary lingered beside him, staring down at him while he removed his clothing. Nothing was said. The only sound was Mutley settling himself back to slumber on his pillow.

Disrobed, Gary stood over Chase, pumping his own cock. Chase felt those sharp eyes on him in pleasure as they studied every inch of his body like a strategic map.

Gary made a show of slipping the rubber on his cock. Another sexy gesture of coating it, sliding it through his own slippery hands.

Chase was rock hard once again. The erotic display was almost as good as the act itself. Almost. Scooting low on the pillows, he bent his body in half, his knees next to his own ears. A low masculine sound of delight soon followed the gesture.

The bed shifted from Gary's weight as he positioned himself. Before he penetrated, Gary used his cock to toy with Chase's genitals, smearing the gel over Chase's balls and ass crack.

Chase reached both his hands to his own bottom, spreading his cheeks wide. Another deep whimper from Gary was his reward.

Gary's hot cock ran from Chase's balls to his hole. Once it made contact with Chase's puckered ring he pushed in. Chase inhaled sharply and his dick jerked in response and grew engorged again.

Drawing closer, Gary slowly burrowed his cock inside Chase

to the hilt, pausing when he couldn't go any deeper.

The pleasure washing up Chase's body was so intense his cock oozed more sticky fluid.

Painfully slow, Gary pulled out to the tip, only to thrust in fast and hard.

"Ah!" Chase gasped, his own hips jutting upwards for more contact.

Again and again, Gary repeated the same move–pulling out slowly to the very tip and jamming inside quick and deep.

Shaking his head side to side, Chase moaned, "Ahh, fuck…" as his head spun.

After a few more thrusts the same way, Gary pushed in as far as he could and used both hands to massage Chase's balls.

The touch made Chase quiver visibly and a long string of pre-cum was now pooling on his abs.

"You ready, lover?" Gary purred.

"God yeah." Chase panted in excitement.

With two hands Gary held Chase's dick, and as he thrust in, he fisted it. Chase reached his arms out to either side of the bed, holding on for the ride. Watching Gary's hands, then his face, Chase was on target for climax number two. "Babe!" he said, "I'm there!"

Gary accelerated his thrusting and squeezed Chase's cock mercilessly. As Chase shot out semen on his own skin, Gary choked in a grunting noise and his cock pulsated deep inside Chase's ass.

Chase could barely moan, the pleasure was so strong. He clenched his jaw and knew he had never had an orgasm even close to the ones he was achieving with Gary.

As Gary ground his pelvis as tightly as he could into Chase, Chase writhed under him in ecstasy. Finally able to speak, he shouted, "Oh God!"

Gary hung his head and gasped for air, sweat running down his face.

"Gary…Jesus Christ, Gary."

"I know." Gary caught his breath. "Chase, I know."

A minute later, Gary pulled out, sitting back to recuperate.

Chase knelt up in front of him and drew him into an embrace. "I adore you."

"I love you too, babe." Gary kissed his cheek. "Let's wash up. I'm wiped out."

Agreeing, Chase followed Gary to the bathroom, peering back to catch a glimmer of Mutley's eyes.

Chapter 11

Wednesday night Gary made the obligatory visit to his parents' house for dinner. Rapping his knuckles on the door before he opened it, Gary called, "Hello?" The house smelled like roast turkey and vegetables.

"Hello, Gary!" His mother's voice came from the kitchen.

Gary closed the front door behind him and spotted her at the stove. "Smells great, Mom."

"Well, I figured you'd miss out on both Thanksgiving and Christmas dinner."

He embraced her from behind and kissed her hair. "Thank you."

"My pleasure."

"Where's Dad?"

"I'm here."

Gary spun around to see his father at the threshold between the kitchen and the hall.

"Are you ready to go?" Bill asked.

"As I can be. In the morning we'll make sure all our gear is packed."

Mary asked, "How early do you have to get to the base?"

"Early. That's why I don't want it to be a late night."

"Dinner's ready. Bill? Could you carve the bird up for me?"

Gary stepped back as his father did the honors. His dad did the carving ritual every holiday. "Anything I can do, Mom?"

"Just get yourself whatever it is you want to drink out of the fridge."

"There's wine," Bill said.

"You want some?" Gary located the bottle and held it up.

"I'll take a glass," Mary replied.

"Dad?"

"Sure, son."

Gary waited as his mother removed three stemmed glasses out of the cupboard. He filled each and placed the bottle on the table. Sitting down, Gary picked up his wine to take a sip as he watched his parents work in harmony filling three plates with comfort food. The scene made him regret missing the upcoming holidays.

Once a steaming meal was in front of him, Gary inhaled deeply with a smile. He'd miss food like this. Big time. "Looks great, Mom."

"Thank you, dear. Eat up."

"I'll wait for you and Dad." Gary had another sip of wine.

His parents joined him at the table a moment later. They toasted the meal and began partaking in it.

Taking the gravy as his father passed it to him, Gary wondered what Chase was eating, knowing he'd love a meal like this. He covered his turkey breast in gravy, and handed his mother the porcelain boat.

"Will you have access to a computer?" Bill asked.

"Yes." Gary nodded.

"Good." Mary dabbed her lip with her napkin. "Keep us up to date."

"I will."

"Do you want me to send you treats?"

"Yes!" Gary laughed. "Put this meal into a box and ship it."

His parents laughed softly.

"I'll make sure you have a steady supply of cookies and brownies."

"Thanks, Mom. The guys will love you." He winked.

She gave him a special smile back.

∽≈

The television offered nothing of interest. Chase slouched on the sofa in the den reading the newest Kage Alan novel. Though the story tried its best to enthrall him, Chase kept glancing at the time. He imagined Gary showing up near seven. That was the plan.

He hadn't eaten. Couldn't force himself to. His stomach was queasy and he felt disconnected and numb. He thought about calling his parents or maybe one of his sisters to kill the time, but that didn't sound exciting either. More annoying than distracting. No. He didn't have much of a support group for this. What were the odds in Dayton there'd be a 'Help for Lovers of Deployed Gay Boyfriends Left Behind' hotline?

Mutley mumbled as he rolled to his side. He'd been sleeping on the floor at Chase's feet. He knew the dog would hear Gary's arrival well before he did, so he didn't bother moving at the sounds of cars passing on the street in front of his house.

Closing the novel, resting it on his lap, Chase relaxed his body as he listened to the clock on the kitchen wall ticking loudly, Mutley's snores, the beating of his own heart, which seemed to be pounding more loudly than anything else he was hearing.

When Mutley bolted to his feet, Chase started. Putting the book on the side table, he got up and walked to the living room. Mutley had his nose to the door, wagging his tail. Chase couldn't hear anything yet. Then a car door sounded.

He checked his watch. Six thirty.

As the man on the other side of the door approached, Mutley began going nuts. So was Chase but he didn't have a tail to wag. Another body part was responding, however.

Though Chase had left the door unlocked, he opened it for Gary.

Seeing his man's big smile, Chase thought wryly, *Yes, my love, you're being greeted by the 'beast' and his dog.* He positively melted at the sight of Gary.

"Hi, babe." Gary pecked Chase's lips as he passed. "Got you something."

Chase noticed him holding a plate covered in foil. "What's this?"

"Pumpkin pie." Gary grinned, dropping his backpack down by the staircase.

"Did you have a nice dinner?" Chase asked, observing Gary's content and slightly tired appearance.

"I did. Mom went all out. I wish you could have been there."

Wishing he could have been too, Chase brought the plate to the fridge and stashed it inside. When he spun around, he found Gary roughhousing with Mutley.

"How ya doin', big guy?" Gary wrestled him, making Mutley growl playfully.

A tidal wave threatened, but Chase bit it back as he watched Gary continue to pet Mutley between his pointed ears. "So. I suppose you're full. Can I get you a nightcap or anything?"

"I'm good," Gary answered, looking around. "Did you eat dinner?"

"No."

"Chase…" Gary admonished.

"I just didn't feel like making anything."

"I would have brought you some turkey."

"It's okay." Chase folded his arms over his chest.

Chase's breath caught in his throat when Gary walked over to him, and grabbed him around the shoulders. "I need to get to bed early. I have to get up at five."

Chase said, "I know."

"Mind if I shower now?"

"No. Why would I?"

"Join me?" Gary purred, rubbing their crotches together.

"Sure."

Gary held his hand and led Chase up the stairs. Mutley sprinted passed them to his pillow in the bedroom.

Undressing as Gary did the same, Chase kept beating himself up to stay in line. No tears. He promised himself.

Watching Gary enter the bathroom naked, Chase savored that manly strut with gusto, burning it on his brain for when he needed to conjure it up later. Chase leaned on the doorframe as Gary started the shower. "Gary Wilson, you are *all man*…"

A smile brightened Gary's face at the compliment. His blue eyes met Chase's while he held his hand under the warming spray. Giving his cock a sensual stroke, Gary asked, "Wanna suck your man?" and vanished inside the shower stall.

Chase was right behind him, sliding the door shut. Seeing

Gary soaking wet, Chase groaned deeply and dropped to his knees. He was in heaven taking Gary's semi-erection into his mouth. The water cascaded over the both of them. Chase's hands seemed possessed as they danced from Gary's balls, to his thighs, to his ass, to the base of his cock, not knowing where to settle. Everything felt so incredibly wonderful.

"Don't make me come."

Allowing Gary's cock to slip out of his mouth, Chase peered up at him.

"I want to come in your ass."

Slowly, Chase rose to his feet, hugging Gary and kissing his soft lips. In the swirling steam Chase rocked with his lover, teasing him, biting him, licking his coarse jaw as he slid his own wet rigid cock against his.

Gary parted from him gently, and finished up washing. Then he shut the taps to stand and drip as they gazed at each other.

Chase couldn't imagine what Gary's thoughts were. Perhaps even the simple act of a hot shower was going to be a luxurious memory now. Nothing would be taken for granted once Gary touched ground at Al Taji Airbase. Chase had no clue what type of facility it was and dreaded asking.

Through dulled senses, Chase took the towel he was handed, and watched Gary rub his hair and back.

On autopilot, Chase did the same, tossing the towel over the shower doors when he was finished. Again, led by Gary's strong hand, Chase was guided to their bed.

The puppet to this man's mastery, Chase was there to serve the man who served his country.

Urged to lay back, coaxed to spread his legs, Chase complied willingly. Gary's tongue went right for his ass and balls. Shivering at his aggression and passion, Chase dug his fingers through Gary's wet hair as his rough jaw scratched the delicate skin of his genitals. Chase's legs were pushed upwards so once again his knees were near his ears. Gary tongue-fucked him vigorously. The ripples of pleasure shot through Chase making him shake his head side to side on the pillows in disbelief. Christ, did this man know how to make love, or what? Chase was forever at his mercy.

Once his hole was slick with saliva, Gary slid his index finger in.

Chase was already entering the stratosphere. His dick was so hard the head was a deep shade of purple and once again, dripping. He only hoped he pleased his lover as much as his lover pleased him.

While Gary fingered his rim, he used his cock to explore Chase's balls and inner thighs. Gary ran his stiff length up and down Chase's sack. Chase could only watch and try to catch his breath. From his trapped position, he could do little else. Offering what he could to the action, Chase again used his fingers to spread his ass cheeks for Gary.

Gary groaned deeply, running his oozing slit between Chase's legs from his puckered rim to the base of his cock before diving back on it to lick some more.

This time when Gary tongue-fucked him, Chase felt his cock pulsate and almost came. A pool of pre-cum juices was forming, matting his dark hair at his lower abdomen. The stimulation was so extreme that Chase had to keep forcing himself to keep his eyes open to watch, as the passion sought to close them. "Ohmy-God…" Chase whimpered.

Gary sat up, wiping his face with the back of his hand roughly. He stretched over Chase to the nightstand and tore open a condom. After sliding it on, he used a generous amount of lube.

The minute three of Gary's fingers entered Chase's back passage, Chase jerked his hips involuntarily and came, spraying cream all over his chest. "*Fffuckk!*" Chase's cock throbbed and more cum shot out.

Gary made a lovesick noise in his throat when he witnessed it, and immediately jammed his dick into Chase. After a few deep fast thrusts, Gary climaxed, his whole body convulsing, nailing Chase to the bed. As if the power of the orgasm was overwhelming him, Gary howled at the thrill.

Chase had never heard him so vocal before and blinked in surprise.

As soon as Gary slowed, he pulled out, dropped down, and licked the cum off Chase's chest. In disbelief, Chase groaned. "I have never had a lover like you before…Jesus Christ, Gary, what you do to me."

Sucking in air deeply, Gary raised his chin from his lapping to reply, "Or you me. Chase…you're a fucking drug. I'm so hooked."

His legs released from their confinement, Chase straightened them out on the mattress, and forcefully dragged Gary up his sweat-soaked body to his lips. On contact with Gary's sticky face, Chase devoured him, lapping his own cum off Gary's jaw.

Gary tightened his grip around Chase's body, whimpering as they kissed, sucking hard, painfully hard as they battled their emotions.

Chase knew he'd never had a love like this before in his life. It was everything. All consuming in its passion. Defied all doubts in his mind that this man was his consummate soul mate. He understood fate had brought them together. And nothing—not time, distance, nor war, would break them apart.

CHAPTER 12

When the alarm went off Gary died inside. It was still pitch dark. He heard Chase hit the snooze button. Aware he had to get up, Gary rolled to the side of the bed and set his feet on the carpet. A dim light illuminated the room. Seeing Chase had turned on the small lamp on the nightstand, Gary whispered, "Stay in bed."

"No." Chase leant up against the headboard and scrubbed at his eyes and hair.

Inhaling deeply, Gary motivated himself to stand and wash up. Once he returned, he found Chase in a pair of gym shorts, his hair sticking up from their rough night's rest.

In silence Gary put on his uniform while Chase watched.

"Let me get you a cup of coffee."

"No. I'll get one at the base." Gary tucked in his shirt. "Thanks, though."

Chase nodded but didn't answer.

After a cursory glance around, Gary finished packing his small kit and shouldered it. Chase and Mutley followed Gary down the stairs. As Gary crouched down to lace his beige boots, he wrapped his boot blousers around his shins to properly puff out the bottoms of his trousers. His ABU utility cap in place on his head, he rose to his full strapping six-foot-two height and looked at his forlorn lover.

When Gary was standing at the front door, he stopped moving. He couldn't say goodbye. He pecked Chase's mouth. "I'll call you. Or e-mail you."

Chase was biting his lip, fighting.

One more kiss and Gary opened the door. As an afterthought,

he spun back. Giving Mutley a good scratch behind the ears, he told the dog, "Take care of him, Mutt."

One last peek at Chase who was barely holding it together, and Gary left.

It was so dark it felt like the middle of the night. He opened the door of his Hummer, tossed his pack in it, and stuck the key in the ignition. Chase and Mutley were standing at the screen door.

Gary gave them a wave he wasn't sure they could see and backed out of the driveway. There was nothing he could do. They would get through it. The time would pass quickly. No reason to be upset or emotional. He was coming back.

Focusing on the drive while he still felt half-asleep, Gary tried not to think about the lover he was leaving behind, and only on the mission ahead. It was the only way he could survive the separation. If he sat and dwelled on it, he'd fall apart.

Chase was so lost inside himself he couldn't focus. Determined to pay attention to his patients, Chase had them repeat things for him when his mind wandered, and apologized at his lack of concentration.

By lunchtime Thomas had joined him in the staff room. "Are you okay, Chase?"

After pouring a cup of coffee, Chase sat across from him at the table. "Yes. I'm fine, Thomas."

"You seem miles away."

"I do have a lot on my mind."

"Anything I can do?"

"No. But thanks."

Thomas took a bite of his sandwich. "No food?"

Waking out of his thoughts, Chase met Thomas' kind eyes. "No. I'm not feeling very hungry."

"I'm here if you want to talk about it."

"No. Thanks for the offer though." Chase forced a smile and assumed it looked like pain and not pleasure.

"No problem."

The rest of their break was silent. Chase kept trying to

imagine where Gary was. Obviously already on a plane. Of that he had no doubt.

∽≈

Chase arrived home, thumbed through his mail and walked straight through the house to the back door to let Mutley in. Mutley danced around his legs as Chase separated the bills from the junk. Once he finished that task, he sighed. "Right. Food for you, Mutt."

Mutley wagged his tail vigorously.

After he had prepared Mutley's meal, Chase set his bowl on the floor and headed to his bedroom to change. The minute he entered the room he caught the scent of Gary's cologne. It felt inviting and familiar. It even made him smile.

Wearing his jeans and a sweatshirt, Chase trotted back down the steps to find Mutley in the process of licking his dog dish clean. Leaving through the back door, Chase kept his mind blank as he did poo patrol in his backyard. Mutley followed him out to sniff around the perimeter.

"I'll bet even shoveling crap doesn't compare to the shit you'll be doing, babe." Chase frowned. Was it deliberate he never asked Gary what exactly he'd be doing 'over there'? Maybe. Gary didn't offer, and Chase never inquired. He had a vision of Gary putting the Iraqi military through various drills, the tough Staff Sergeant Wilson barking out orders. Chase was betting his thoughts weren't too far from reality.

"He's safe. He's fine." Chase shoveled up another pile of doggie doo. "Jesus, Mutt. You sure crap a lot." When he peered up, Mutley had the Frisbee in his mouth.

"Okay, let me just finish up." Chase remembered them playing together at the high school and grinned again. "He'll be back before I know it. No reason to get upset."

Once he had finished clearing up the yard, Chase grabbed the Frisbee out of Mutley's mouth and tossed it for him. He tried to relish in the fact that he was deeply loved, and also was deeply in love, that alone should be celebrated, not mourned.

∽≈

It didn't hit until ten o'clock. Chase was slouching on the sofa watching *Frankenstein* in the dark room. His lap was horribly vacant of his lover's warm head.

Staring down at where Gary should be but wasn't, Chase felt a lump finally form in his throat. Swallowing it down, he fixed his eyes on the television screen. The monster was throwing a little girl into a lake. Even though the movie was made in 1931, it still creeped him out. He didn't like horror movies. Despised slasher/ gruesome films, and thought excessive violent genre movies like *Saw* should be banned. "They allow that kind of sick vulgarity on the screen. But God-for-fucking-bid you show a penis or men kiss…gasp! Censors would be all over that, thinking it's morally wrong. What a fucking world we live in, huh Mutt. A sick, sad world."

Mutley didn't even raise his head from his paws for all the soapbox ranting Chase was doing.

The argument Chase was making in his head was getting him incensed. He was railing over nonsense. "Can't buy a goddamn film with gay sex in it unless it's pornography. God help an actor who comes out of the closet…but cut off a body part? Eviscerate a human body? Sure! That's fine!"

He was shouting, waving his hands. "Look!" He held up the television listing to Mutley who barely raised an eyelash to all Chase's fervor. "Count the fucking blood and guts movies, Mutley! *Halloween V*? *Friday the Thirteenth*? *Scream*? *Nightmare on Elm Street*? You want horrific gore, Mutley? Take your pick! What kind of animal goes to see these disgusting movies? Hmm? Oh, but wait! You want a gay romance? Ha! Good fucking luck!" He threw the newspaper down in a flurry of pages.

When the phone rang it scared the crap out of him. Catching his breath from the fright, he muted the television and picked up the cordless. "Hello?"

"Hi, Chase, it's Mom."

"Hi." Chase felt his heart still pounding under his ribcage.

"Are you okay?"

"No." He leaned over and began gathering up the newspaper he threw. "I'm a mess."

"Oh, no. Chase, talk to me."

Managing to fold the guide with one hand, Chase set it aside, and flopped down on his back on the sofa. "Gary left for a tour of duty in Iraq this morning. I'm a wreck."

"Oh, sweetheart."

"He'll only be gone for three or four months, but I'm falling apart at the seams. I miss him so much."

"The months will pass very quickly, Chase."

"Mom. Iraq? He's in fucking Iraq!"

"Okay, calm down. Many men are in Iraq and come home just fine."

"Yeah?" Chase said sarcastically, "and how many didn't come back fine? How many came back in a fucking box or with pieces missing?"

"Chase, calm down."

Rubbing his forehead in agony, Chase felt Mutley's wet nose on his cheek. He nudged it away but kept petting him to reassure him. Mutley always knew when he was upset.

"Are you rational?" his mother asked quietly.

"Yes. Sorry. I've never been in this situation before and I'm not coping well. And that's an understatement." He said to Mutley, "Sit." Mutley plopped down and leaned against the couch beside him.

"Look, honey, he just left this morning. Give yourself some time to adjust."

"I know." Chase exhaled a deep stressful breath.

"How are his parents dealing with it?"

"I don't know. I met them once at dinner in a restaurant but they don't know Gary's gay. So I was his friend. I can't call them."

"That does make it tougher."

"No kidding."

"Will there be contact between you and Gary while he's gone?"

"Yes. I can write him, and even e-mail. He'll have access to a computer once he's there, and I think I remember him saying he can even phone me on occasion."

"That's helpful. You'll get to see how he's doing."

"Mom."

"Yes?"

"I'm petrified."

"It sounds like you and Gary grew very close very fast."

"We did." Chase dabbed at a tear before it fell. "I'm head over heels, Mom."

"And he feels the same?"

"Yes."

"Well, I think you're going through what many spouses and partners are enduring over this war. I don't think you're alone in your feelings."

"I know. It doesn't make it any easier." Chase peered at the television screen. The villagers were gathering with torches at the evil scientist's lair to burn it down.

"Do you want to come out for a visit?" his mother asked. "Take a long weekend? I'll mail you the tickets."

"No. Not yet. Gary is going to be gone over both Thanksgiving and Christmas. Why don't I come out then?"

"All right, dear."

"How are you and Dad?"

"We're fine. Other than missing you."

"I was going to call Stella and Kim but I just didn't. I should talk to them more." Chase thought about his sisters affectionately.

"Yes, at least once a week you all should touch base."

"Anything new with them?"

"No. Kim is still busy at work, and Stella is getting through graduate studies. Pretty much the usual news."

"Good." Chase caressed Mutley's ears gently as the dog rested his muzzle next to him.

"Anytime you need a sympathetic ear, Chase, call."

"I know. Thanks, Mom."

"And when you can, send Gary my best wishes."

Chase smiled. "I will."

"Goodnight, dear."

"Night, Mom." Chase disconnected the line and stared at his dog. "You miss him too, don't you?"

Mutley tried to lick Chase's face but he dodged that pink

tongue, laughing.

"You want a milkbone?"

Mutley hopped to his feet and wagged his tail.

"Go on, I'll meet you."

In a flurry of fur, Mutley raced out of the room. Chase could hear his nails tapping the kitchen tiles. Slowly sitting up, placing the phone back in its cradle, Chase shut the television and made it to his feet. He dug two treats out of the box in the cabinet and said, "Sit."

Mutley did, his ears twitching.

"Shake."

That big paw slapped Chase's hand. Chase gave Mutley one milkbone, dropping another on the floor near him.

Chase hadn't eaten since the day before, living on nothing but coffee all day. Opening the fridge, he stared at the contents without interest. Instead, he poured a shot of brandy for himself and leaned against the sink counter sipping it, as Mutley licked up the biscuit crumbs from the floor.

Taking his time to finish it, Chase rinsed the glass when he was done. He let Mutley out for his last pit stop before climbing the stairs. Washed up and in bed, Chase set the alarm and gazed at the ceiling. Reaching his arm out to the empty side of the bed, Chase imagined Gary with him. He couldn't get to sleep.

Chapter 13

Saturday morning Chase was so relieved to see the crowd gathering for football he almost cried. "Come on, dog." He jogged with Mutley to the larger tree he had previously secured him to and tied him up. They had completed their run and Mutley instantly lay down on the cool grass, panting. After a pat on his head, Chase jogged to where the gang was lingering.

"Hey!" Sam greeted him warmly.

"Hi, Sam, Dev." Chase waved at the other men, catching Kevin's eye.

"Have you heard from Gary?" Chris asked, tossing the football up in the air.

"No. Not yet. It's only been three days." Chase noticed Kevin staring at him boldly.

Dev patted Chase's back. "He'll be fine. We didn't know if you'd show up."

"I need to give you my phone number. Remind me after the game." Chase met Sam's gaze.

"Yes. Please." Sam smiled at him.

"Now we're uneven again," Jerry said.

"Oh," Chase replied, "sorry. I can leave."

"No! Don't be stupid." Dev shook his head. "We were playing four against five before you showed up."

Kevin, hands on his hips, pushed out his pelvis in a sexual come on. "Who gets Chase now?"

"Not you," Chase teased playfully.

The other men cracked up.

Dev touched Chase's back. "He'll just stay with us."

"Good." Kevin's eyes brightened.

Chase gave Kevin a reprimanding glare, but it did nothing to stop Kevin from licking his chops at him.

"Did you already toss for the ball?" Chase asked.

"Yeah, they receive." Dev raised his arms and Chris threw the ball to him.

Lewis brushed up against Chase as they walked down the field. "I'd tell you to block Jerry, but my guess is Kevin's going to be all over you like flies on shit."

"I'm getting the same feeling." Chase sighed heavily.

"Just punch him in the face." Dev smiled. "It worked last time."

"No." Sam laughed. "Chase's dog attacking Kevin worked last time."

They had a good chuckle over the memory. Once they were down field, Dev shouted to the other team, "You girls ready?"

"Yeah!" Joe hollered back.

"You guys ready?" Dev asked the three men standing with him.

"When you are." Chase smiled, very glad to be with Gary's buddies.

"Here we go!" Dev threw the ball high into the air.

Kevin caught it and crouched over the ball to protect it as

he ran.

Chase tackled Kevin only after he managed to avoid being blocked by Barry and Joe. Together they slammed to the soft damp earth.

Turning his head, Chase met Kevin's stare

"Don't start." Chase got to his feet as Kevin handed the ball to Chris.

Jerry hauled Kevin to his feet. As he was set upright he licked his lips seductively at Chase. He ignored it and walked back to his group.

"I knew it," Lewis said. "Sorry, Chase. There's no way to completely avoid it."

"Don't worry about it." Chase waved him off.

"He's just trying to get a rise out of you," Sam said.

"He's an ass." Dev sneered. "How can he do that with Gary over in Iraq? I swear he pisses me off."

Chase touched Dev's arm. "I appreciate it. But believe me, it doesn't mean a thing."

"How sweet is that?" Sam smiled.

"You idiots ready?" Joe asked them.

They dispersed into a defensive line as Chris reached between Kevin's legs for the ball. "Hep one, hep, two, hike!"

As Chase tried to block Chris's pass Kevin body slammed him. Twisting away, Chase raised his arms high over his head trying to prevent Chris from throwing downfield.

When Kevin grabbed Chase's balls, Chase roared and shoved him down to the ground in fury.

The game action halted and Chris glared down at Kevin in anger. "Nice one, dipshit. Can't we just play without you doing something stupid?"

Kevin made it back to his feet slowly. "I didn't do anything."

Chase puffed up his chest and approached Kevin in rage. "The man I love is over in Iraq-hell right now!" Chase pointed his finger into Kevin's face. "If you think just because he's out of my sight means he's out of my mind, you've lost it." Chase tried to calm down. "One more unwanted touch from you, and I'll kick the crap out of you. I've been trying to be patient but you're wearing on my fucking nerves at the moment."

Dev and Sam finally caught up after running down field.

"Kev', come on. Chase has it bad enough right now with Gary gone," Sam said, "Leave him alone."

Brushing off his legs, Kevin replied under his breath, "All right. Let's just play."

"Finally!" Chris said, "Replay of down."

"It shouldn't be!" Dev snarled.

Sam grabbed Dev's arm and dragged him back behind the line of scrimmage.

Chase followed Lewis so they were all standing together again.

"He'll stop now, Chase," Sam said.

"If he doesn't, I'm going to fucking kill him."

"All right, buddy." Dev rubbed Chase's back. "He won't do it again."

Sam caught Chase's eye. "We need to go out for a beer. Talk about Gary."

A lump formed in Chase's throat. "Yes. I would love that."

Sam winked at him.

❧❧

An hour and a half of elbows to the ribs, getting slammed to the ground and racing up and down the field, Chase was beat. With Mutley's leash around his wrist, he wrote down his home information for Sam and Dev as they reciprocated. Chase handed his piece of paper to Sam, then knelt down to wipe the mud off Mutley's paws before letting him inside the car.

"Here ya go, Chase."

"Thanks, Sam." Chase took the note.

"So? You up for a beer and a burger over at Max and Irma's?"

"Is that's over by the mall?" Chase thought he remembered seeing the restaurant there.

"Yes. Would you rather have us pick you up?" Dev read over the information Chase provided. "You're on the way. Christ, Chase, you're really close to my condo."

"Okay. If you don't mind. I'm still finding my way around." Chase checked to see Mutley sitting patiently on the passenger's seat.

"Not a problem. How about six thirty."

"Perfect."

"Good. See you then." Dev and Sam climbed into Dev's car together. It seemed with the cooling weather the motorbikes were left behind.

Waving as they backed out, Chase was about to sit down behind the wheel when he caught Kevin walking towards him. He hadn't noticed him, but assumed Kevin had been waiting for Dev and Sam to leave before he approached.

Leaning over the roof of his car, Chase asked, "What do you want?"

"To apologize."

Chase paused to see if that was all Kevin had to say.

"Look, Chase, Gary and I had a bad breakup. I don't know if he told you."

Yes, you asshole, he told me you cheated on him and lied. Your loss is my gain. "And?"

"And…I guess there's still some bad blood between us."

"What's it got to do with me?"

"I don't know. Maybe it's tough to see Gary's moved on finally." Kevin bit his lip and gazed around the parking lot. "And that he met such a great guy."

Assuming Kevin was simply trying to make amends, Chase softened his expression. "Apology accepted."

"Good." Kevin hesitated, then smiled and said, "See ya next week?"

"See ya." Chase climbed into his car and stuck the key in the ignition. "How do you like that, Mutley? An apology. Not a bad start for a Saturday morning." He headed home, anxious to check his e-mails to see if anything showed up from Gary yet.

~∂∾

Chase was coming out his front door when Dev's car pulled up. He double-locked the deadbolt, and walked over to the low-slung two-door coup as Sam climbed out and pushed the passenger's seat forward to allow him access to the back seat.

"Thanks." Chase ducked inside.

"No problem." Sam resettled into his place and fastened his safety belt.

"Where's the dog?" Dev asked.

"I keep him in the backyard while I'm gone."

"No doggie door?" Sam turned around and smiled at Chase.

"You kidding? A doggie door big enough for Mutley will be big enough for a burglar."

"True." Dev chuckled.

"Have you heard from Gary yet?" Sam asked.

"No. I expect it may take some time for him to make contact."

"My brother Rusty is in Iraq."

Chase gazed at Sam in surprise. "Shit."

Nodding, Sam replied, "Full active duty. He's there for two years so far but he will get a break soon. Unfortunately he'll go back again."

"Christ, Sam." Chase sighed. "That has to suck."

"He didn't think he'd be there as much as he is. I think because they feel they're short on personnel, he's been called up more than usual."

"I am so sorry." Chase felt sick.

Sam shrugged. "He wanted to do it."

"How do you and your family cope?"

"We just do. You get used to it."

Chase didn't think he ever would. Looking out the window as they headed down Route 725 to the restaurant, he tried to feel reassured by Sam's story. But it did little to ease the knot in his stomach.

When they finally reached their destination, Chase walked with them to the entrance. He smiled noticing his friends wearing their leather motorcycle jackets. To him, the two appeared to be such an ideal couple. He gave Dev an appreciative nod, when he held the door for him and Sam. Once the hostess had them seated, he barely had time to inspect the menu before their waitress showed up.

"Can I start you guys with something to drink?"

"Beer," Chase replied in unison with Sam and Dev. The

waitress grinned and left.

"Okay," Chase said as he opened the menu. "What's good here?"

"Burgers," Dev answered flatly. "I haven't ventured anywhere else."

"Burgers sound good." Chase made his selection in his mind, setting the menu down.

It was a loud boisterous eating establishment, rough and ready; a cross between a fast food chain and an East Coast style diner.

The waitress placed a beer in front of each man. "Are you ready to order?"

They nodded, asking for their choice of hamburgers and fries.

Once she vanished, Chase sipped his beer, and then asked, "How did you guys meet?"

Sam exchanged wry smiles with Dev. "At a biker rally."

"No," Dev corrected, "we actually first met at a meeting for our motorcycle club, then went to the rally as a group."

"Ah." Chase nodded. "Love at first sight?" His tongue was planted in his cheek.

Again Sam gave Dev a look that Chase could not immediately decipher.

"More like love at first punch." Dev laughed.

"You punched him?" Chase asked Sam.

"No. I'm not the one who punched him. It's a long story, Chase. Let's just say Dev thought coming out at Sturgis bike rally was a good idea."

Having heard a little about the event, Chase shook his head. "Now I know why you were punched."

Dev shrugged indifferently. "Better than hiding my ass."

"No. It wasn't." Sam glared at him.

Chase held up his hands for calm. "I didn't mean to start an argument."

"I hate that closet shit." Dev snarled. "If you don't like who I am, fuck off."

"Almost got him a trip to the hospital," Sam said. "You have to use discretion, Devlin. A little common sense goes a long way."

"Never mind. Change the subject." Dev waved his hand. "Are you out to your family, Chase?"

"Yes." Chase had to wonder if they knew Gary wasn't.

"How are they about it?" Sam asked.

"Good. No problems." After taking another sip, Chase turned the point, "How about you guys?"

"Both of our families seem to have accepted it pretty well." Sam tipped the remainder of his beer from the bottle into his glass.

"That's great." Chase figured they did not know about Gary.

"It does make it easier," Dev said. "I'd hate to hide it from family. That has to be the worst."

A smile appeared on Sam's face. "You should see Dev's mother when we're around her." Sam glanced at Dev to give him a wink before he added, "She's this sixties flower child who loves it when I give Dev a hickey."

That made Chase laugh.

Dev's cheeks grew red. "Yeah. They're very cool about it."

"What's Gary's situation like?" Sam leaned his elbows on the table as if speaking more confidentially.

"You guys know him longer than I have. I'm surprised you need to ask me."

Dev looked around first, and said, "My guess? He's not out."

Both men stared at Chase for his reaction. Chase wondered what he was at liberty to say.

"Never mind," Sam replied quickly, reading the awkwardness.

The meals arrived. Once they began eating the discussion morphed to politics and hobbies, safe places. Chase was glad because he didn't want to betray any of Gary's confidences.

"Kevin actually came up to me today after you guys left and apologized to me." Chase wiped his mouth with the napkin.

"No kidding?" Dev shoved a french fry into his mouth.

"I'm glad." Sam met Chase's eyes. "He and Gary had a really bad break up."

Dev finished chewing before he said, "You know Kevin cheated on him."

"Yes. Gary told me about it."

"Then," Dev sipped his beer, "Kevin has the fucking balls

to come on to you in front of Gary. What a jerk."

"I'm glad he said he was sorry, Chase," Sam said, "It was getting really awkward, and I could tell how unhappy it was making you."

A sudden wash of emotion hit Chase. Seeing so much understanding in Sam's sweet brown eyes, Chase said, "I love the guy."

"We know." Dev glanced at Sam, smiling broadly.

"Is it that obvious?" Chase felt so good talking about it.

"Just a little," Dev teased, showing a tiny amount of space between his index finger and thumb.

"I'm so happy for you both." Sam ate his last french fry. "You seem so good for one another."

"I hope so." Chase finished his beer, wondering if he should ask for another. "I mean, he's my ideal man."

"What's not to love?" Sam grinned. "He's gorgeous, fit, and a soldier. Hello?"

Chase felt a stirring in his crotch at the description. "God, I miss him. He's gone three days and I'm going out of my fucking mind." Pushing his plate aside, Chase slumped in the chair. "How am I going to last until he gets back?"

"You mean cheating?" Dev asked in surprise.

"No!" Sam whacked Dev's shoulder.

Chase just smiled. "No, Dev. Missing him. Not cheating on him."

"Keep busy," Sam said, "Just find things to occupy yourself."

"I do most of the time. It's the hardest at night."

"Poor thing." Sam pouted.

Chase sat up in his chair. "I didn't mean to get maudlin."

"We understand, Chase," Dev said, "I'd go nuts if I didn't have this hottie in my bed every night."

"Oh!" Sam blinked, wiggling in his chair. "Nice!"

"What do you guys do for a living?" Chase thought they were adorable.

"I design websites. This horn-dog writes erotic novels." Sam grinned widely.

"No!" Chase replied, stunned.

"Yeah. Gay ones. You'd like them." Dev dug out his wallet

and flipped his business card over the table.

Chase picked it up. "D. Young Author of Erotic Gay Romance. My oh my!"

"Buy my books." Dev grinned mischievously.

"I will." Chase pocketed the card. "Will I be reading about your secret love life?"

Sam grew bright red while Dev laughed at his expense.

Shaking his head in amusement, Chase said, "Never mind. Don't answer that."

"How embarrassing." Sam rubbed his cheek. "I never thought about it that way. It makes no difference if strangers read the stuff, but...man."

"Will you relax?" Dev nudged Sam and then addressed Chase, "You have any idea how much of a chicken shit Sam is about things?"

"Don't start," Sam warned.

Dev ignored him. "We were at Mount Rushmore surrounded by a gay bikers group and Sam ran and hid instead of greeting them warmly."

"I wasn't going to kiss a man in public at that rally." Sam obviously still felt very strong about the topic.

"How about here?" Dev wrapped his arm around Sam, purring.

The expression on Chase's face softened to a sad smile as Dev and Sam pecked lips affectionately. Even if Gary was with them, he never would have allowed Chase to kiss him that way in public.

"Are you guys having another beer?" he asked.

Sam turned to Dev, "Do you want to stay or head somewhere else?"

"Let's have one more here." Dev looked around for the waitress.

As they waited for him to flag her down, Chase began to sink again. How was he supposed to last three or four months? He was a complete A-type personality. A goddamn New Yorker! Patience and calm weren't in his vocabulary. Life would be torture. And though it was pleasant to spend time with Gary's friends, seeing them kiss and exchange loving smiles, only made him miss

Gary more.

❧❧

Once he was dropped back off at his home, Chase stood at his porch to wave to Dev and Sam as they drove off. Just as he put the key into his lock he heard Mutley's 'woof' from the backyard. Immediately coming through the house to allow the dog in, Chase greeted him warmly as Mutley spun in circles in his happy dance. "Hey, Mutt. It's just us again tonight."

Chase checked the dog's water dish, before tossing down a few treats for him. After washing and refilling the bowl, he took off his jacket and headed upstairs to his bedroom. Tossing it on his bed, he sat down to boot up his computer. Impatiently, he waited for his e-mail box to open. However, it was empty. No new e-mails.

"Gary!" he shouted in vain. He was going completely insane.

Mutley whined in the hall, peering in at the tone which sounded like discipline. Chase reached out. "Come here, dog."

Mutley rushed over and rested his muzzle on Chase's lap.

"Why hasn't he e-mailed me? Hm?" Chase scratched the dog's ears vigorously. In reflex, Mutley sat down and raise his large back paw to mimic scratching at the soothing rub. When Chase quickened his hand, Mutley's foot went into action thumping on the floor rapidly, making his master laugh. "Silly pooch."

Drooping back in the chair to look at the computer screen with its vacantly depressing lack of communication, Chase closed the mailbox down and sighed. He'd send one to Gary, but he didn't know his address yet. He did however have a postal address.

Bringing up the word format, Chase composed a letter; not too mushy in case it was opened and read before Gary got it. It just asked how he was, and if he needed anything. Chase even refrained from adding, '*Love*, Chase' on the bottom, just as a precaution. He signed it, 'Chase'. That was it.

Rereading it a few times, he went ahead and printed it off, then set it aside to mail on Monday.

After shutting the computer down, he stared at Mutley as he curled up on his pillow.

Chase checked his watch. It was nearing ten. He motivated

himself to wash up and get in bed. Propped up on pillows, he read until his eyes grew too heavy and he fell asleep.

Chapter 14

It was odd. The busy days in the clinic seemed to be passing relatively quickly, but the weeks moved slowly. Something that Chase felt was against some law of nature or physics. But just the same, the time at work flew, and the moment he got home it dragged.

One week had past and still he hadn't gotten an email. He posted the letter, but would have no way of knowing if it would find his man–way over there–in the war zone.

After dinner that night, he was washing his dinner plate when the doorbell rang. Quickly drying his hands, Chase followed Mutley to the front of the house. When he opened the door to peer out the screen, he found a small group of children in costume, holding out their sacks.

"Trick or treat!"

Shit! He had forgotten Halloween was tonight. Thank God, he remembered to buy candy. He held up his index finger. "Hang on!" Chase left Mutley sniffing through the door as he ran to the kitchen to get the large bag of miniature Reese's peanut butter-cups he had bought. He ordered the dog to sit before he opened the screen to dole out the sweets. "What have we got here?" he asked, smiling.

"I'm a fairy princess!"

"I'm a zombie!"

"I'm a pumpkin," the tiniest one whispered shyly.

Chase waved to the mom standing a few yards away. He popped a chocolate into each bag and watched as they walked off.

He sighed as he closed the door, and made sure his outside

porch light was lit. "Three more holidays to go." *Thanksgiving, Christmas, and New Years. The biggest and the worst for being on my own. Oh, well. What doesn't kill you makes you stronger.* Sitting in the den, trying to read prove to be a challenge, having to get up every few minutes to answer the door. Even Mutley was growing bored, walking calmly beside him instead of bolting every time he heard it. Chase hoped the flow would let up soon. He was getting low on candy.

When the bell rang again, he opened the door and his heart sank. Two young boys stood on his porch dressed in military outfits, they were little carbon copies of the men in Iraq. "Hey guys. Nice costumes." Chase dropped a candy into each bag.

"My dad's in Iraq," one boy boasted proudly.

"And he's my uncle!" the second one added loudly.

"Good men! My best friend is there too."

"Cool!" They saluted and spun around, jogging to the next home.

Chase watched them leave, feeling some comfort. No, he wasn't the only one going through this. It seemed here in the mid-west, everyone was.

By nine-thirty he was out of candy. He'd shut off the porch light since the volume of trick-or-treaters had dropped off by then anyway. Though, he remembered they had a curfew in *these here* parts that only permitted trick or treating between certain hours. And it was a day early, which Chase thought was very odd indeed.

"Welcome to corn country." He threw the empty candy bag out and stared at Mutley, who was watching his every move. "What now, dog?"

Mutley tilted his head, his ears like two satellite dishes.

"Come on. I'm sure there's something horrible to watch on television." Just before he entered the den, he veered off, feeling compelled to climb the stairs to his room to check one more time. *Yes, I'm becoming compulsive, so sue me.*

Sitting at his desk, he turned on the computer and tried to be patient as it connected to his Yahoo mailbox.

As he opened his inbox, he read the subject line. 'Trick or Treat'.

"Gary!" he cried, clicking it to open.

Hey, lover. I'm here. A little worse for wear but in one piece. How are the goblins treating you? You now have my e-mail address, though I have to say I may not get to check it regularly. But I will try my best. Did you play on Saturday? What did Kevin do? You know I know he did something that would piss me off…

Chase laughed.

…gotta go. Wish I could sit and type all day to you, but I can't. Miss ya like hell, Chase. Hang in there. Gary.

His eyes filling with tears, Chase typed back in reply:

I'm so glad you made it there okay. I'm going nuts, as you would expect. Kevin did act like a jerk, but actually apologized after. I had a beer with Sam and Dev, and Christ, it felt good talking about you with them. You don't worry about me. You got that? I am here for you, period. So you focus on your job and don't be distracted. I hope you have some privacy where you are because…I LOVE YA, LOVE YA, LOVE YA!

Chase wiped at his eyes, even as he laughed tears rolled down his cheeks.

I just sent you a letter in the mail. Not mushy, sorry. I had no idea who would open it prior to it getting to you. Lover, just be safe, please. You mean the world to me.

He used his sleeve to clear the water from his eyes, before adding, *all my love, Chase. PS. Mutley misses you too.*

Rereading it once, Chase sent it off. He printed Gary's e-mail and held it in his hands to look over. "Baby…" He blubbered, his bottom lip quivering.

It took a moment for him to gain control of his emotions. Once he did, he logged off, and set the letter on the nightstand by his bed before going to the bathroom to wash his face. When he saw his red eyes in the mirror, he sighed sadly. "He'll be okay," Chase told his reflection. "He'll be fine."

Shutting off the light in the bathroom, Chase announced, "Ten o'clock, Mutt. Let's give you your last pee break." Mutley led the way down the stairs, his tail wagging. Chase tried to feel warm and secure now that he had heard from his partner, but the heat of love quickly dissipated to worry. Leaning against the back door frame, Chase waited for Mutley to do his thing. He was tired.

Tomorrow was Sunday and there was nothing he wanted to do but lie in bed and sulk.

Allowing Mutley back in, Chase shut off the downstairs lights and locked up the house. He dragged himself back to his room to wash up for bed. The entire time he undressed he stared at the piece of paper on his nightstand. His baby. His lover.

Once in bed in the dark, Chase curled into the clean sheets and sighed deeply, hoping he would dream of his soldier.

CHAPTER 15

Chase prided himself on how well he was coping with the sporadic correspondences he got from Gary now. Once a week he would get an e-mail from him about his exploits, or a letter a month with a photo of him in either his dress blues or khakis.

He had sent Gary everything he had hinted he lacked: including socks, t-shirts, briefs…if Gary had a need, Chase filled it even before an actual request was made. In Gary's e-mails Chase found out Gary's mom was supplying him with plenty of food and even some novels to keep him busy. Though Chase had purchased several of Dev's erotic gay books, he didn't dare mail them off to Al Taji. Those he and Gary would share in bed.

Thanksgiving had come and gone. He'd spent it in New York with his family, and though he had been preoccupied with his thoughts of his lover, he was glad he went. His sisters, Stella and Kim allowed him his need to discuss Gary in detail, making Chase feel as if Gary was with him, if not physically, at least spiritually.

As the weather turned icy cold, Christmas began lurking. Even though the retail stores had Christmas items for sale as early as the first week in October, Chase couldn't wait for yet another milestone holiday to pass behind him. It brought Gary that much closer to his embrace.

Sitting in the den with Mutley the Sunday before Christmas Day, the phone rang. Chase set the newspaper he was reading aside and picked up the cordless expecting his mother, not checking the caller ID.

"Hello?"

"Hey."

At the sound of Gary's voice, Chase felt his body explode. "Gary!"

"Merry Christmas, hot stuff."

Cupping the phone to his ear tenderly, Chase replied, "Merry Christmas to you too, babe."

"I hope it's not too early. I had the chance to make this call so I grabbed it."

Chase checked the time. It was seven so that meant it was one in the afternoon Iraq time. "No. I was up."

"Already had your run?"

"Yes, I ran, showered, and I'm in the den sitting with the funny papers on my lap."

After a groan, Gary sighed. "Sounds so wonderful."

"How are you, babe? Your e-mails make it sound like you're going non-stop."

"At times I am. But it's making the days go by fast. We do get some breaks and Mom sent me out those stupid mystery novels so I have something to do when I'm bored."

"I don't want to talk about novels. I want to talk about how much I love you."

Gary laughed softly.

"I take it you're surrounded by people?"

"A few."

Chase could hear very little in the background, but assumed Gary wasn't on a private phone.

"Everyone wants to call home this time of year," Gary said.

"I know, babe." Chase felt his emotions swell. "Any actual date of your homecoming?"

"I think February second. That's the rumor."

"Good. At least I have a time frame."

"Mom wrote telling me Lyle is coming in for the week. You should hear from him any day."

"I can't wait. I love talking about you."

"Hey! Be careful about that. He's my kid brother and God knows what he'll tell you." Gary laughed.

Chase's chest warmed at the sound. It was pure heaven to hear. "I love you."

After a pause, Gary whispered, "And you."

Aware the time was growing tight, Chase tried to find meaningful things to say. But all his yearning was to keep declaring his true love. "How are you, Gary? I mean, really."

"Tired. Ready to get out of this shithole."

"I can't imagine. I try, but I can't."

"I just want to be with you again. My dick is going crazy." Gary hissed quietly.

"Me too. Christ, our reunion will melt the whole house down."

"Augh! I can't wait."

"Me neither, lover."

"I have to go. Other guys are waiting to use the phone."

"I know. Are you getting the stuff I'm sending?"

"Yes! Thanks for the care packages. I love it."

"You just tell me what you need and I'll send it."

"I need you."

Chase's eyes filled with water. "You have me."

"Okay. Let me go. I'll e-mail you again soon."

Tears running down his face like rivers, Chase replied, "Good. I look forward to it. You just keep taking care of yourself."

"I will. Merry Christmas, baby."

"Merry Christmas to you too. Thanks so much for the call, I love you, Gary."

"And you. See ya."

"See ya." Chase listened until he heard it disconnect. Even after, he held onto the phone as if it were his lifeline.

Finally he set it back in its cradle.

Taking a long moment to come back from the sound of Gary's voice in his ears, Chase gazed at nothing, sitting perfectly still, the moisture from his tears cooling his cheeks. Wiping at them roughly with the back of his hand, he came around from his dream and found Mutley looking at him. "That was Gary."

Mutley's ears twitched.

"He'll be home soon." Chase swallowed back a choking sob. "Soon, Mutley."

When the phone rang again, Chase lunged at it and picked

it up. "Hello?"

"Chase?"

At the sound of someone other than Gary, Chase paused.

"Did I get the right number? Is this Chase Arlington?"

The voice rang familiar but he couldn't place it. "Yes, this is Chase Arlington."

"It's Lyle."

Lyle?

"Lyle Wilson, Gary's brother."

"Lyle!" Chase felt like an idiot. "I'm sorry. I just got off the phone with Gary two seconds ago. I suppose I was on another planet when the phone rang. For some reason I thought it was him calling back."

"Wow. Great timing on my part. How is he?"

"He sounds good, but tired. I think he's ready to be home."

"No doubt."

"Where are you? Are you here or in LA?"

"I'm here. I'm actually hiding in my old room and using my cell phone. I didn't want my parents to know I was calling you."

"Ah." Chase nodded. Mutley relocated to sit next to Chase, leaning on his knees. Chase stroked his head gently. "So? Can you escape for an hour?"

"I can do better than that. I told them I have some last minute Christmas shopping to do. So? What's a good time for you? Do you want to meet at a café or something?"

"A café?" Chase laughed. "You're not in Kansas anymore, Dorothy."

After a chuckle, Lyle agreed, "I know. Silly me. Gee, Chase, which chain restaurant do you find the least revolting?"

Roaring with laughter, Chase felt relieved to hear Lyle's opinion of the area was identical to his own. "Just come here. I'll fix us a light lunch."

"Perfect. Where the hell are you?"

Chase gave him his address. "Did you rent a car?"

"No. I'll use Mom's. She rarely goes anywhere without Dad anyway."

"Okay. How about noon?"

"Perfect. See you then."

Chase hung up and shook his head. "Son of a bitch, Gary. I'm thrilled to meet your brother." He patted Mutley's head and rose up to get the house straightened and vacuumed so it was dog-hair free.

Almost as if he were preparing for a date, Chase wanted to impress Lyle. There were a few reasons for his rationale: one, he wanted to be accepted by a member of Gary's family, and two he was very nervous about meeting a man who modeled in LA. He had no idea what Lyle looked like now even though he'd seen an old photo of him at Gary's condo. If that picture was any measure his appeal, Lyle would most likely be amazing.

A shrimp and crabmeat quiche in the oven, a tray of vegetables and dip, a carafe of fresh squeezed orange juice and a large bowl of strawberries and sliced pineapple was prepared and displayed on the table. Chase stopped fussing with the tableware and looked at his dog as he watched every move he made with rapt attention, hoping for a morsel to hit the floor.

Leaning back on the counter by the sink, Chase rubbed his jaw stubble trying to think. *Food, drink, house cleaned, dressed, dog brushed...what else?*

The doorbell rang. Mutley went racing.

Chase ran his hand back through his hair and held his breath.

The man standing on his stoop blew him away. Tanned, electric green eyes, long wavy brown hair, and a movie star smile. Yet the resemblance to Gary was unmistakable.

"Come in." Chase opened the screen door. Mutley instantly went for a crotch sniff.

"Well, hello there!" Lyle petted Mutley's head.

"Mutley, go lay down." Chase pointed.

"He's okay," Lyle assured Chase, reaching out his hand. "So nice to meet you."

Chase shook that firm grasp and was glued to Lyle's features. He was astonishingly handsome. Seeing Mutley not letting up on his nose prodding, Chase told him, "Go!"

Mutley slunk off and lay down with a groan.

"Sorry about that. Gary is convinced he's gay." Chase closed the front door.

Lyle laughed sweetly.

"Can I take your jacket?"

"Sure." Lyle removed it and handed it to Chase.

As Chase hung it in the coat closet he said, "Bet it feels cold here."

"Fucking freezing. It ain't LA." Lyle rubbed his arms dramatically.

"Come in, please. Are you hungry?"

"I am. It smells great in here. I hope you didn't go to any trouble."

"No trouble at all." Chase led him to the kitchen. "I like to cook."

"Lucky Gary!" Lyle stood at the threshold of the kitchen as Chase washed his hands.

"I have fresh squeezed orange juice there." Chase pointed to the pitcher on the table. "But you're welcome to add vodka."

Flashing Chase a smile, Lyle replied, "Just the juice is fine."

"Sit. Relax." Chase poured the liquid into a tumbler. "Did you just get in?"

"Yesterday. I'm only staying until the twenty-eighth. I hate leaving David during the holidays." Lyle sipped the juice.

Chase opened the oven, and poked a knife into the center of the quiche to see if it was done. "Sucks being in the closet with your family, doesn't it?"

"Yes. I just don't see telling them."

"No. Gary obviously agrees with you." Chase took the quiche out and let it set on the stovetop. "Don't wait for me." He gestured to the cut up vegetables and fruit.

"Okay." Lyle picked up a carrot and stuck it into the dip, munching it.

Letting the quiche cool down, Chase sat in the chair across the table from Lyle and tried not to stare too boldly at him. "So. Tell me about David, your partner."

Lyle's expression turned to mush instantly. "My David..." He smiled. "Where do I start?"

"How did you guys meet?" Chase took a cauliflower floret

off the tray and dipped it, popping it into his mouth.

"On a scaffolding six stories above the ground."

"Huh?" Chase didn't get it.

"I was working with a construction company at the time. They were doing an upgrade of David's office building."

"Oh?" Chase grinned.

"Well, I took one look into his window, found him seated at his desk looking like a diplomat and that was it." Lyle smiled wickedly, picking up a blanched stalk of asparagus and slathering it in the dip.

"You seduced him through a six-story window?"

"Yup." Lyle appeared satisfied with himself as he chewed. "Wow!"

"I wish you and Gary could meet him. He's unbelievable."

"If you don't mind my asking…how old is he?"

"Forty-two. But he's got the body of a fricken god. I swear, he's hot. Kind of like Richard Gere, only better."

"He must be exceptional to have netted you." When Lyle stopped chewing and met Chase's eye, Chase blushed. "Sorry."

"Don't be. I took it as a compliment." Lyle winked.

Feeling slightly embarrassed, Chase checked on the quiche and began slicing it up. He put two wedges on plates and served them, relaxing again at the table. "Got everything you need?"

"I do. This is great. Thanks."

"My pleasure."

After a quiet moment of eating, Lyle asked softly, "Seriously, Chase. How are you holding up?"

Chase finished chewing and swallowing before he let out a deep stressful breath. "I have good and bad days."

Lyle nodded sympathetically.

"I miss him like hell. I'm petrified something will happen to him."

"We all are. Me, Mom and Dad."

Chase met Lyle's eyes. "I don't want him over there."

"No. None of us do."

Making an effort to stop being so angry, Chase stared at his plate to compose himself. When he felt a light touch he looked up. Lyle had laid a hand on his arm.

"Don't worry."

"It's impossible not to." Chase completely lost his appetite.

"This is his third time over there. He's really becoming an old hand at it. It's us that are left behind that suffer."

"No." Chase shook his head. "You're wrong. He's the one in that hellhole. Do you think he'd rather be there, or having quiche and salad on a Sunday afternoon here with us?"

Lyle bit his lip. "Point taken."

"Why did you hide your sexuality so long from your brother?" Chase forced himself to keep eating though now his stomach felt tight.

"Mr. Air Force man? Are you kidding? I figured he was just like dad. I didn't want to take the chance."

"How on earth have you managed to keep it hidden?"

"It's not that hard. I just keep coming here to visit and putting them off if they ask to come to LA. I only gave them my mobile phone number, so David never picks up."

"What if they just show up at your door one day?"

"They won't. It's not their style."

"I feel terrible for both of you. My parents are very cool about it."

"Are you the only child?"

"No. I have two sisters."

Lyle nodded in understanding. "Are you going to be on your own for Christmas?"

"I am, but I don't mind. To be honest, the holidays don't really mean that much to me. It's all just commercial nonsense."

That made Lyle chuckle. "True."

"But saying that," Chase grinned, "I did go back to New York for Thanksgiving."

"Families. What can you do?" Lyle finished his quiche.

"Another slice?"

"Yes, please."

Chase rose up, taking Lyle's plate and refilling it. When he returned it to the table, Mutley was sitting next to Lyle with his begging face on.

"Go lay down."

Mutley's ears went flat and he dropped back to the threshold between rooms.

"He's so sweet." Lyle looked back at him. "I bet Gary loves him."

"He does. Mutley goes nuts when he hears the Hummer coming down the street."

After another moment of silence, Lyle asked, "Are you sure you don't want me to ask if it's okay for you to join us for Christmas dinner?"

Chase gave Lyle a strained expression. "No. How on earth would you explain that? No. Don't. I don't want any suspicion falling on Gary."

"Okay. I just hate the idea of you here on your own."

"I won't be. Got my Mutt." Chase tilted his head towards the dog.

Giving Mutley a quick glance, Lyle turned back and met Chase's eyes and said, "My brother is very lucky he met you."

Instantly Chase blushed. "It's me that's the lucky one, Lyle."

"Yeah?" Lyle teased, "Hooked up with my big macho soldier brother? Are you nuts?"

"Certifiably insane." Chase grinned.

"When he gets back, both of you need to come out to LA." Lyle pointed his fork at Chase like it was a warning.

"Believe me. We will."

≈≈

Clearing up the remnants of the dishes and leftover food, Chase smiled. Lyle was a delight and he shared wonderful stories about growing up in Vale, Oregon with his older brother.

For most of the visit Chase was content to gaze at Lyle as he spoke. Chase didn't know if Lyle had changed over the course of his career, but he was articulate and refined, not the type Chase could ever imagine working on a construction job site or roofing.

Perhaps the swanky top gun lawyer, David Thornton, had managed to rub off his high-class style on Lyle. Because not only did Lyle's looks impress the heck out of Chase, his manner and class did as well.

As they parted ways at the door, Lyle gave Mutley a good pet on the head, and Chase was given a nice peck on the cheek.

"Soon," Lyle said, "The minute Gary gets back, we'll plan your trip out."

"Yes," Chase replied, feeling an attachment to Lyle like to a brother. "The minute he gets back."

"Call whenever you need to vent."

"Thanks, Lyle. I may take you up on that."

Watching Lyle climb into his mother's Ford sedan, Chase waved at him and closed the door.

Finishing up getting the kitchen back to its original clean state, Chase missed Gary all the more. A couple of weeks playing in LA sounded so fantastic. He wanted to buy the tickets now.

Wiping his hands on a towel, Chase looked down at Mutley who was riveted to Chase's actions. "Do you need to go out?"

Mutley walked to the back door, wagging.

Chase let him out, feeling the icy cold wind blowing. Closing the door, he watched Mutley do his thing, knowing he'd want to come back in quickly to get out of the cold weather.

Once he took care of his dog, Chase imagined writing an e-mail to Gary to tell him about the visit. He knew Gary would be excited that he and Lyle had met.

Chapter 16

New Year's Eve Chase sipped hot chocolate with his feet up on the hassock in the den. Christmas, and now New Year's finally getting behind him, he zoned off at the television set watching the news before the ball dropped in Times Square.

He'd done the same thing for both holidays; sat in his den with a hot drink, thinking and trying not to think. The waiting for Gary's return had gotten harder as it had grown closer. It seemed as if the hours had ground to a halt and time would not move on.

And with all the days off for the holidays, Chase had too much time to ruminate.

Yes, he'd seen Sam and Dev a few times, went out for a beer and dinner with them. The Saturday and/or Sunday morning football games had vanished with the icy cold weather and snow flurries. Chase had to be satisfied bundling up and running the street with Mutley in the frosty air for his exercise.

Several people at work were battling colds. Even after his flu shot Chase avoided contact with them, hating being sick.

The last correspondence he'd received from Gary had been nearly three weeks ago and he was growing anxious to hear from him. He dreaded getting an e-mail stating the tour had been extended. He'd heard so many men were being used and abused in Iraq, he wouldn't be surprised to hear Gary was being held back for another three or four months. The enlisted men were serving three year terms, and the thought was excruciating to Chase.

Nothing surprised him anymore. It simply depressed him. Even the new president did nothing. More lies and broken promises. Oh, well. It was what he expected.

When the phone rang Chase checked the time. It was nearing eleven p.m. and it seemed too early for a family member to be calling to shout Happy New Year to him from New York.

He thought of Gary, but calculating his time zone, that would equate to almost six in the morning in Iraq. Could it be him?

Thinking it might be he dove at it and said, "Hello?"

"Chase."

At the tone of Lyle's voice, Chase's heart stopped in his chest. "No, Lyle no."

"He's not dead, Chase."

Chase tried to find relief but dread had a hold of him.

"You there?"

"Yes, Lyle. I'm here." Chase sank both mentally and physically.

"He was in an accident. His truck rolled over. He's got a few broken bones and a possible head injury."

"Oh, Christ…" Chase rubbed his eyes in agony.

"This is everything I know…" Lyle took a deep inhale before he continued, "After the accident he was airlifted to Balad airbase in Iraq. I was told by Mom he was only there for around three hours. From there he was brought to Ramstein Airbase in Germany. They kept him there until he regained consciousness…"

Chase was about to vomit he was so distraught.

"They kept him in Germany for around eight hours, then he was flown to Dover Air Force Base in Delaware…you still there, Chase?"

His throat about to close tight, Chase squeaked out, "Yes."

"Mom and Dad were about to head out to Dover to be with him when they got news he was flown back here to Wright Pat's medical center. They have him in the critical care ward, but I don't know another thing about it. Not even the extent of his broken bones. But the good news is, Mom said they wouldn't have brought him here unless he was relatively stable."

Chase couldn't reply. He was so sick he couldn't form words.

"Chase?"

He managed a grunt and stared at the wall.

"You work at the base so you should be able to figure out where he is pretty easily. Mom and Dad are going to see him in the morning. The staff told them they couldn't see him until tomorrow. You believe that? Their son just got back from being airlifted from the Middle East, injured in a war and they have to wait to see him? I never heard such a load of crap in my life. I'm flying in first thing in the morning so I'll be there ASAP…Chase?"

Managing to get a sentence out, Chase said hoarsely, "If I go see him when your parents are there, they'll know."

"Fuck them. Go see him."

"Is he well enough to talk to anyone?"

"I don't know. You'd be amazed how sketchy all this info is. Like it's a top military secret or something."

"Lyle…" Chase died he was so petrified.

"I'm worried, Chase. David said brain damage was the most common Iraq war injury. I swear I'm going insane."

Chase checked the time. He wondered with his clearance if he could get in to see Gary now.

"I just wanted you to know. I knew there was no other way you would find out what had happened."

"Yes. Thanks, Lyle."

"Let me go. David is coming with me, so we have to pack."

"K."

"We'll see you tomorrow."

"Yes." Chase's throat went tight again.

"Bye, Chase."

"Bye." Chase disconnected the phone and stood. His legs were shaking. He shut the television and climbed the stairs to get changed into a decent shirt and slacks. Taking his ID with him, Chase wrapped up in his winter coat and gave Mutley a last caress on the head and he closed the door behind him.

It was nearing midnight when he arrived at the base. He stopped at the gate and showed his credentials. The young guard paused as he read it. "Why are you here after hours on New Year's Eve?"

"A soldier, a close friend of mine, has been injured."

"Were you summoned for his medical care?"

Cognoscente of the fact Gary wasn't exactly up for physical therapy at the moment, Chase lied, "Yes." He hoped the young man didn't spend too much time reading his occupation on the tiny photo card.

"I bet they pulled you away from a cocktail party." He shook his head. "Why am I not surprised? Sorry, Doc. Happy New Year."

"Thanks. You too." Chase took back his identification card and drove through the gate. Parking near the emergency entrance, Chase got out and jogged to the information desk.

"Yes, I'm Dr. Arlington. It's my understanding you have a new patient, Staff Sergeant Gary Wilson, in your critical care unit. He was just flown in from Iraq. Err, actually from Dover." He flashed the woman his medical ID quickly, praying she wouldn't inspect it. He wasn't an MD.

"Yes, Doctor. Sergeant Wilson is right down the hall in room 2B. Did someone call you out tonight? On New Year's Eve? The patient is stable. There was no reason for that."

"It's no problem. Thank you."

"He's probably completely out of it from the pain killers, Doctor. Just so you know."

"Yes, thank you." Chase hurried away before she uttered another word. It was minutes away from the stroke of midnight and there were very few staff members around, and luckily the hospital wasn't Fort Knox. It seemed any Wright Pat ID worked to get him in. At least it worked on midnight during New Year's Eve.

The room was almost dark. Chase noticed two beds, both with curtains around them. He checked the clipboard and read Gary's name. "Baby…" he sobbed softly, struggling to mentally prepare himself for the sight of him, and failing miserably. Chase pushed through the light curtain.

Gary was lying on his back with intravenous tube attached to his arm. Taking off his coat, Chase crouched next to him and caressed Gary's coarse jaw. After a quick glance behind him, Chase kissed Gary's forehead. At least he wasn't burning with a fever. In the dimness Chase noticed the tip of a bandage sticking out from under the blankets. Taking a look, he could see Gary's arm was in a sling and his fingers were swollen and bruised. Chase tucked him in again, located a stool to sit on and drew it up to the bed. He sat with him, caressing his hair back from his forehead. "You're okay, Gary. You're okay."

A brain injury? Chase cringed at the thought. That meant anything from learning how to walk and talk again, to memory problems, to bursts of rage, or depression—anything at all. There was no way for him to know if Gary would suffer any long term problems.

And even though his lover was with him finally after three excruciating months, not knowing if Gary would suffer from post traumatic stress, or any other devastation from the accident, was killing Chase.

Resting his head on Gary's side, he listened to his partner's heartbeat, thanking God he still had one.

~~

"Chase?"

His name was called from a far off place, stirring him from a deep sleep. When he opened his eyes he found Gary lying on a hospital bed, still out of it, and sunlight pouring into the room.

Just realizing he had slept on the stool next to his lover's bed all night, and to his astonishment, been allowed to by the staff, Chase stretched his stiff neck and back to be able to turn around.

Gary's parents were gaping at him as if he had grown horns overnight.

Shit.

Chase stood clumsily. "Mr. and Mrs. Wilson." He nodded slightly in greeting.

"What are you doing here?" Bill asked, moving to the opposite side of Gary's bed.

"I was checking on him."

A nurse poked her head in. "Good morning, Doctor. These are Sergeant Wilson's parents."

His face blushing hotly, Chase said as she left, "Thank you."

"Doctor?" Mary asked curiously. "I thought you were a physical therapist. Isn't it a bit premature for you to be treating Gary?"

"I'm not here as his doctor. I'm here as his friend." Chase

wondered when they were going to notice their fucking son lying still on the damn bed. Was his presence more important than their eldest son's health?

Mary snorted. "I'll go out and see if we can find his real doctor, Bill."

"Fine." Bill expression appeared pinched.

Chase assumed he looked as if he'd slept on the stool all night. Heaven knows he felt like he did. He tucked in his shirt, then ran his hand through his hair and scrubbed at his unshaven jaw, anything to dodge eye contact.

Bill didn't say a word. Chase thought a 'thank you for caring for my boy' would be nice. Then a notion occurred to him. Lyle was bringing David with him. Did they just find out Lyle was gay? And now their macho soldier son had a man sleeping in his room all night watching over him? *Oh, dear.*

A man in scrubs entered the room with a chart. He met Chase's eyes curiously.

Wanting to act courteous and casual, Chase extended his hand to him. "Chase Arlington. I work over at the clinic in PT. Gary is a good friend of mine."

"I'm Dr. Rhabi, Gary's neurologist."

Mary broke off their connection as if irritated. "This is my husband Bill, doctor."

Dr. Rhabi moved to shake Bill's hand. After he had he read his notes on the chart he began, "Yes. An MRI scan was done of Gary's brain while he was in Dover and the results show a slight swelling in the frontal lobe, which is to be expected after an accident where the head was involved. He also suffered a broken right shoulder, collar bone, and a fractured right knee cap…"

Chase was trying not to wince in agony.

"Until we can put him through some tests there's no way to know how much damage has been done to his brain. So, at this time, we can expect anything and hope for the best. The good news is, he's responsive and alert."

"How long has he been in and out of consciousness, Doctor?" Chase asked softly.

Dr. Rhabi checked the chart. "Just shy of thirty hours."

Chase nodded, avoiding any eye contact with Gary's parents.

"Are there any questions I can answer for you?" the doctor addressed Mary and Bill.

Chase knew he had to get home to let Mutley out. Poor thing must be going nuts holding his water. He waited as long as he could to hear what the doctor said, but it was the same thing over and over. 'We won't know until some time passes and we can take more tests.'

"I'll let you take over now." Chase tried to make it sound normal.

Mr. and Mrs. Wilson didn't even smile.

Regardless of the scowls, Chase grabbed his coat and waved at Gary's parents.

The lot was almost vacant. New Year's Day. He had to scrape the frost off his windshield.

When he got home he jogged through the house to open the back door. "Sorry, Mutt."

Mutley dashed out, his stream causing a steam cloud in the chilly morning.

While the dog was doing his thing, Chase checked his messages. There were several. He picked up the phone, glancing at his watch. It was nearly nine-thirty.

"Chase!"

"Hi, Mom."

"I thought you were staying home for New Year's Eve. Did you decide to go out after all?"

"Gary was injured in an accident. He was flown home. I spent the night over at the base's hospital."

"Oh, no. Chase... How serious is it?"

"His truck overturned and he suffered some broken bones and a head injury. They don't know how serious it is until he has more tests." He felt numb explaining it. Like it wasn't his Gary he was talking about.

"I am so sorry."

"I knew this would happen. He was weeks away from returning. I knew it." A lump finally formed in his throat. "And the worst part is, since he's not out to his family, they gave me murderous looks this morning when they found me asleep at his bedside."

"You give me their phone number!" his mother shouted. "Let me have a word with them!"

Loving her loyalty, Chase had to smile. "I think when his brother Lyle and Lyle's lover David show up, they'll have to deal with it."

"Ohhh…" his mother whispered, "They have two gay sons?"

"Yeah. Tough luck, huh, Mom?" Chase tried to see the humor but it was rapidly retreating. "Look. I just came home to let Mutley out. Once I get him taken care of, I'm heading back to the hospital. I don't give a shit what they think."

"Good for you!"

"I love you, Mom."

"You too, sweetie. I'll say a little prayer for Gary."

His mother was anything but religious. Even still, Chase was touched. "Thanks. I'll call you later and let you know how he is."

"Yes. Please, Chase. I'm worried sick."

Feeling encouraged by her support and strength, Chase said, "Thanks, Mom. See ya," and disconnected the call. He stood at the back door seeing Mutley waiting to get inside.

"You done?" Chase let him in. "I can't let you sit out there all day. It's too cold. I need to buy you a dog house for that." He rubbed Mutley's back briskly, feeling the chill on his fur. "Come here." Chase grabbed a handful of milkbones and a rawhide chew. "I'm going to be gone for another few hours, but I'll come back at lunchtime and let you out again. Okay?"

Mutley crunched a milkbone, wagging as he listened.

"Good boy."

Chase took a quick pit stop, washed his face, brushed his teeth and left.

When he stood at the threshold of Gary's room he noticed a few attendants around him. Growing concerned, he rushed over. To his astonishment, Gary's eyes were open.

"Gary!"

The male attendants spun to look at Chase.

"Chase." Gary reached out weakly.

"We were just moving him to out of the critical care ward to a regular room. Are you a family member?" one of the orderlies asked.

"No. I work PT on the base over in the clinic. Gary is a good friend." After a glance around, Chase asked, "Where are his parents?"

"They went for a cup of coffee. They were going to come back after that to his new room assignment."

"Let me help you guys."

"Chase…" Gary's voice was weak, but determined.

All Chase wanted to do was wrap him up in an embrace. He clasped Gary's hand. "How do you feel?"

"My head is killing me but they drugged me up." Gary squint his eyes in the bright light.

Chase figured that was why Gary was holding his hand. He must be high.

"What can I do?" Chase asked the orderly who was preparing another cot for transport.

"We'll move him on three. Hang on." Two men stood opposite from where Chase and the first orderly were.

Once they had the intravenous solution packed on the new cart, the orderly counted off, "One, two, three…"

They hoisted Gary over to the new bed.

"You okay?" Chase asked him after the shift.

"The pain killers are wicked." Gary gave him a silly smile.

"He's on a morphine drip," Chase was told by one of the men.

"Did you just wake up?" Chase gripped Gary's hand again wishing he was there at the time Gary opened his eyes.

"I've been awake for a little while. They really got me drugged up, Chase."

"We gotta move him," the orderly said. They began wheeling him out.

"Stay with me?" Gary asked Chase.

"I'm not going anywhere." Chase felt the eyes of the other men boring into him. He ignored them.

Once Gary was loaded onto an elevator, Chase stayed quiet. The suspicious glances were already pissing him off.

He was wheeled down the hall which was still sparsely staffed because of New Year's Day. Once more on a count of three Gary was settled in his new bed.

After all his tubes were hooked up, the orderlies left.

Finally Chase had him alone. He drew the curtain around the cot and cradled Gary's head in his arms. "Hello, baby. Welcome back."

"I'm in pieces, Chase."

"I don't care. Kiss me." Chase closed his eyes and pressed his lips against Gary's. Hearing Gary moan was worth everything he owned, plus a million bucks.

Parting from their kiss, Chase found a chair and scooted it up close, gripping Gary's good hand. "Do you remember anything from the accident?"

"The truck flipped," Gary said, "I hit my head on the windshield. Broke my damn shoulder, collarbone, fucked up my knee…"

Stopping himself from asking about a seatbelt, as if that were ridiculous for army personnel, Chase hushed Gary. "You'll be fine."

"They said I had some brain swelling." Gary peered around as if he were embarrassed.

"It's normal with that type of accident. But Gary, your speech is perfect, and you're reacting well. You will recover fully."

Gary didn't appear convinced. "I heard rumors you don't know how sick you are until later. Then it's like you're having a nervous breakdown or suffering post traumatic stress…"

"Don't worry. You'll be fine. You have me. I'm going to get you all the way to your perfect self."

"Yes, my private physical therapist." Gary's smile softened.

"You do know your parents are suspicious now." Chase peeked behind him nervously.

"They told me Lyle came out to them over the phone. That he's coming here with David. I think it shocked the heck out of them, Chase."

"I know. That's how I found out about you. Lyle called me yesterday. Do you know what made him bring David with him?"

"No, but I assume he just thought he needed the support from him. Are you saying my parents now suspecting we're both gay?" Gary rolled his eyes tiredly.

He looked exhausted and pale. Chase tried to remember this man was nearly unconscious for almost two days. "Have you tried to eat yet?"

"Yes. They've been giving me some clear soup and bread." Gary eyed the intravenous tube. "I assume that's my supplement meal."

"They put your meds into it, Gary, and keep you hydrated." He paused, staring at him. "Do you need to rest?" Chase caressed his hair back from his forehead.

"I wouldn't mind closing my eyes. It's just this bad headache. And the light seems very bright for some reason."

Chase reached back, shutting off the lamp by the bedside.

"Thanks, babe."

"You just tell me what you need." Chase cuddled Gary's hand to his chest.

"You."

"I'm not going anywhere."

"What about Mutley? How's my big furball?"

"I was just there to let him out. He's fine."

"Just there?"

"Yes. I slept by your bedside last night. Your parents found me and woke me."

Gary blinked. "You did?"

"I did."

"I love you."

Chase leant down to Gary's lips again.

"Excuse me!"

At the sound of Mary's voice, Chase jumped back and spun around.

"Get away from him." Bill sneered.

"Dad…" Gary tried to sound forceful, but he was obviously weak.

Chase did nothing, having no idea what the right thing to do was.

"I said get out before I have you removed!" Bill puffed up.

"Dad!"

Chase knew the shouting was using up Gary's last reserves of strength. "Don't upset yourself," he whispered to Gary.

"No." Gary struggled to see his father. "Dad, get your stubborn homophobic ass over here so I can speak without yelling."

"Gary!" Mary chided, "That's no way to talk to your father."

"Dad!" Gary ground his jaw.

Chase released Gary's hand with the idea of backing up to allow Bill closer access.

"Where do you think you're going?" Gary gripped his fingers tight.

"I was just—" Chase pointed behind him.

"Stay still." Gary implored once again, "Dad…"

Chase could see plainly that Gary was in pain. His head must be killing him.

Bill walked closer with great reluctance. When he did, Gary closed his eyes as if to ease his discomfort. "Can you hear me, Dad?"

"Yes, Gary." Bill exhaled loudly, as if to blast his irritation away.

"Good. Because I'm too fucking tired and in too much agony to repeat what I'm going to say." Gary took a deep breath. "I know you just found out Lyle has been living with a man. I know. Okay? But that has nothing to do with me. Lyle has always done his own thing." Gary flinched, pausing to catch his breath as everyone waited.

Chase grew upset at seeing him so uncomfortable.

When he regained his strength, Gary continued, "I don't care about Lyle right now. Dad, I almost died two days ago. And lying here busted up with a possible brain injury, guess what?" Gary managed to squint at this father. "I don't give a fuck. I'm alive. Okay? And I decided to be me. Me. I love Chase. I don't give a crap if you think me and Lyle will rot in hell. Screw ya. Now either leave us alone or get over it. I need to rest."

Chase's heart burned with affection for him. He sat next to him on the bed, stroking his hair to comfort him.

"That feels great, baby. Thanks." Gary moaned.

Forcing himself to peek, Chase found Mary and Bill appearing rather perplexed by their new situation. He tried to sympathize, but he'd always been in favor of love, not war. To him this information was a no-brainer. He knew who he'd support.

"We'll come back a little later on to see you, Gary," Bill's voice was weak and sheepish.

"Good."

Chase didn't even force a smile at them. Once they left he scooted lower so he could kiss Gary's cheek. "I missed you, soldier boy."

"I know." Keeping his eyes closed, Gary smiled.

"I never thought time could pass so slowly."

Gary nodded.

Chase massaged his temples.

"That feels good," Gary barely whispered.

"Sleep. I'll be here."

"I want to get out of this place and stay with you."

"I know. Soon." Chase kissed his face a few times.

"You'll be here when I wake?"

"Unless I have to let Mutt out. But even then, I'll be right back."

"Mutt." Gary grinned. "I miss my Mutt."

"He misses you too." Chase was so happy Gary was home, he felt his eyes burn. "Sleep. Rest and recover."

"Thank you, babe."

"Don't mention it." Chase stroked Gary's hair and face until he was breathing softly. While Gary was asleep, Chase whispered, "You're home. You're back…that's all that counts."

It was the pain that woke Gary. Despite the drugs diluting in his blood, he felt every inch of his battered body and the throbbing agony that came with it. The dreams from the morphine were nightmarish and disorientating. Forcing his eyes to open even though he had to fight the urge to keep them shut, Gary peered out of narrow slits to see Chase dozing on the chair beside him. Chase's arm was resting on the bed on top of Gary's side. Gary hadn't a clue what time it was but the florescent light was bright in the room.

Going over the maneuver that landed him here, Gary was so angry with one of his fellow officers he was grinding his jaw.

"I said slow down, Fred!"

"I know what I'm doin'!"

"The fucking ground is nothing but ruts and holes up ahead. Do you know that?"

"Christ, Gar', chill! I want to get this done so we can eat and call it a night."

"You're driving too fast! Why won't you listen to me?"

It was right at that point that they hit a ditch and rolled. Gary recalled being thrown first into the windshield, then the passenger's side door. The massive five ton M939 flipped over on its side, finally resting on the roof.

He remembered nothing after that until he gained consciousness in the airbase in Germany. After that everything was a blur until he woke this morning to find his parents sitting near him. The pain in his head made it impossible to think or do anything else but cringe in agony. Then his baby appeared, like an angel of mercy.

Staring at Chase's unshaven face as he slept, his head resting on the back of the chair, Gary smiled but it soon slid to a frown.

He could barely move the fingers of his right hand, his right leg was in a splint and he felt like it would take years to be himself again. That didn't even begin to factor the damage to his brain. Did he want to saddle Chase with that? An invalid?

As a hot tear ran down his face, Gary struggled to free his left hand from the blankets to wipe it off.

When he stirred, Chase woke.

Chase drew closer, embracing him as much as he could. "Are you in pain?"

"Yes."

Instantly Chase pressed the call button summoning a nurse.

"I'm sorry, Chase." How could Gary explain it was so much more than the physical pain he was feeling? It was guilt. Chase didn't deserve a cripple.

"Sorry?" Chase snuggled up, pecking Gary's cheek.

"You don't deserve to be burdened with this crap."

"Shut up. You're being ridiculous."

The nurse appeared at the door.

Chase sat back to advise her, "He's awake and in pain."

"I'll be right back."

Once she left, Chase gripped Gary's good arm. "Do you think I'm some kind of shallow asshole who will desert you when you need me the most?"

Feeling emotional from the worry, the guilt and the excruciating pain, Gary began to sob. "I can't do this to you."

"Why don't you calm down? Do you have any idea how much I love you? You are here with me. Alive. I wouldn't care how you came back to me, Gary. I'm just thrilled it was in a cot and not in a pine box."

Gary tilted his head to see two rivers of water rushing down Chase's cheeks. He didn't deserve this man. Gary knew it may take a good year or more of therapy, convalescing to get back a halfway normal life. No one should have to deal with that.

The nurse returned. She pushed a syringe into the saline drip and said, "You should feel better very soon."

"Thanks." Gary tried to brush away his tears.

"Are you hungry?"

"I suppose I should eat."

"I'll be back with something for you."

"Thank you," Gary replied, smiling at her.

Once she left, Chase cuddled around Gary again. "If it were up to me, I'd get you out of bed. Now. Today."

"Ask the doc. I need to get out. My ass is numb."

Chase smiled wickedly. "How I've missed your ass."

"Mine?" Gary began to feel slightly better as the morphine kicked in. "You're my bottom, baby."

"Oh, yes." Chase purred.

"Is the soldier boy awake?"

Chase spun around in his chair.

Gary could see his brother and a handsome well-dressed man standing in the room. "Son of a gun."

Chase stood, shaking both of the men's hands and giving them a chance to move closer to Gary.

"Nice to finally meet you, Gary." David extended his hand.

Gary touched it awkwardly with his left one. Well, his brother had good taste. David Thornton was gorgeous, dripped of money and class, and smelled divine. "Nice one, Lyle."

Lyle sat on the bed next to his brother. "How you doing? You look like crap."

Gary laughed softly. "Then you know how I'm doing."

Lyle tapped the intravenous tube. "Are they at least keeping you high?"

"Yeah. Morphine."

"Nice!" Lyle winked at David. "So? Was the accident your fault or some other schmucks?"

David hit Lyle on the shoulder lightly. "Will you behave?"

"Some other schmucks," Gary replied, smiling. "David, how the hell'd you get this punk under control?"

"Who says he's under control?" David answered in amusement.

Gary peeked around the two men. "Chase? Get the fuck over here."

"Ah, the meds have kicked in. Good." Chase drew closer.

Gary reached for him. Chase stood on the opposite side of Lyle and petted Gary's hair.

"So?" Lyle asked, "When do you get out of here? You guys need to spend time in LA on the beach."

Gary groaned. "Ohh. Let me go now."

"Chase?" David asked, "Have the doctors given any indication of time frames?"

"Not to me. Maybe they have to Mary or Bill."

Lyle snorted. "Mom and Dad?" He rolled his eyes. "I take it they're not speaking to you either. They gave us the cold shoulder. We're staying at a hotel."

"No!" Gary bristled. "That's complete bullshit."

"You think I want Mom and Dad hearing us humping all night?" Lyle choked at the absurdity.

"You can stay at my place," Chase said.

"It's not a problem, Chase," David spoke calmly. "But thanks for the offer."

Though the pain killers were easing his physical discomfort, Gary began to sink thinking about his situation. *Christ, how long before he could walk again? Go to LA? It seemed impossible.*

"You okay?" Chase touched his arm. "Do you need to rest?"

Gary rubbed his forehead tiredly. "I can't believe I'm so battered up. I am so angry."

"Hey," Lyle said, "Calm down. Gary, you're lucky you're alive."

"Don't push yourself, Gary," David said. "LA's not going anywhere." David touched Lyle's shoulder. "Maybe we should let him rest."

Nodding, Lyle said, "Okay, big brother. We'll give you a break for a little while. We'll come back in a few hours."

Gary barely acknowledged him, his eyes cast down as he began to grow upset.

Lyle kissed Gary's forehead, held David's hand and said, "See ya later, Chase."

"Bye. Nice meeting you, David."

"You too, Chase. Take care of him."

"I will." Chase waited until they left, before returning to the chair on the opposite side of Gary. He gripped Gary's good arm to his chest and asked, "Tell me what is going on in your head other than excruciating pain."

Gary turned his face away in shame.

Chase stubbornly turned it back. "Gary."

"You want to know?" Gary asked like a threat.

"You know I do." Chase didn't flinch.

"I left here whole. I've returned as damaged goods, Chase. What the fuck am I? I can't even get out of bed."

"You will. Give it some time."

"I don't even know if I can get an erection." Gary clenched his teeth.

"Stop tormenting yourself. You will heal."

"Will I?" Gary felt his heart break. "You want to be stuck with half a man, Chase?"

"Half a man?" Chase appeared genuinely surprised at the assessment. "Is that what you think you are?"

"I don't fucking know." Gary turned away again.

Gently, Chase urged Gary's gaze back. "You are not half a man, lover. You are *all man*. Now, before, and forever. Yes, you're injured. You could have gotten into a car wreck here too, you know. Any one of us could. You will get yourself back again. Just be patient."

Gary thought about it. It was true. He could have rolled his Hummer right here in Ohio. But here he would have been belted in. Not like he was in that truck, freefalling into the windshield.

"Baby, look at me."

Gary allowed Chase to tilt his jaw toward him again.

"I adore you so much, I want no other man."

Opening his mouth, Gary went to object, but Chase put his finger to Gary's lips.

"No other!" Chase made it clear. "It's you and me. You got that?"

"What did I do to deserve you?" Gary's tears spilled down his cheeks again.

Chase wrapped his arms around his neck and held him.

With his good hand Gary rubbed Chase's back, sobbing like a baby from the relief and the groggy effects of the medication. "Thank you."

"Shh. No need."

Chase parted from the embrace when someone came into the room.

The nurse had a tray of food, smiling softly at them.

Gary brushed off his cheeks and tried to sit up.

"Stop moving." Chase held up his hand and used the control on the bed to raise Gary's back upright.

As the bed elevated Gary felt some relief to his back muscles. The nurse rolled the tray table, placing it in front of Gary.

Soup, bread, jello, crackers…all the right things for an injured soldier. "Thank you."

"If you're still hungry after, I'll get you seconds." She winked and left.

Chase moved close again. "Can you manage lefty?"

"Yeah." Gary took a sip of the soup while Chase opened the package of crackers.

"Is it good?"

"Not like your home cooking." Gary smirked. "But it's not bad."

"Good. Eat up."

Trying to find comfort and not be a complete frustrated mess, Gary ate awkwardly with his weak hand, feeling embarrassed when he dropped things or spilled. But Chase was there by his side to right the wrongs immediately.

"I feel helpless," Gary said with remorse.

"If I were ill, would you help me?"

Gary met Chase's brown eyes. That line said it all, didn't it? "Yes."

"Then shut up and eat." Chase nudged him.

"I'm shutting up," Gary said.

"I'm going to find the doctor. You need to get out of the bed."

"Thanks, Chase." Gary gnawed on the roll.

"No problem, hot stuff."

As Gary watched Chase leave the room, he was filled with a mixture of gratefulness and sorrow. He just wanted to be whole again, not half a man.

❧

Chase asked a nurse where Gary's doctor was. As she left to find him, Chase rubbed his jaw stubble anxiously. A few minutes later Dr. Rhabi appeared.

"Doctor," Chase asked quietly, "don't you think we should be getting Gary out of bed? I'm a physical therapist and I think the sooner we get him upright the better."

"I want another scan done first. Just to see if the swelling in the frontal lobe has gone down. How is his pain level?"

Chase bit his lip. "Still quite high, I think."

"That's an issue. And with a fractured patella…"

Nodding, Chase sighed as he said, "Yes. I don't want to push him."

"He's eager to get back to normal. I know." Dr. Rhabi smiled. "Let me get the scan done so we can see what we can do. I'll get his orthopedist in on the discussion."

"Thank you." Chase touched the doctor's arm.

"Don't worry. We all want the same results. Getting Sgt. Wilson back on his feet."

"Yes." Chase was very glad Dr. Rhabi didn't take offense.

"Let me get things arranged and I'll be right with you."

"Thanks again." Chase returned to Gary's room seeing him done with his meal, but staring off with a very deep frown. The sight broke Chase's heart. He didn't know what else he could do but be supportive. He already decided to take time off. Screw it. Yes, the clinic was short staffed. But when wasn't a clinic short of what it needed?

Gary didn't react until Chase was almost right next to his bed. It was then Gary glanced up and Chase was treated to those spectacular baby blues. It melted him instantly. Moving the tray aside, Chase sat on the bed next to him. "Good boy for finishing your food."

"Wiseass." Gary nudged him.

"The doc wants one more brain MRI before we move you."

"Okay."

"Gary," Chase spoke in a serious tone.

Gary met his eyes.

"You will get there. Will you trust me?"

Gary peeled down the blankets to show off his black and blue fingers poking out of his sling. "Look at this." He jerked the covers lower to point out his Velcro and metal knee splint. "And this." Putting his finger to his skull, Gary growled, "And this!"

"Gary…" Chase urged the blanket back up, but before he did, he lightly cupped Gary's crotch over his hospital gown. "Trust me."

Gary closed his eyes and his face seemed to lose some of its anger. "Thank fuck."

"What?" Chase smiled.

"You're giving me a hard-on."

"I know." Chase massaged him naughtily.

"Thank fuck, thank fuck, thank fuck…" Gary moaned.

"Still works, see?" Chase heard someone coming in and quickly covered Gary, standing up.

"Chase Arlington, this is Sgt. Wilson's orthopedic physician, Dr. Bradley," Dr. Rhabi said.

Chase shook the older man's hand. "Nice to meet you, sir. I work over at the clinic as a physical therapist, and I'm as anxious as Gary is to get him back on his feet."

"Good. Very good. We've got him set up for an MRI and then we'll see how to proceed. I do agree getting him up is imperative."

Chase was so relieved he felt his eyes burn with tears.

A group of orderlies filed in.

"You ready, Sergeant?" one asked, wheeling a trolley with him.

"Yes. Let's get this show on the road." Gary tried to sit up.

"Stay." Chase nudged him back and used the switch to get the bed to recline to level again.

"What am I, Mutley? Stay?" Gary teased.

"Your face is almost as fuzzy as his is." Chase laughed.

"Look who's talking!" Gary pointed his finger at Chase's two-day growth.

"On a count of three…" one orderly said. They moved Gary to the transport cot and settled him in.

"Will you be here when I get back?" Gary asked.

"I'm not going anywhere."

"Speaking of Mutley?" Gary said as he was rolled out of the room.

"He'll be fine." Chase waved.

Once Gary vanished around the corner, Chase checked his watch. Mutley needed a piss break and a doghouse so he could be left out on winter days.

As he waited, Mr. and Mrs. Wilson approached from the hall. Mary instantly turned up her nose at the sight of him. Bill, looking resigned, asked, "Where's Gary?"

"They've taken him for an MRI."

Bill nodded but did not engage him further.

Mary stood out in the hall. The coldness was nauseating Chase.

Now would be a good time for David and Lyle to show up. Get me off the hook.

It was cold as ice in that room, waiting for Gary with his

moronic parents there. Chase couldn't deal with it. He left and asked the nurse, "Where do they do the MRI scans?"

"Down that hall and to the right."

"Thank you." Chase strode quickly and stood right outside the door. As luck would have it, Gary was just being wheeled out. Chase walked along side of him. "Your parents are here. Let me go let Mutley out and I'll come back in a bit."

"Okay, babe." Gary squeezed his hands.

"Any results yet?" Chase looked around but didn't see either doctor.

"They said it would only be a minute. You want to hang around?"

Chase did but was growing anxious. "Yes. I can."

"Poor Mutley." Gary pouted in exaggeration.

"I have to get him a doghouse so I can leave him out in this cold weather."

The minute they entered Gary's room, Chase stood back as the orderlies replaced Gary on his bed.

It only took a moment for Dr. Rhabi and Dr. Bradley to return, holding paperwork.

Chase stood by as Dr. Rhabi shared his findings with everyone in the room.

"The swelling had gone down substantially," Dr. Rhabi said, "So we see no reason not to begin Gary's rehabilitation." He turned to look directly at Chase. "Both you and Dr. Bradley can confer on how to proceed. If you have any questions for me, just let me know." With that, Dr. Rhabi left the room.

"That's great news, Sgt. Wilson." Dr. Bradley approached Gary. "I'll get you a pair of crutches and Mr. Arlington can begin your program."

"Good." Gary smiled, but Chase could see he was in pain again.

"Do you need more morphine, Gary?" Chase asked in concern.

"No," Dr. Bradley said, "We're stopping the morphine. He'll be on Vicodin and then we're going to drop that to ibuprofen. No one leaves this medical center a drug addict."

Chase got the impression Dr. Bradley was himself a war veteran. He certainly looked and acted the part.

"He's in pain," Chase said, gesturing to Gary.

"I'll get the nurse to give him something."

As Dr. Bradley left, Mary approached Chase. "I resent you trying to guide the doctors. Stay out of it."

"Mom…" Gary moaned weakly.

Chase hurried to him, massaging Gary's head gently.

"Mom," Gary repeated, squinting his eyes from his discomfort. "*You* stay out of it. Leave Chase alone. He's the one who knows what's best for me."

"Gary!"

"You at it again, Mom?"

Hearing Lyle's voice, Chase breathed a sigh of relief.

"Give it a rest!" Lyle entered the room, boldly holding David's hand.

If Lyle had meant to antagonize his parents by hanging onto David, it worked like a charm.

"Let me let Mutley out. I'll be back." Chase was just as brazen as Lyle and kissed Gary on the lips.

"I wish I could build him a doghouse. That would be a blast." Gary smiled despite his agony.

"I'll buy a cheap one and we can build him a luxury penthouse when you're well."

"Deal." Gary reached out. "Kiss me one more time."

Chase did gladly. Behind him he heard Lyle sigh. "Aww, aren't they adorable?"

As Chase left he winked at Lyle and David. "Thanks guys. Just in the nick of time."

"We got it covered," Lyle said and patted Chase's arm.

Grabbing his coat, Chase threw Gary a kiss, and passed the nurse in the hall. "He's in bad shape," he informed her.

"These will help." She held up a cup of pills.

"Thank you."

"Don't worry. We'll take good care of him."

Smiling, knowing they would, Chase left, rushing to get home to his hound.

CHAPTER 17

Gary was moved to an upright position on the bed and took the water and cup of pills from the nurse. After he swallowed down the painkillers he asked her, "How long does this thing have to be in?" He gestured to the IV.

"Now that you're eating regularly, I think we could remove it. Let me check with the doctor and I'll let you know."

"Thanks." Gary handed her the two empty paper cups.

The minute she left Lyle sat on his bed with him, peering over at his parents. "If you're going to look like you're in as much pain as Gary's in, leave!"

"Lyle," David said quickly. "Don't be disrespectful to your parents."

Gary chuckled at the irony. "Forget it, David. They won't get over it. They'd rather I was dead than gay."

"Gary," Bill said, stepping closer. "Don't say things like that. You know it's not true."

"No?" Gary waved at his mother who wouldn't leave the safety of the doorway. "She must think we all have a disease. Look where she is."

Lyle and David took a quick glance over their shoulder.

"Fuck her, Gary," Lyle said.

Bill drew closer, standing on the opposite side of Gary's bed from where Lyle and David were. "You have to understand it's just a shock to us. Lyle is twenty-six and you're twenty-eight and yet this is the first time we have any indication you both…both…"

"Are gay!" Lyle finished the sentence in exasperation. David gripped Lyle's shoulder to calm him down.

"Did you really think we felt comfortable telling you?" Gary tried to shift on the bed, dying to get off it he was so stiff. "Look at your reactions."

"Bill."

The four men looked to where Mary was.

"I'm going home. Are you coming with me?"

"Yes. Hang on." Bill bit his lip, annoyed. He addressed Gary, "Just give us some time."

Gary knew Lyle was gearing up for a biting parting word. Both he and David gave him a warning look. "Okay, Dad." Gary sighed.

"We'll see you later." Bill met Mary by the door and they vanished.

Lyle found Gary's good hand and held it in his. "Forget them, Gary. Mom is Mrs. Christian ethics, what did you expect?"

Gary had already stopped worrying about his parents and sank thinking about his own misery.

David walked to the opposite side of the bed, pulling a chair closer. "What is it, Gary?"

Removing his hand from his brother's grip, Gary rubbed his face. "I just hate doing this to Chase."

"Doing what?" Lyle tilted his head confused.

"Saddling him with a goddamn cripple."

"You're not a cripple." David stroked back Gary's hair from his forehead. "You're injured. And even if you were disabled, do you think Chase is the kind of man who would desert you?"

"No. He's too good." Gary glared at David in anger. "That's why I need to cut him loose. I can't put him through months of my rehab, have him play nursemaid to me. It's unfair to him."

David gripped Gary's shoulder to speak seriously to him. "This is your pride talking, not your worry for Chase. Be honest with yourself, Gary. Do you think you'll lose his respect if he sees you weak?"

Gary fought back his emotions with every ounce of strength he had. Meeting David's intelligent eyes, Gary forced the words to come out of his strangled throat. "The attraction Chase has for me is for my strength, David. My aggression, my power. Look at me." He waved to his condition under the blankets. "And to top that off, I could have a permanent brain condition. How could I put him through that?"

Lyle hissed out a breath of air loudly. "You do say the stupidest things, Gary."

"Lyle," David admonished sternly before he gave his attention back to Gary. "Look, I'm coming from the outside. I don't know either of you well enough to make a sound judgment on it, but I do have an opinion."

Gary nodded weakly for him to go on.

"From what I've witnessed, Chase is completely in love with you." David stopped Gary from interrupting him. "And no matter what the results are of your recovery, he will be there."

"Because he's obligated!" Gary cried.

"No. Because he adores you."

"I wouldn't want to be burdened with a fucking mess the rest of my life, why would I do that to him?"

Lyle was about to whack Gary but stopped himself. "You'll recover, you jerk. So you'll have a few months of limping around. Big fucking deal. Will you get over it?"

"Lyle!" David appeared exasperated. "Don't trivialize this. It's very important that Gary feel whole inside his head as well as his body. So, be quiet for a minute."

Gary grinned at David. "Man, are you good for my bratty brother or what?"

Lyle stuck his tongue out at Gary.

"Yes. And if two men as opposite as Lyle Wilson and myself can make it work, then for you and Chase, it's simple. Do you get my point?"

That struck something deep in Gary. He glanced from one man to the other to see indeed, how incredibly different they were. Like in *Pretty Woman*, David had taken his rough-hewn younger brother and turned him into a sophisticated LA model. If Gary hadn't witnessed the change in Lyle himself, he wouldn't have believed it. And that didn't even factor in the age gap of sixteen years between the men.

"Don't cut Chase off now. Lyle told me he was going mad these last few months without you. Don't break his heart, Gary, by telling him he can no longer be in your life. Let him get you where you should be. He's a physical therapist. Who better to do it than Chase Arlington?"

After gazing long and hard at David, Gary stared at his brother's green eyes for a moment. "You better realize how lucky you are, punk, to have a guy like David in your life."

"I do. And you better realize how lucky you are to have a stunning hunk like Chase Arlington in yours!"

Feeling drowsy from the meds, Gary allowed his body to settle into the pillows. "I am lucky. Right?"

"Right," was replied in stereo.

CHAPTER 18

A new milestone presented itself when Chase helped Gary out of his car and, with the help of crutches, Gary made his way to Chase's front door.

"Woof!"

Smiling, Chase said, "Guess who's waiting to see you?"

"I've missed him." Gary waited as Chase turned the lock.

"Let me calm him down. He'll go completely nuts when he sees you. I don't want him knocking you over."

"All right," Gary replied, laughing.

It'd been nearly a month of rehab at the hospital and clinic, and Gary, after weeks of arguing with the staff, finally was cut free of the confines of the base's hospital. Lyle and David had returned to LA, and the visits from Gary's parents were few and far between.

Chase had to get back to his work and patients, so the option of having Gary live with him full time while they continued his therapy appealed to them both.

"Sit!" Chase warned Mutley as he whined and wriggled as if he were in agony holding back his hello to his favorite human.

Assisting Gary inside the living room, Chase could see Gary was as eager to greet Mutley as his dog was to go for a big lick of Gary's face in welcome.

"All right," Gary said, "let me say hello." He handed Chase his crutched. "Come here, big guy." Gary managed to crouch down.

Mutley went nuts, licking his cheek and spinning in his happy dance as Gary gave him a good scratching, sending hairs floating in the air.

"I've missed you, ya big furball." Gary's eyes teared up and Chase had to turn aside so he didn't have a meltdown of his own.

Chase gave Gary back his crutches and helped him into the kitchen to sit down. Once he was settled, he returned to the car for Gary's suitcase.

After he put the case in his bedroom, Chase bounded back down to see Mutley resting his long muzzle on Gary's lap and Gary's big contented grin staring down at the dog as he petted him.

Well, if that's not good therapy, I don't know what is.

"Lunch." Chase washed his hands at the sink. "Let me see what I can whip up."

"God!" Gary said, "I am so happy to be here."

Mutley made a strange 'waawaawoo' sound that sent both Gary and Chase roaring with laughter.

Dabbing at his eyes, Chase said, "That's his version of what you said."

Gary wrapped his good arm around Mutley's neck. "I'm so glad I'm home."

Hearing Gary say he was 'home' while at his house made Chase's heart beat faster. He wanted this to be Gary's home.

Moving to stand behind Gary, Chase hugged from behind. "You are home, lover." He kissed Gary's head.

Gary reached up to touch Chase's arm. "Thank you. I don't know what I would do without you."

"You won't have to find that out." After another peck on Gary's hair, Chase returned to fixing lunch.

"Chase?"

"Yes, babe?"

"I want us to make love tonight."

Chase knew Gary's therapy was going well, but the poor man was still so battered. "I'll make sure we're both satisfied."

"I haven't come for months. I didn't want to jack off in Iraq. It just felt awkward doing it there."

"Today. I promise." Chase felt his emotions well again. He had missed Gary so much.

Once he prepared sandwiches for them, Chase set them on the table and helped Gary to the sink to wash his hand after messing with Mutley.

Once they were both at the kitchen table, Chase asked, "You need an ibuprofen?"

"Soon. I'm not too bad at the moment."

"You do realize how well you're coming along, don't you?" Chase asked.

Gary pointed to his sling. "Hate this fucking thing. I can't wait for it to come off permanently."

"At least it's not a plaster cast. It could be worse. You can remove it for a shower."

Nodding as he chewed, Gary met Chase's eyes slyly. "Shower with me after lunch?"

"Mm." Chase grinned wickedly.

"I love you." Gary leaned across the table.

Chase met him halfway and pecked his lips. "Ditto, hot stuff."

As they finished their meal, they smiled at each other in anticipation.

❧

Gary was nervous. He was both dreading and dying for their first sexual bout after he had returned. The fear of wondering if he could do it, could come, was unnerving him. An evil voice in his head kept whispering that he was half a man, not capable any longer of fulfilling Chase's demands.

As Chase helped Gary remove all his wrappings and bind-ings, Gary began to sink mentally. *I'm a wreck. Look at my hand. I'm purple. For crying out loud. Look how bruised I am. He'll take one look at me naked and cringe in disgust.*

Sitting on the bed, his body on the verge of being completely exposed, Gary almost chickened out and stopped Chase out of fear.

"There's my gorgeous man," Chase crooned.

Gary blinked in surprise. *What?*

Lowering to knees, Chase gently parted Gary's thighs and moved in between them.

Feeling Chase's mouth on his genitals after nearly four months of missing it, Gary closed his eyes in a swoon. He thought he would gross Chase out with all his horrible bruising and discolorations.

"How I've missed you. Missed sucking this cock."

Gary reached out to caress Chase's head. A sharp pain in his right shoulder reminded him to use only one hand. He stroked Chase's hair gently. "Are you just saying that?"

"Mm mmm," Chase moaned 'no', Gary's dick deep in his mouth.

Feeling his cock thicken in the wet heat, Gary was so relieved he was growing hard as a rock he felt a weight rise off his shoulders. Yes, he'd been semi-hard in the hospital with Chase's hand massaging him when he could cop a feel, but now he actually felt like he could come.

Chase paused to ask, "You want to come in my mouth, or my ass?"

"How about your mouth? I don't think I could kneel at the moment."

"No problem." Chase slipped Gary's cock back into his mouth.

"Chase…" Gary whimpered as Chase brought him up quickly. *How I have missed this! Dreamed of it! Craved it!* "Ahh!" Gary's body tensed up, and even through the pain of his injuries he reveled in the glorious pleasure of an orgasm.

Chase deepened his sucking, moaning in ecstasy. When he drew back to look into Gary's eyes, Chase said, "Gary…Gary… how I have missed the taste of your cum."

Gary laughed softly. "And I've missed your mouth."

Once Chase got to his feet, he reached out. "Ready, lover?"

Hauled up gingerly by Chase, Gary wrapped an arm around him and tried to put pressure on his sore leg.

"You okay?"

"Yeah. Not too bad. My shoulder feels much worse than my knee."

"Okay." Chase directed him to the bathroom, allowing Gary to hold onto the wall while he started the shower.

Gary laughed and Chase spun around. Mutley was standing in the bathroom with them. "Dog!" Chase said, "Go lay down."

"I swear he feels left out." Gary watched Mutley slink to his pillow.

"And he'll remain left out of our private contact." Chase helped Gary get into the tub slowly.

"We need to get him a fuck buddy."

"One big hairy dog is enough." Chase closed the shower door and stood with him as Gary wet down under the spray.

"Christ, that feels good." Gary groaned. "I feel like I haven't had a proper shower in ages."

"Sponge baths not good enough?" Chase teased as he swapped places with Gary carefully.

"No. You weren't giving me them." Gary kept trying to use his right hand and cringing at the pain.

"Will you slow down?" Chase asked in exasperation. "Let me do it. Jesus, same old Gary."

"Not quite." Gary pointed to a purplish blushing bruise on his shoulder and collar bone.

"It only makes you more rugged and masculine." Chase purred.

As Chase shampooed Gary's hair and washed him from head to toe, Gary closed his eyes and groaned in pleasure. "Spoiled, spoiled, spoiled."

"Tough. Get used to it."

"I want to do you." Gary touched Chase's cock.

"Here." Chase held out Gary's good hand and squeezed a blob of soap into it. "Do me."

Gary instantly went for Chase's dick. "I suck jacking off lefty."

"Who cares?" Chase widened his straddle and thrust out his pelvis.

It felt wonderful to be playing with Chase's cock again. "God, I've missed you! Missed this!"

"No shit." Chase moaned, thrusting his hips into Gary's slick palm.

Inadvertently reaching with his right hand, Gary inhaled sharply from the pain. Stopping Gary, Chase held onto him tightly. "Let's rinse. Come on."

"Chase…" Gary felt horrible he didn't make him come.

"Out. On the bed where we'll be more comfortable."

Relinquishing his hold reluctantly, Gary felt like the worst charity case in history.

Chase dried Gary off first, rubbing him briskly with a towel before he tended himself.

"I hate this feeling!" Gary roared. "I can't stand being so helpless."

"I know. But look how far you've come." Chase tossed the towels over the shower door. He practically lifted Gary out of the tub and held onto him as he walked him to the bed.

The whole time Gary was fighting with his emotions and the pain. Once Chase had him horizontal, Gary lay facing him as Chase joined him on the bed.

"Bring that here," Gary ordered, pointing first at Chase's cock, then his own mouth.

"Yes, sir!" Chase laughed. He shifted on the bed to sit near Gary's face.

Gary had to give Chase an orgasm. It was a matter of principle.

Scooting closer, wincing but trying not to show Chase his pain, Gary rested over Chase's lap and took Chase's soft dick into his mouth. The relief he felt to have Chase's body to enjoy was palpable. Soon Chase's cock was fully erect and Gary tasted his delicious pre-cum. He had to move faster. Gary withstood pain that was morphing into agony, but wanted Chase to come in his mouth.

"That's it, babe. I'm there." Chase's cock hardened to stone and Gary tasted his delicious juice as he climaxed.

Swallowing it down, milking it out, Gary was very glad Chase had come for so many reasons. Allowing Chase's cock to slip out of his mouth, Gary rolled to his back and gasped for breath.

"God. Lay still, babe…" Chase could obviously read the pain in his expression. "Let me get you an ibuprofen."

"Okay." Gary held his shoulder still as it throbbed in excruciating pain. Once Chase jogged out of the room, Gary cursed at his own injuries in anger.

≈≈

Grabbing a bottle of water out of the fridge, Chase found

Gary's meds and felt terrible for him as he jogged back up the stairs. To Chase's surprise, Mutley was sitting steadfast at Gary's bedside instead of making the trip down and up the stairs with him. "Son of a gun." Chase assumed Mutley could tell Gary was hurt. It amazed him.

Once he gave Gary the pills, he helped him back into his shoulder splint and under the blankets. "You know," Chase said, smiling, "that dog is now your guardian angel."

Gary peeked over at Mutley, as if he just realized where he was in the room. A big smile found Gary's face. Chase was thrilled to have put it there.

He climbed into the bed and cradled Gary close to his body.

When they felt a weight shift the mattress, both men raised their head off their pillows to look.

Mutley was lying at the foot of the bed, his long muzzle on Gary's shins.

Just as Chase was about to scold him, Gary said, "Don't. Let him stay there."

"Just this once." Chase kissed Gary's cheek. "You do realize you give him an inch he'll take a mile."

"I know. But he's warm and he feels good on my bum leg."

"Okay, baby. Rest." Chase snuggled against Gary, hearing Mutley release a loud sigh as he too closed his eyes to sleep.

EPILOGUE

The silky white sand of Redondo Beach sliding through his toes, Chase sat up on the blanket as David coated Lyle's back with sunscreen beside him.

Staring at the curling white surf, the seagulls and bathers, surfboards and body boarders, Chase wondered how he could go back to Dayton after this.

And standing on his own, without a cane or crutch, was his amazing soldier boy.

Staff Sergeant Gary Wilson, in his swim trunks and Ray Bans, stood tall gazing out at the water. Seven months of rehab, and Gary was very close to being fully recovered.

Laughing, Lyle warned, "Don't do too good a job, Chase, or the air force will send him on tour again."

That threat stuck in Chase's head. He made sure on Gary's medical forms it indicated he would never be one hundred percent ready for active duty. No way. His baby would be at a desk from now on, not overseas.

Gary spun around, looking back at him, Lyle, and David, a satisfied smile on Gary's gorgeous face. Chase couldn't help but respond, both with his sexual urges and his love. He reached out his hand, beckoning.

Watching Gary's masculine movements as he returned to their blanket, Chase licked his lips in desire. Unaware he was being observed, Chase felt Lyle's playful punch on his shoulder.

"You hungry, Chase?" Lyle's smile was pure wicked delight.

"Famished." Chase humored him.

"That's what months of going without will do to a man."

Lyle's gaze moved to his brother.

Gary knelt down, somewhat carefully, mindful of his healed wounds, and asked, "Why don't we live here, Chase?"

"I was thinking the same thing." Chase caressed Gary's arm. "Just thinking about getting on that plane to Ohio makes me cringe."

David laughed softly, capping the lotion and wiping his hands on a towel. "Ah, the hypnotic draw of California strikes again."

"You think Mutley would like it?" Gary asked, as if the dog's opinion counted for something. "It's very hot for dog as furry as he is."

"Who did you get to watch him?" Lyle asked, reclining on the blanket.

"Our friends Sam and Dev," Gary replied. "Bet he's getting overfed."

Chase groaned. "He does have a way of giving you those big brown, 'I'm starving' eyes."

"Sam's a sucker for that stuff." Gary smiled.

Lyle reached for David, urging him to rest beside him.

Gary picked Chase's leg up off the blanket and placed it on his lap, massaging it.

"Hey, I should be doing that to you," Chase teased, "as part of your rehab."

"This is part of my rehab." Gary grinned. "Getting my sexuality back on track."

"It is, babe, it is!" Chase chuckled, recalling Gary back in prime form, hammering his cock into him on demand. "You're giving me a hard-on."

"Good." Gary's eyes darted to Chase's crotch.

"You see, you asshole!" Lyle shoved Gary with his foot, nearly knocking him over. "All that whining you did when you came back from Iraq…I'm a cripple! I can't do this to him!"

"Lyle!" David said, "What's wrong with you?"

Gary threw a handful of sand on Lyle in retaliation. It made Lyle jump up, cursing as he brushed it off his sweaty, lotion coated skin.

"I just didn't want to stick Chase with half a man, all right?

Shut up Lyle," Gary's tone wasn't angry. He was obviously used to his brother's taunting.

Chase moved to embrace Gary where he sat, wrapping his arms around his torso. "Oh no, big fella. You're all man, make no mistake about that." After checking out their immediate surroundings, Chase whispered, "Feel brave enough to kiss me, soldier boy?"

Without hesitation, Gary cupped Chase's face and planted a good kiss on his lips.

"Hey!" Lyle laughed. "Whoever would have thought my straight-laced air force sergeant brother would kiss a man on a public beach. I'm in shock."

Once Chase and Gary parted from their kiss, Gary replied, "And whoever would have thought a man as fantastic as David would put up with you?"

"All right, you two," Chase scolded playfully, dragging Gary down on the blanket beside him. "Behave," Chase whispered into Gary's ear.

Gary reached out to hold Chase's hand as they soaked up the LA sunshine.

Smiling contentedly, Chase knew he found a good one. All man? Yes. His man.

The End